S e

SEEFORGE

Marian O'Neill

Pillar Press

Copyright © 2005 Marian O'Neill

Seeforge
First published 2005
Pillar Press
Ladywell
Thomastown
Co Kilkenny

The author has asserted her moral rights.

ISBN 0955082102

British Library Cataloguing in Publication Data.
A CIP catalogue record for this book is available
from the British Library.

Printed in Ireland by ColourBooks

10 9 8 7 6 5 4 3 2 1

For Maeve, Eileen, Aine, Antoinette and Damian

CHAPTER 1

Tracy Sheehy ran The Continental Café in Seeforge, and she was famous for it. "Best food in the South West," people said, but Tracy knew better. She knew that her cooking was simply the best; it was just that her clientele couldn't fully appreciate what she served them because most of them hadn't travelled beyond the South West. But Tracy didn't mind that. She didn't want any higher praise. She didn't want her talents advertised. She reckoned that life was too short for that kind of pressure. Who needed more money? She already started work at five and finished at midnight six days a week, and who had the time to do more than that? Who would want to? Not Tracy. She knew what she wanted and she was already halfway there. She wanted a solid little business and a young, handsome husband. She had the former and she was confident that, in time, it would attract the latter.

Trouble was there weren't that many men to choose from in Seeforge. It was a small town, less than two thousand people, but its tourist trade was growing by the year. Three years ago, when Tracy turned thirty-five, she cleared out the rooms over the cafe that she had, up until then, used for storage, and hung a "rooms for rent" sign in her window. And that was how she got to know Tom Hamilton.

Tom arrived in Seeforge one Wednesday afternoon in April looking dusty, thin and full of city swagger. He came on the three-thirty train and strolled into town on the crest of an easy spring wind. With his shirt and jacket crumpled from the journey, his bag slung over his shoulder and his cowboy boots kicking up little puffs of dirt Tom looked just as he imagined he should, like a stranger come to town. He was just twenty-four but he felt as worn and as wise as the blue hills behind him; he was still that young.

Tom Hamilton had never been to Seeforge before and had chosen it purely because of its location. It was as far from home, and as far into the wild South West, as he could go without reaching the sea and the summer crowds that that would draw. Tom was looking for somewhere quiet, somewhere he could write but, because he only had enough money to last him six to eight months, he didn't want to waste too much of it on accommodation or on travel. So that really ruled out going abroad, or moving to another city, or spending the summer in one of the more fashionable inland towns. And so Tom was left with Seeforge.

But, from the very beginning, he was well pleased with his choice. As soon as he stepped off the train and down onto the gravel of the empty station platform, he knew that he was in the right place. The air, the view, the rustle and hum of the countryside touched him immediately. He nodded to himself; he'd be able to do some good work here. This was what he had been searching for, some place simple and pure. Somewhere men let the sun govern their days, not their watches.

"Do you know how I spell mediocrity?" Tom had shouted at his father over last Sunday's roast. His father had just helped himself to some more meat; it was his mother who had politely answered.

"How, dear?"

"S.U.B.U.R.B.I.A."

"Really, dear," his mother said. "Would you like some carrots?"

And that was it. Just there! That was why Tom had to leave. No one could write in such a crippling environment. How could even one truth be recorded in such a hypocritical atmosphere?

And truth, honesty, the word, that was what Tom was about. That was all he had ever been about. The last three years working in the telecommunications industry had just been a means to an end. During all those years Tom had been saving and now he had enough money to take some time off to record his truth. He was going to write a new landscape for his generation. He was going to put a mirror up to all those millions who were happy to just mindlessly exist within their fabricated realities behind their chosen stereotypes; the housewife, the mother, the golfer, the Lexus driver, the weekend drinker, the office joker.

He was going to kick them awake, push them out of their semi-ds, force them to face each other over their garden fences and really look at each other for the first time, and then what would they say? Then, knowing what Tom knew, how could they talk about the lawn, or the mortgage, or the holiday in Spain? They couldn't. Faced with the truth, the only questions they would be able to ask each other would be, "When did we die?" And, "When do you think they'll get around to burying us?"

But Tom knew there was no point in trying to explain this to his parents. Not yet anyway, not before his great truth was recorded. And so he just nodded that, yes, he would like more carrots and, the following Wednesday, he left the comfort of his South County Dublin suburb and headed for the South West, and Seeforge.

And so here he was, with his bag slung over his shoulder

and the sun in his face and everything looking just perfect. From the height of the station he could see the small spread of the town clustered along the banks of the river See, bounded to the north by gently sloping hills and spreading out into the straggle of a planted pine forest to the south. He was close enough to the sea to feel the tingle of ozone in the air and it was quiet, quiet and green. Tom walked down into the town on the click of his cowboy boots and everything he saw just added to his deepening sense of satisfaction.

Seeforge is bigger, more substantial, than most rural small towns. Its main street, Hephaition Way, is well proportioned; broad, long and lined with mature trees all neatly wrapped up in railings. In summer these trees fill up and screen off the buildings behind them but in April they just throw the upper storeys into dappled shade. Or at least that's what Tom thought as he started off down Hephaition Way but he hadn't gone very far before he noticed that the delicate filigree that spread over every building was in fact a combination of light, shadow and some very fine ironwork.

Every façade in Seeforge is decorated with some kind of metalwork. It creeps over every lintel, runs along the eaves, drips like lace from window boxes and dainty, decorative balconies. And it doesn't stop there. The windows of the shop-fronts below are all framed by iron shutters, some rusting and falling limply off their hinges, some brightly polished or painted up. But the condition of them doesn't matter: they still unify the whole street, giving Seeforge a sense of identity that both historically and geographically it lacks.

Because, although there always seems to have been some settlement in the area, there is no real reason for Seeforge. The name does suggest that the town grew up around some navigable point on the See, but no proof of this has ever been found. On the contrary, any research that has been done shows that the See runs very deep and fast through Seeforge. Its currents make it dangerous for swimming and it is a dead area for fishing. Of course the river's nature could have changed dramatically since the first people settled in the area, but usually such settlements would move to suit the river's changes. Usually towns grow up around something more substantial than habit, but habit seems to be Seeforge's only reason for existing.

It has never been a centre for commerce. It has never needed to be as it is bordered by two, much larger, towns; a substantial port town and an agricultural town, which still boasts a large monthly fair. It is in a hollow and so doesn't command any strategic position in relation to the surrounding countryside. It doesn't skirt any great estate and so didn't grow up around the needs of the aristocracy, and it has no natural resources; no mining, no quarry, no rich farming land, no reason to attract any settlers. But still Seeforge does exist and so, at some stage, it must have either supplied a service or filled a need.

With Tracy in The Continental the locals didn't have to look very far for that service or that need. They joked that the service was supplied by Tracy and that the need was their hunger.

"A town has sprung up around worse things than a good breakfast," they said and Tracy was more than happy to encourage the myth.

"You're right there," she would say. "There was nothing nor no one here before the Sheehy's came looking for a place to lay their pots and pans. But it's a known fact, you put a Sheehy right bang slap in the middle of the desert with a knob of butter and an egg and before that egg's fried there'll be someone there asking to eat it. You may have out-grown your animal skins but we Sheehys know that you're all still led by your hunger."

And she would wink, letting her listener know that she had a broad definition of hunger.

Tracy's facts may have been confused but she was right about some things. Of course the Sheehys weren't the first to settle in Seeforge, but they had been there for generations and they had always made their living by cooking.

The first Sheehys arrived in the already busy town of Seeforge with pots, pans, recipes from all over Europe and a very sick grandmother. It was because of their grandmother that they stayed, otherwise they would have moved on, because that's what they did, move and camp, and move again. They weren't quite gypsies, they didn't align themselves with any group, they were just a family who had been displaced and so had taken to the road. That was a common enough story back then but what was so unusual about the Sheehys was that the road had taken to them. Took them off and tramped them through cities and countries, led them around wars and famines, riches and tragedies, before finally depositing them down on the banks of the river See.

This had all happened generations ago but, because the Sheehys had stayed so close to the origin of their story, its details hadn't become as diluted as most family histories. So, for the most part, Tracy did know what she was talking about. She also knew that, although the Sheehys had contributed to the town's growth, they hadn't instigated it. But, Tracy reasoned, that kind of honesty didn't make for such a good story, that wasn't what her diners wanted to hear and, because a person needs to feel easy with their company if they're going to feel easy with their food, she made it her business to tell them all exactly what they wanted to hear.

For instance she told Dean Kelly that his hair was still as thick as it was when he was thirty and she told Robert

Hardy that the Russians were monitoring us all by placing chips in our mobile phones. She told Mavis Bradley that the unmarried mothers were ruining the economy and the race by having all those dirty-skinned babies for the illegal refugees and she told Jill Daily that it was far easier to conceive during a waxing moon.

On that Wednesday in April, Tracy was leaning by the door of The Continental when she saw a skinny young man come strutting down the street towards her. He was too young to have grown into himself yet but Tracy could see beyond his youth and on into his potential. She was a cook and that was her business, recognising the finished product in the raw materials, and she was well pleased with what she recognised in Tom.

By the time he stepped up to The Continental she was ready to tell him just what he was wanting to hear.

CHAPTER 2

Tom always remembered the first time he saw Tracy. He wasn't to know that all men did, that Tracy knew the power of first impressions and knew how to maximise their effect. For Tom she stayed quiet, letting him approach her; she figured that it was only polite to allow such a young man the pretence of control.

The Continental wasn't very big, just two storeys at the front and three at the back but, even so and even though it was at the far end of Hephaition Way, it still dominated the main street. Its heavy red roof fell low over its three crookedly spaced upstairs windows which seemed to rest their sills on a trellis that served as a narrow metal porch. Three delicate, fluted pillars held this trellis up and behind those pillars there was just one long plate-glass window that continually advertised all the glory of that little café.

The café floor was quite narrow: a bar counter ran the length of the wall facing the door, and so the tables were all pushed tight against the front window. It was an arrangement that Tracy was very proud of, as it put every diner and every dish on display. For the most part of every day the window of The Continental was filled with all the joy that is associated with good food – deep, rich smells, warm clots of colour and the comforting hum of companionship.

The tables in The Continental were too small to allow for reserve; they pushed the patrons together, elbow to elbow, plate to plate, mouth to ear – they left no room for constraint. Each table was covered with a plain, cream cloth and lit with its own fat candle, all throwing out their own little pools of light, all flickering off glass and chrome, all playing over golden roasts and rich red sauces, deep green vegetables and light pink desserts. And over every meal happy, eager heads were bent in appreciation or conversation. As it got later the heads leaned back and the candles picked up on flashing smiles and eyes glinting with animation. Then, as the night wore late, the warm smell of roasting coffee would thicken and thicken until it gradually blanketed first the conversations and then the lights. The people of Seeforge knew the nightly drill: once Tracy put the coffee on they started winding down their evening. Sometimes she didn't even have to serve it – the smell of it was enough to send her customers home.

But you didn't have to eat at The Continental to live by its rules. Most of Seeforge followed Tracy's timetable without even knowing it. It was her rooster, kept out back, that started off every day. It was the smell of her freshly baking bread that got most people out of bed and eating breakfast, and it was the smell of her roasting coffee that warmed them all to sleep.

And it was the smell of afternoon cakes that first attracted Tom Hamilton.

Wednesday was early closing day in Seeforge and so, when Tom first arrived, Hephaition Way was very quiet, almost deserted. A few cars were parked on either side of the road, a newsagent's was open and a few teenagers were hanging around outside it. A couple of old men were standing in the porch of a pub opposite and a dog, keeping one eye on Tom, slowly crossed the empty street.

Tom was just heading for the pub that the old men were guarding when he caught the smell of apple tart. He never remembered actually smelling apple tart before but he was positive that that was what he was smelling now, apple tart and more. He raised his head, breathed a little deeper and, just as if he were tasting it with his nose, the warm aroma separated into its different components. Tom could smell cinnamon, cloves, nutmeg, caramelised sugar and cream whipped through with the zest of a lemon. He turned away from the pub and walked slowly on down to The Continental and to Tracy Sheehy.

On the way he passed a rather lumpy adolescent girl. He didn't notice her, Melissa wasn't the kind of girl that attracted notice, but she noticed him. She turned as he passed her by and watched him as he headed straight for The Continental. She watched the way he stepped up onto the kerb, the way he dipped his head in greeting and something about the sad lift to his smile made her eyes water.

Tracy Sheehy was standing in the doorway of her cafe, leaning against a rusting metal gate, smiling. She looked old, at least to Tom she looked old. Her skin was red raw from constant exposure to ovens and steam, and the echoes of all her expressions were written deep into her face. She was wearing a white blouse, cut low, exposing a loose, pink cleavage, and tucked tightly into a full red skirt. A wide black belt made the most of her thick waist and a long gold necklace fastened Tom's attention on her chest. Her hair, shoulder length, lank brown and graying, was caught up on one side in a slide decorated with a flower. She was standing openly, one hand on her hip and the other playing with the fabric of her skirt. Her head was thrown high and cocked to one side, watching Tom's approach She didn't say a word until he had stepped up onto the path and was standing right in front of her and then she pitched herself forward a little and asked, "You new in town?"

"Yeah," Tom answered hitching his bag up higher onto his shoulder. "Yeah, I just came in on the train."

"The three thirty?" Tracy asked turning away and walking into the café.

"Yeah." Tom answered as he followed her inside.

The café was quiet although quite a few people were scattered through it. Six tables were occupied and the other five were still cluttered with delph and glasses and covered over with crumbs. There was just a low a hum of conversation that ran under the more immediate clatter of eating.

"You must be hungry then." Tracy continued working her way through the tables, picking up some dishes as she went, flicking at some crumbs with a cloth she had pulled out from her belt. "Can I interest you in a slice of apple tart? Bet it's just as good as anything your mum ever made, no offence to the lady of course." She was behind her counter now and Tom was facing her.

"Yeah," he answered but his voice had lost its non-chalant edge, his hunger was forcing him to be enthusiastic. "Yeah," he said again and this time he sounded like a child. "With cream please and can it be hot. And I'd like some coffee too and –"

"I'll put some cream in that and all will I?" Tom nodded. "Right you are then. You go and sit over there," and she pointed over to the far table, "and I'll bring it down to you."

It was only then, only after Tracy had dismissed him, that Tom noticed his surroundings. He walked slowly to his table taking everything in, and everything was very far removed from anything he had expected to find in a provincial backwater.

The interior of The Continental, though narrow, was high and bright; the long front window did away with any enclosed feeling. The polished wooden floor glowed with a rich, honey-coloured varnish and where the thick, cream cloths, that swamped every table, touched the floor they crumpled onto it, falling into deep, piled folds. The chairs circling these tables were all wrought-iron and heavy. In places they settled awkwardly on to the warp of the floor but they were beautiful, worked through with birds, plants and wild, fluid detail.

The walls of The Continental were painted a dark red and the woodwork was picked out in green. The ceiling was white and where it met the walls it seemed to have bled into the red, streaking it through with trickles of lighter red and pink and, although the effect was obviously accidental, it worked well. It seemed to both highlight and lighten the darkness of the walls.

The bar, that stretched almost the length of the restaurant, was wooden and varnished to match the colour of the floor. Its counter top was stained a darker brown and was covered with an assortment of terracotta bowls filled with black and green olives, grated cheeses, assorted salads, sundried tomatoes, slices of plain, fruit and herb breads and anything else that might add that finishing touch to a meal. The door to Tracy's kitchen was at one end of the bar and the hatch that let her out onto the floor was at the other and so, whenever she swung out of her kitchen ready to serve, she had to walk the length of the bar. While carrying up to three plates, and without hardly breaking her stride, she could dip in and out of the bowls she had lined up there, adding whatever extra each dish needed to make it perfect.

The area behind the bar was shelved from floor to ceiling and filled with glass and colour. But all those jars and bottles, tins and boxes, were just there for display and bore no relation to whatever ingredients Tracy used in her cooking. The real workings of The Continental went on behind the heavy chrome door that separated Tracy from her public. Nobody had ever seen into the kitchen of The Continental and no one had ever seen Tracy cook. She employed no help; she never had. She could manage the place well enough on her own and so what if sometimes some people were left waiting for their meals? They never complained: they knew it would be worth it in the end.

Tom was left waiting for his apple tart for fifteen long minutes. He thought that maybe it was the fresh air, or maybe it was the fact that he hadn't eaten anything since a bowl of cereal at breakfast time, but he had never been more aware of his sense of smell, or his appreciation of food. Sitting at the back of the café, at the table furthest from the door, he was enveloped in second-hand air. Air that was all warm from use and fragrant with food. Every breath Tom took separated into its different components and worked on his ever-growing hunger.

He could smell goat's cheese melting over sweet red peppers, and whole soft green olives, and eggs frying in deep golden butter, and freshly cracked black pepper, and chives, and dill, and the perfume of Earl Grey tea, and the tang of lemon, and the green freshness of mint, and the clawing, earthiness of roast lamb. To take his mind off his own hunger he started to look around him, to see what the other diners were eating. He was certain that his nose was right, that someone would be eating a roast, another a quiche, another a delicate afternoon tea but, although Tom tried, he couldn't recognise what was smeared over every-one's plate or what dripped from everyone's sauce- soaked bread and so he gave up and instead started to look at the people themselves.

There were twelve people besides him in that enclosed

space but there was no conversation. The occasional murmur or request but nothing more – there was no room for anything more. Tom started by casually glancing around him but he finished by staring. Everyone was too engrossed with their plates to notice him looking, and so he looked on, fascinated. He had never seen a gathering so devoted to food. Everyone ate deliberately, as if in slow motion, sucking and chewing, working their tongues over and under their lips, savouring every crumb and every drop before swallowing and then, as soon as they had done that, they ladled another forkful into their mouths. It wasn't until their plates were wiped clean that they shifted their attention on to each other, but by then Tom's apple tart had arrived and so he was in no position to notice. He didn't even notice them taking their turn to stare at him.

CHAPTER 3

Tracy Sheehy had a certain way of serving her food, not quite with a flourish, she was too confident of her cooking to have to stoop to theatrics, but with pride. She held her plates high, set them before her customers with precision and responded angrily to their immediate reactions. Her food was always simply displayed – she had no respect for presentation just for presentation's sake.

"You can fool the eye easy enough but sure what's the point of doing that when it's the stomach you want to impress?" she would ask whoever was brave enough to compliment her cooking before tasting it.

"Looks lovely!" She would snort at them. "Do you want it framed?"

And so her regular customers often appeared rude to outsiders. They would accept their plates, piled high with colour and fragrances, with barely a nod to the cook and, in many cases, this led to the passing trade being more vocal in their praise to make up for what they perceived to be the local diners' lack of appreciation.

"This smells gorgeous," they would say as soon as their plate was placed before them.

"This looks wonderful."

"Oh, doesn't this look just great?"

And Tracy would bite them down to size before storming off, back to her kitchen, swinging the door shut with a clang behind her.

This had been going on for so long that it was a part of The Continental's tradition, a bit of harmless fun at the tourists' expense, but still something worth looking out for. And so everybody in The Continental was looking out for Tom's reaction to his apple tart.

They saw him watch it pass along the bar, saw him follow Tracy's movements as she sprinkled some sugar over the pastry and stirred a spoon of chocolate into the coffee, before walking on through her hatch and slowly down the length of the room. She kept her eyes fixed on Tom's as she moved towards him, swinging her hips around chairs and tables, holding her shoulders back and her chest out. She carried his coffee high in one hand and the plate, with his apple tart on it, high in the other, and she smiled when she noticed his adam's apple move rapidly up and down his thin, pale neck. His throat was constricting with hunger and, as Tracy swung into position beside him, she could sense that he was becoming confused as to what it was he was hungering after.

"Your coffee," she said, as if she was reminding him, and he nodded. "Yes," he said. "My coffee." As if he had just remembered.

Tracy set the cup down in front of him and Tom gasped. The coffee was swirled through with a double helix of cream and milk chocolate that slowly began to fray at the edges, melting into the thick, black liquid that supported it. Tom watched it, fascinated. He could almost smell the bitter-sharp coffee being softened and sweetened and he knew to wait before touching it. It wouldn't be ready until it had settled.

"And your apple tart," Tracy said while Tom was still staring into his cup. "Oh, yes," he said and pulled back to allow her room to set the plate before him. This time he did more than gasp. "Oh, my goodness!" he said. "This looks amazing!" And the low murmur that had been buzzing around the café was immediately silenced. Tom was silent too, staring down at his plate, lost in appreciation. And there was a lot to appreciate.

The crust of the tart was light golden, thin at the edge and flaking on top, bursting through in parts with bubbles of thick, red syrup. A dusting of fine white sugar lay over the apple-shaped patch of soft, dark sugar that had been caramelised to a deep, almost black, brown, and then there were the apples. Barely holding on to their wedge shapes, they were melting into each other. The flesh of the fruit was relaxed and oozed steaming white and pale-pink streams of juice that spread across the plate and licked at the base of the cream. The cream was whipped stiff and yellow; it smelled of mint and lemon and wild summer fruits and was topped by an intricate lattice of curled chocolate.

Tom looked up eventually, noticing that Tracy was still there; everybody else had noticed that too. They all assumed that she was thinking of a smarter than usual put-down, but then why was she smiling?

"It looks almost too good to eat," Tom said and then repeated "almost" in an exaggerated tone, as a joke. The café waited but all Tracy said was, "There's nothing looks that good."

"Well, then I'll just have to eat everything," Tom answered and Tracy hit him gently with her cloth as if he had said something cheeky. He had started eating by then though and so was beyond paying her any more attention. But even so, she hovered close for another minute or two and, when she did finally walk away, she was still smiling.

Jason Last, sitting at the next table, watched her pass. She walked smartly through the café and on out to her kitchen without as much as a glance at him, and he wasn't used to that. He didn't join in with the whispers of surprise and conjecture that sprang up as soon as Tracy was deemed out of earshot; instead he turned a little in his chair, pushed his empty plate to one side, and stared over at the thin young man in the corner.

Tom ate. Without being aware of it he ate deliberately, in slow motion, sucking and chewing, working his tongue over and around his lips, savouring every crumb, every drop before swallowing. At intervals he dropped his fork and turned his attention to his coffee, but even then he didn't raise his head, he didn't notice the café thin out and he didn't feel the intensity of Jason Last's glare.

Poor Jason couldn't work it out. He had seen Tracy make a fool of herself before. He had grown up with her and so had witnessed, or had heard about, all her romantic affairs. They usually involved some outlandishly handsome tourist covered over in fine blonde hairs and thick bulging muscles, or else some city type, clean shaven, sweet smelling and suited, and they were usually bounded by the first round of drinks and a free breakfast. Jason sensed that this was different, this young man wasn't Tracy's type and coy little flicks with a cloth wasn't Tracy's way. Jason just couldn't work it out and he was worried.

He was an ironmonger by trade; he owned a small hardware shop just a few doors down. All he had ever dealt with was the finished product and so he couldn't see what Tracy saw in young Tom Hamilton. All he saw was the raw material and that didn't seem to be enough: a curly head of dark hair grown too long and wild, a pale hollowed-out face still flushed pink with youth, eyes too close to a nose that was too large, and a mouth that was screwed tight over his food now but when he spoke or smiled it seemed to run all over his face. The boy might be charming but Jason couldn't see anything more in him, and that was why he was worried: he liked to know what he was up against.

Tom ate. He just sat and ate and for that length of time the world receded. When he had finished, when he finally looked up from his plate, he felt completely refreshed, as if he had just woken up after a good, deep sleep and, just as if he had been asleep, it took him a moment to place himself, to adjust to this suddenly sharp reality. He looked around him slowly, yawning and arching his back. The café had thinned out since he had started eating, and that seemed strange to him; he felt as if he had lost some time. He hadn't noticed any movements, hadn't heard the door or seen anyone go, but they had gone.

The café was empty now except for three men. It was nearly five o'clock and, although Tracy wasn't rude enough to actually close between four and six, it was assumed that she would not be taking orders during that time. For those two hours she was very rarely even seen on the floor, but she could be heard clattering around her kitchen, preparing for the evening. The local people who remained, finishing their late lunches, knew to leave their money behind them when they went, and any new customers were watched by Jason who, in return for as much coffee as he could drink and a generous slice of whatever cake Tracy thought he could use, sat in The Continental every afternoon between four and six looking over some paper-work or else just looking over his paper. If anyone wanted anything from his shop during that time they knew where to find him.

Jason was waiting for Tom when the young man finally reached for his jacket and started rumbling for money.

"You can settle up with me," he said, and though he

tried to sound disinterested, his voice grated over the words giving them more of an edge than he had intended. Tom immediately reacted to the older man's tone.

"Why?" he asked in that voice that always irritated his father. "You own this place?"

The older man stood up. Moved to his feet slowly and then just stayed where he was, allowing his size settle the argument. He was a big man, built to a scale that dwarfed his dainty surroundings. Tom, sitting down, had to lean his head right back to maintain eye contact, but he didn't do that for too long. Jason pulled his mouth taut and his pale blue eyes narrowed. His bushy golden eyebrows closed over the bridge of his nose and, as he moved his head forward slightly, a lock of light red hair fell across his forehead. Tom looked away; he understood that his question had been answered, that he had overstepped the mark by asking it, and so he backed down completely.

"How much do I owe you then?"

Jason moved around his table and slowly stepped up to Tom. He rested his two huge hands palms down on Tom's table and stayed there, staring at the boy. He no longer knew what the argument was, but he knew that he didn't want to let go of it yet.

Tom, pressed back into his chair, tried smiling, and then tried looking around the bulk that was blocking his view of the rest of the café, but finally he had to stare straight into that angry face that was looming too close. So close that Tom could see individual hairs, open pores, cracked lips, and he could smell the traces of food and sweat and some kind of detergent.

"What do I owe you then?" Tom asked again, working at keeping his voice level.

"What have you got?" the man growled, leaning forward, and then everything melted into normality. Tom heard a door thud closed and the man stood up straight, extended his hand and laughed.

"I mean, what did you have? Name's Jason Last. I'm just keeping an eye on things for our Tracy here." And, just as he finished speaking, Tracy joined them.

"Everything OK?" she asked and Tom nodded and stood up, eager to leave now that he was finished.

"You going?"

"Yeah," Tom answered but, although Tracy was looking at Tom when she spoke, Jason understood her question to be directed at him. He didn't answer; he just walked away, picking up his jacket as he passed his table. Tracy didn't even wait until he was out of earshot.

"Don't you worry about him," she told Tom. "It's just his way, marking his territory. If he was a cat he'd have sprayed you but he's an ape so he's just shown you his stupidity." Tom laughed, relieved. "Sit yourself back down there," Tracy continued. "And I'll fetch you another coffee, one for the road, to settle your nerves and then you can decide what you're up to. Sure if the natives prove friendly perhaps you'll stay on to your dinner." And Tom nodded and sat right back down.

Joe Hardy and Dean Kelly, the two other men in the café, hunched lower over their game of chess as Tracy walked past them. Three or four afternoons a week they played chess in The Continental and they had never seen Jason walk out, nor had they ever seen Tracy out on the floor after half past four. This was high drama and they were curling up with the excitement of it all.

27

CHAPTER 4

Jason Last had his eye on Tracy. Since they were kids together he had kept his eye on her, but she had always looked beyond him. Her sights had always been set on the whole world, while his world had always been set on Tracy.

When they were children Tracy had always dreamed of travelling. She used to collect maps, and would open them out on her bedroom floor and trace the lines of the roads that ran across them with her finger, imagining that she was walking them. Sometimes she used to take Jason with her on these journeys. He remembered leaning over the edge of her bed, staring at her finger inching its way over those coloured sheets of paper, and he would listen and listen and sometimes catch enough of her enthusiasm to understand it, but he never caught enough to share in it.

Tracy would lose herself totally in her imaginary world. She would talk her way around fantastical cities populated with fairy-tale characters caught in eternal, legendary conflicts. Or through wild forests filled with noises, night fears and fierce mythical creatures. Or over ice-blue mountains that stretched so high their summits were always lost in darkness. She explained how real maps needn't be bound by geographical details, how they should primarily be portraits of the land. How real cartographers should be able to catch a cultural expression as well as a factual likeness.

"It's an art," she said. "Travel is a big, scary art form and before modern transport and photography fecked it all up everyone knew that. Everyone knew that there be monsters!" And she would fling her arms up, bare her teeth and lunge for Jason.

As they grew up Jason waited and waited for Tracy to leave Seeforge, but she never did. She said that there were always reasons for her to stay but, it seemed to Jason, those same reasons could have been used to go. First her mother died, then her father drank and the weight of The Continental fell on to Tracy's shoulders when she was still just fifteen. Her father died when she was eighteen and she felt it her duty to continue the family tradition that, by that stage, was what The Continental had grown into.

And as for holidays, there was never time. Never anyone to run the place, never a good time to close up for a week, never enough money, never enough energy, no one to go with, and on and on. And so Tracy never left Seeforge. In all of her thirty-eight years she had never travelled more than fifty miles from her kitchen.

Jason used to think that perhaps it was because she had never travelled that Tracy was so easily impressed with everything, and everyone, that wasn't from Seeforge. But lately he was beginning to think that it was the other way around. Maybe Tracy didn't travel because she knew that she was too impressed by everyone she had never met, and everything she had never seen. Maybe she still believed that there were dragons, and kings, and wizards in the world. Maybe she didn't want the world to prove her wrong.

Jason knew that most people would see this as cowardice, but he thought it was brave. He thought it was brave to limit your life in order that you could preserve your dream. He believed that his bachelorhood was an act of bravery. That his love for Tracy was a daily proof of his courage. But even he knew that there was nothing noble in being called an ape.

That Wednesday afternoon Melissa Taylor watched Jason stride down Hephaition Way, anger driving his steps wide. She saw him push the door to his shop open and she watched how the door snapped back shut immediately after him. From across the road, from two doors down and from behind her bedroom window she could almost hear the slam. Then she leaned forward a little and she watched Tom finish his second cup of coffee, but then that's what Melissa Taylor did. She watched.

Downstairs her mother was busy. Even though it was early closing Jean Taylor was working hard. That's what she did; it was what she always had done and it had worn her thin and wretched. Drudgery had long since honed her expression into sharp, clear lines and then it had attacked her spirit. Once Jean believed that the world had turned into a mean place she turned on her world, and then she turned in on herself. She took to muttering to herself. In the little back room that she used as a workshop she sat hunched over her table, working her mouth over pins and bitterness.

"... and I wouldn't mind but they don't pay a penny in taxes and them milking the system for every bit ..."

"... and she won't thank me for it let alone pay me for it, you can be sure of that, and her with more money than sense ..."

"... and that selfish lump upstairs again. When I think what I had to be doing at her age ..."

"Melissa, I could do with a hand!" Jean called out crossly. Melissa heard the call and sighed heavily before she slowly responded. She was bored and lonely but she hated working with her mother and usually tried to avoid spending time with her.

Jean Taylor, as her name suggested, was a dressmaker and owned a little business almost directly across from The Continental. For generations her family had been dressmakers and for generations they had lived in Seeforge. The coincidence between the trade and the name was so great that people said that the trade came first, that the Taylors had been named for their talent, but Jean never liked to hear that. She didn't like the thought of being descended from some nameless tribe. It seemed indecent to her; it smacked of illegitimacy, and illegitimacy was too personal a topic for Jean Taylor to ever want to discuss. It was common knowledge that, for generations, the Taylor women had managed to keep their name because none of them had ever managed to keep a man. But still, Jean reasoned, that didn't mean that you had to go around talking about it. There were certain things that people should be allowed forget about and Jean was still hopeful that, in time, they would forget about her one disgrace.

And so she always maintained that the name Taylor was just a coincidence. That the Taylor women were dressmakers because it was one of the few trades available to them, and because it could be easily passed from mother to daughter. But the people she told knew that there had to be more to it than that because the Taylors weren't just dressmakers: they were artists. It was obvious to everyone who had ever owned one of their creations that the Taylors were dressmakers by vocation rather than necessity, and so it seemed logical to claim that the trade came first. The people who once said this to Jean had meant it as a compliment but they soon learned that she didn't appreciate it as such, and so they stopped saying it, and then they stopped thinking it because, although Jean still produced quality clothes, that was all she did.

When she was younger, before her mother had died and before Melissa started swelling up inside her, Jean had produced pieces of magic. Back then she had been pretty and had laughed a lot. She had gone to school with Tracy Sheehy and Jason Last and, although she had never been friends with Tracy, she had gone out with Jason for almost one full year, and that was a long time back then.

As soon as she had left school Jean started working with her mother. She always knew that that was what she would do, that that was what the women in her family had done for as long as any of them could remember, and she loved it. She loved her mother, and Jason, and the way her legs looked in summer skirts, and the way her hair fell softly into big, fat, natural curls, and the way her needle could run along a length of material shaping it into something more than its parts. Back then Jean Taylor understood the power of clothes. She knew which fabrics suited which cut, and which cut could influence which occasion.

Cotton, for instance, was suited to purity, to honesty, to a day's work in the fields or to a young woman's summer best and silk was, more often than not, associated with decadence, with seduction and false impressions. But still Jean liked working with silk. She wasn't there to judge her creations, or her commissions, her job was just to create without question. She liked to know what she was creating though. She liked to know if she was working on just one more frock for just one more dance, or the one frock for the very first dance. There was a difference. Jean never told anyone this, not even her mother, though she suspected that her mother already knew, but you had to sew a dress up with something more than thread if it was to properly suit its purpose.

Another dress, for just another occasion, had to combat its wearer's apathy; it had to be all weaved through with originality and enthusiasm. Whereas a first dress had to be

32

whispered through with wishes and hopes. Even if these two dresses followed the exact same pattern and were cut from the exact same cloth they would still have to be very different creations if they were to succeed.

And, for a while, all of Jean's clothes did succeed; they only started failing when life started failing Jean.

First her mother died suddenly, leaving her alone and so deeply hurt that she couldn't stop crying. For weeks tears ran down her face continuously, dripping on to her work, turning everything she sewed into mourning weeds, curtaining her world in misery. She had broken up with Jason a few months earlier but, because he was still fond of her, and because he felt guilty about leaving her in the first place, he offered her his companionship and she finally dried her eyes on his thick, linen-clad shoulder.

Jean had never understood why herself and Jason had broken up. She remembered him talking about commitment and youth, about having to know yourself before you could love someone else, about having to set people free, about giving them the space they needed to find themselves. She had listened to everything Jason had said and she had agreed with him, and then they were broken up. But that was OK. Jean knew that they were too young to marry or settle down yet, but she never stopped believing in their wedding and so she was quick to misinterpret Jason's shoulder for his heart. Eventually she forced him to be honest with her; eventually Jason had to hold Jean away from him as he spelled it out.

"It's not you," he said. "It was never you. I love Tracy and I always will. I was never going to marry you, never, and I never will. I don't love you."

"Tracy!" Jean spat back at him.

"Tracy," she repeated to herself long after he had gone.

Poor Jean just couldn't believe it. Tracy, with her lank

hair and her unsociable habits, had never been either pretty or popular. But it wasn't just that: it was the name Sheehy that really galled the recently orphaned Jean.

Jean's mother had told her all about the Sheehys. About how they had stolen the site of The Continental from the Taylors and how the Taylors had set up shop just across the road to keep an eye on their property and to always remind the Sheehys of their wrongdoing. Jean's mother would whisper this much to her daughter, the pair of them peeking through their blinds watching the lights and life across the road, biding their time. And for a long time Jean didn't question her mother but, as soon as she started to, the gaps in her mother's story stretched wide enough to swallow up any facts that may have once supported it.

"When did we own The Continental, Mammy?"

"Years and years ago."

"And when did we lose it?"

"Ages ago."

"Who lost it?"

"One of your ancestors."

"How?"

"Through misadventure."

And that was all Jean got, and that was no story at all. So, as Jean grew up, she forgot about the reasons why she shouldn't have anything to do with Tracy – she even ate at The Continental when her mother wasn't looking. But now, once she realised that Tracy owed her a husband, she remembered that she owed her a premises as well and so, although she still made Tracy's clothes, she stopped eating her food.

For a while after Jason finally left her, Jean closed herself away, limiting her reality to her own wretchedness. She took her orders over the phone and, from behind her closed shopfront, she sat and planned, working through her days, stitching away, making tight, sculptured garments that bristled with angry potential; shirts with crisp, sharp collars and dresses with tight bodices and firm shoulder pads. It was during this time that she met Melissa's father.

No one ever knew who he was. Jean never referred to him, never called him into being in conversation or confession. He was no one and that was all Jean would ever tell Melissa.

"No one," she would snap crossly. "A ne'er do well. A nobody. None of your business."

As soon as Melissa reached any understanding she assumed that her mother had good reason to refer to her father with such violence. Once she had asked her mother about this. One afternoon she had tentatively reached for her mother, while they were both busy in their dull workroom, just before the lights were turned on for the evening.

"Mammy," she whispered, forcing the words out through her tightly held breath. "Mammy, were you raped?"

Jean had reacted violently. She hit out, landing her hand hard across her daughter's head.

"What a dirty question!" she had shouted. "Dirty! Dirty girl!" And then she had cried. Cried for the question she had forced her daughter to ask and cried for her own reaction. Later she managed to convince Melissa that she hadn't been raped, that she had just been stupid. That she wasn't angry with the man, that she was just angry with herself. But she never fully explained the real reason for her shame – no one ever knew that except Jason.

The truth was that Jean had developed a plan. Locked inside her grief, hiding in the gloom of her workroom, she had decided on what to do and, although she blamed her behaviour on loneliness and a broken heart, she knew it had more to do with anger and hurt pride, because hers was a nasty little plan bred out of mean motives.

One night she had dressed herself up a little and took the bus to the neighbouring port town. After that it was easy and, for a while, even enjoyable. There were a lot of compliments, a lot of drink and a lot of men – all Jean had to do was choose the most palatable of them. And then came the sordid part; the grit of the sand digging into her buttocks, the smell of whiskey and sweat, the grunts, the way he called her Jane. But Jean never allowed herself dwell on those aspects of the affair for too long; even at the time she had distanced herself from it.

Even at the time she had superimposed Jason's head on those strange shoulders, had dropped Jason's words into that ugly mouth, had rounded out the moon and had brushed up the stars. She had even added some rose petals, a clear head and a glass of sweet, sparkling wine. Later, at home, she added her own bed and all sorts of whispered endearments. By the time she rang Jason up she had almost convinced herself of her version of conception: now all she had to do was involve Jason in her interpretation of reality, and she was confident that she could do that. After all she was pretty, and he was a young man, and neither love nor commitment need ever be mentioned until duty was called into question. And so Jean dressed herself in plain cotton, in flat shoes and thick curls, in wide eyes and sweet dependence, and then she called Jason and asked him to come over.

"Just as friends," she said. "I miss you. No one is rich enough to lose a friend, not even you," she whispered, and so he came, but he didn't touch her. And after two months of casual calls and no contact Jean began to panic; she was losing time and so she launched an offensive that drove Jason out of her house for good.

"I told you," he shouted at her. "I want nothing to do with you like that."

And so it had all been for nothing. Jason had finally lost all respect for Jean and, once he saw her swell up and realised what she had been doing, he lost all pity for her as well, and Jean, locked inside her pregnancy, finally lost herself.

First she tried to lose the baby. She drank cups and cups of sage tea, she took hot baths and chewed sloe berries and, finally, she went swimming in the curve of the See that was known locally as the Dell. It was said that if a pregnant woman swam there her baby would drown. It was said that the faint trace of salt that washed through the See up to that point came from the tears of those lost souls. But as Jean dived through the water all she felt was the force of the life within her; she knew her baby wasn't drowning and, just for a few moments, she wondered if she might. She wondered if she wanted to. Lying on her back, floating on the reflection of a clear night sky, she felt very close to death. But not close enough. She got out, slipping on the muddy bank, dried herself off and went home.

She still sewed but only because she had to now. She hated it. It drained her eyes, stiffened her back and grew more and more awkward as she had to stretch her arms over the huge bulk of her belly. She hated most things now. She hated the town that filled her world and kept her shackled to its poverty. She hated that she had no capital to work with, and that if she charged too much for her commissioned pieces she wouldn't be paid. She hated that her clients kept her talent limited to cheap materials and provincial social occasions. She hated her clients and, when the time came, she hated the sex of her child. She had been hoping for a son. She believed that a man, no matter what his relationship to her, would eventually rescue her but that she would always be responsible for a daughter.

And she hated Tracy Sheehy, and The Continental, and she remembered all her mother's stories and embellished them for her own daughter, but Melissa never listened. Melissa never seemed to listen to anything; the world just seemed to bounce off of her.

CHAPTER 5

Jean's version of the past rounded all her mother's vague
accusations into a package that implicated Tracy's more
immediate ancestors. Jean claimed that it was Tracy's
grandparents who had initially done the Taylors out of some
settlement, that Tracy was all too aware of this and that as
soon as she, Jean, was able to afford legal representation she
was going to have the whole mess looked into. Melissa just
nodded; she didn't listen and she didn't question and so Jean
never had to defend her position. Soon she found that she
didn't have to look beyond it, that she believed it herself.

"It was that Tracy's grandfather who started up The
Continental, out of what I'd like to know?" Jean whispered
close to Melissa. It was an old question and one that Melissa
had long since stopped listening to. She was sitting opposite
her mother, in front of a thick spread of fabric, and was
working on some girl's going-away suit while her mother
was working on the bridesmaids' dresses.

"Out of someone else's hard work I'd say." Jean answered
her own question and, although Melissa and everyone else
knew that the Sheehy's had cooked food on the site of The
Continental long before the café was opened, Melissa didn't
remind her mother of this: there was no point.

"There's them that say that the sins of the father

shouldn't be taken out on the child and I'm all for that but there are times when, if the sins of the father can be atoned for by his family, they should be. There's some say that to live off the fat of a sin is a sin in itself."

And Melissa flinched seeing the words "sin" and "atoned" being embedded into what should be such happy dresses. This was why Melissa hated working with her mother; she loved sewing so much it cut her to see how her mother worked her needle and thread through other people's dreams. Because Melissa understood more about clothes than her mother ever had. She understood that they were all there was. She hadn't found the words yet but she knew that clothes were every bit as important as religion and as flesh. She knew that they housed our bodies just as our bodies housed our spirits but that they could be used to express the spirit – they could be used to free us from the awkward, sick, frail lumps of mortality that were allotted to us.

Melissa sensed all this without ever being able to express it, but she worked her wonder into everything she made. Everything she created reflected personality and hope; she managed to catch something vibrant in even the smallest garments, the least consequential ones. She was always aiming at the spirit, trying to wrap it up in the material, and sometimes she managed to do just that.

Sometimes she managed to curl a skirt just over the ankles in a sweep that perfectly described a shy flirtation. Sometimes she fixed a collar just so high under a chin that it caused its wearer to raise his gaze and look his world straight in the eye. Sometimes she cut a bodice just tight enough to remind some matron of her life as a girl. And everything she sewed she sewed in stitches that spelled out what she hoped her work would help achieve.

Melissa had met the lady whose going-away suit she was working on now three or four times and had liked her. She had liked her confidence in her future, her optimism that marked her with a deep, continuous smile. Jean said that she was going foolishly into marriage.

"She doesn't know what she's in for at all if she goes up the aisle with that stupid grin still on her face."

But Melissa liked her and stitched every blessing she could into the seam of her skirt. "Happiness" she wrote with her needle, "health", "continuing love", "comfort", "companion-ship", and there was her mother sinking "sin" into the dresses that were going to be up there on the altar. That was why Melissa didn't like working with her mother. That and her mother's constant moan against life, and the workroom itself.

It was a dark room anyway but its clutter highlighted its sense of gloom. Bales of material blocked the one small back window. The length of the room was shortened by a long worktable that barely fitted into the space and the one bare bulb, that dangled overhead, just served to illuminate all this dinginess without ever brightening it up.

The room in front, the one that opened on to the street, was brighter and cheerier. Melissa could never understand why her mother used it for fittings and not the smaller, more private, back room. She always thought that it would be nice to work out there, separate from her mother, at her own table, facing out on to the street, watching it pass through its day, instead of being cooped up away from it all. At times it seemed to Melissa as if her mother was ashamed of more than her illegitimate daughter: at times it seemed as if she was ashamed of herself and her work as well.

"... and her always so late to pay and not just to me. Oh no, she owes to everyone, running that business into the ground she is." Jean was still talking about Tracy Sheehy, still working her bitterness around the pins she held in her mouth and deep into the fabric of the dresses she was snarling up with too many small, tight stitches. "There's no good comes from greed. No good can ever come from any sin and that's what she's yet to learn."

Melissa curved her needle around the "t" of "respect"and sat back for a moment trying to work out what the opposite of sin could be; just then Jean looked up from her work.

"Finished already?" she snapped, although she knew that Melissa couldn't be more than halfway through,

"No, no not yet." And Melissa returned to her work, bowing her head low over it. "Grace", she thought to herself. "Grace" would do as an antidote to sin. Jean sighed heavily to show her frustration, but she got no response. She was used to that; she was well used to no conversation, and to sullen looks, and to awkwardness, and to social ineptness, but being used to it never made it any easier to live with.

"Sit up straight," Jean ordered and Melissa automatically moved her shoulders back. "For God's sake child can you not act a bit more ladylike? If your grandmother could see you now and she was such a lady. Take your hair out of your eyes at least," and Melissa half-heartedly pushed her heavy hair to one side, but it didn't help. Jean returned to her own work, defeated. She had tried everything and nothing ever worked.

"No, no good can ever come from any sin," she repeated to herself, finding her way back to the comfort of her familiar complaint before continuing with it.

If Jean saw the connection between her logic and her daughter she never admitted it. Although she frequently acknowledged them, she never implicated herself in Melissa's failures. She always said that she couldn't understand how they had come about. She couldn't understand how her daughter had grown so large, why she had no friends, why she glowed red and damp all the time and why she was clumsy with absolutely everything except needles. Jean didn't accept Melissa's talent at dressmaking as anything other than her birthright, and so she looked beyond it for signs of her daughter's brilliance and was continually disappointed.

Because, to women like Jean, Melissa was a disappointment. She had been quite a charming child, smart and sweet, with dimpled cheeks and thick black curls. But then, around the time when Melissa turned twelve, a horrible thing happened to her or, to be more precise, a beautiful thing failed to happen.

While her friends grew little roundy breasts, long midriffs and brittle, gangly limbs, Melissa clung tight to her childish shape. Her flat chest sloped into the swell of her belly, her knees and elbows stayed in their folds of flesh, her thighs rubbed together when she walked, a light dusting of hair, clustering in places into darker, denser patches, appeared along the length of her limbs and she began to sweat. Wherever flesh met flesh she sweated, whenever the temperature rose to bearable she sweated, whenever a social occasion pounced she sweated. Her mother said, "Perspire. You perspire." But perspire didn't come close to describing what Melissa's body did, and Jean knew that every bit as well as Melissa did.

Around the time when Melissa turned twelve it seemed to her as if her world turned against her, and she wasn't prepared for that. Suddenly her academic achievements meant nothing, suddenly her charm stopped working and suddenly her best friend, Louise Hardy, failed her.

At one time and for years Melissa and Louise had been best friends. All through dolls and make-believe they had been inseparable but, at the first sign of adulthood, Louise had joined forces against her friend, slipping into that larger social pool that included boys, and dances, and tight, body-hugging fashions. A place where Melissa couldn't follow. At first though she did try to fit in with everyone else. She tried to glance at the boys and giggle with the girls, but soon it became apparent that she just couldn't maintain that existence. Soon, in various subtle ways, it was made obvious to her that she was too different to be tolerated. Her peers were never intentionally cruel towards her, though. They never bullied her – they just presumed upon her failure and, in doing so, ensured that Melissa achieved it.

One such instance was during a gym class way back when Melissa still enjoyed games. It was decided that they were to play leapfrog and Melissa, who had never played before, was as eager as anyone else to give it a try. Mags, one of the smaller girls, was made stand in the middle of the hall, bent over with her hands resting on her knees, and one by one the rest of the girls in Melissa's class all flew over the crouching girl, spreading their legs wide, squealing with joy and landing in a blurr of gracefully flailing limbs.

When Melissa's turn came she ran forward, just as she had seen all the others do, confidently anticipating that short flight that would end with a laugh and a slight stumbling as her legs hit the ground. And so she ran with her arms outstretched, placed them flat on Mags' shoulders and trusted in her body to glide above and beyond. It didn't happen. Her arms had to tighten and strain to drag the sudden weight of herself forward. Her hands turned claw like, grasping Mags' shoulders and pushing them down. For a brief moment Melissa sat astride Mags and then she lay sprawled on top of her on the ground.

It was funny, of course it was funny – even the gym teacher had laughed after she had first checked that Mags was all right – and so Melissa had laughed along with everyone else before taking her place at the end of the long line of girls. On their teacher's signal they set off again. All flying through the air, all light and jangly collapsing onto the floor before running, head forward with enthusiasm, to the end of the queue. Girl after girl jumped clear and then it was Melissa's turn again. She was nervous about her jump now but she was also determined. She ran as fast as she could towards Mags – she was guessing that speed would be an asset when trying to leave the ground.

Now Mags was a lovely little girl. She had a wide round face with dimples in her cheeks and a cute little birthmark on her chin that made her look as if she had just eaten chocolate. All the girls liked Mags and not just because of her dimples but because she made them laugh. And she was planning on making them laugh again. When she saw Melissa come thundering towards her she sprang up, gave a pretend yelp of terror and ran straight towards the open door at the other end of the room squealing, "Help! Help! She's after me!"

Everyone laughed. Melissa could see their open, jiggling mouths as she ran past. She knew it was a joke. She knew that she should stop running and she was trying to – it was just that she had picked up such momentum she couldn't quite manage it. Eventually Mags stopped and Melissa stopped and the gym teacher put Melissa in the middle of the hall. She was never given another chance to try to leap-frog. Instead, for the rest of the class, she was made feel all the feathery fingers spread lightly on her shoulders and was made watch all the delightfully jumbly limbs bounce down in front of her. That evening, when she went home, she wrote "light, fast, delicate" into the hem of her gym shorts.

It took maybe a year of being subjected to that kind of good-natured torture before Melissa stopped trying. She took to expecting a little less out of life and to staying home most afternoons and evenings. She didn't mind too much. She found it much easier to watch this strange world that excluded her, rather than have to involve herself in it. She began reading and she loved it. The Taylor house was filled with generations of women's fiction; it took Melissa years to wade through everything. And she also liked television, she liked the view from her bedroom window that allowed her watch everything that went on in The Continental, and she loved sewing.

She helped her mother a lot and, when she was finished doing that, she worked on her own clothes.

She tried very hard to fashion her spirit into the reams of cloth it took to cover her body. She sewed her wishes into her seams and she wished her appearance into something as light and as delicate as she felt her spirit to be. Five years on and she was still trying, still wishing. Nothing Melissa made for herself seemed to work. It seemed that no material, no sweetly sewn stitches, could hide the awkwardness of her bulk, the broadness of her shoulders, the deep flush on her cheeks, the spots that cluttered up her chin and the thick blanket of hair that blurred her edges.

It worried Melissa. At times she thought that maybe all the ugliness that oozed out of her skin was just an out-pouring of what was inside her. She worried that she couldn't fashion her spirit into her clothes because her spirit was just as ugly as her face, and then she would try that little bit harder. She would get up a little earlier in the morning, try a little harder to please her mother, work a little harder around the house, but she knew that none of this would save her because all of these good deeds were motivated by one of the ugliest vices of all, vanity. By the time she was seventeen Melissa was close to believing every-thing she saw in the mirror and everything that lurked behind her mother's sighs, but she still worked late into the night sewing up clothes for herself, working "light" and "sweet" and "beauty" into their seems and hems, always hoping for the right combination.

She was due to leave school soon. Soon she would sit her final exams, and soon she would come home to work beside her mother full time. She was an intelligent girl. She knew that she would do well in her exams and that she was more than capable of going to college but she also knew that that wasn't what the Taylor women did. It wasn't anything that she had ever really thought of doing. Occasionally she did dream of what it would be like to study fashion, to travel and see other styles of dress; old folk costumes heavy with forgotten history, wild tribal wear ripped free of all western intervention, tight Chinese clothes fiercely bound to some ancient laws of etiquette. She knew that there was so much to see, so much to experience, but she also knew that her confidence could not be stretched that far into the world. And so she prepared herself to stay at home with her mother.

Jean sighed again. These days she could hardly keep her breath from continually gushing out in frustration. She couldn't bear her grown daughter's apparent lack of excitement or enthusiasm for life. She couldn't bear to see those shoulders slowly fold forward again. Surely they couldn't sit like this for the next forty years, bending over their work, the one sighing and the other sullenly respectful? Surely there had to be more to life than this?

"And can you not get your arms waxed!" Jean finally barked out into the silence. "For God's sake, child, you look as if you're wearing a woolly jumper."

Melissa looked up at her mother and the expression of hurt in her eyes caught Jean unawares.

"I'll bring you with me the next time I go," she said in a much quieter, kinder voice and Melissa smiled. She didn't want to get waxed, she didn't see the point, but she knew better than to argue.

"So soon we'll be doing this full time," Jean said still using her quiet, girls-together kind of voice. "Soon it'll be you and me working side by side, day by day. What do you think of that?"

"It'll be fine," Melissa answered without raising her head. Jean's enthusiastic smile slipped a little.

"We'll be able to take on a lot more work," she said, struggling to keep the anger out of her voice. "You'll be earning money of your own." There was no reaction from Melissa's bent head. "What'll you do with it?" And this time Jean waited out the silence, demanding an answer. Finally Melissa looked up from her work.

"Save it, I suppose," she said.

"Save it! At your age! Is that all you plan or hope to do?" Melissa shrugged and Jean lost all pretence of composure. "Save and work and work and save! Good God, child, can you not even imagine having a hobby, or a friend come to mention it? Well if you plan to do nothing about it I don't. I'm not having you sit opposite me growing older and duller by the day. I'll fix you up, you wait and see. There must be plenty of things out there to interest a young girl." And just then the street door jangled open and Mavis Bradley called through.

"How de do de, only me! Come to remind you about my cake sale."

Jean smiled at Melissa, "For instance Mavis Bradley is always looking for someone to help her." Melissa reacted to that all right.

"Oh no," she said but her objection hadn't the strength of defiance about it and that annoyed Jean even more. She knew that at Melissa's age she would have fought tooth and nail against the ignominy of being sent to help the spinster of the parish with her good works.

"Oh yes," Jean said and then, with one eye fixed on Melissa, she answered Mavis enthusiastically.

"Come on through," she said, "we're in the back and we were just talking about you."

And that was that. Mavis, complete with headscarf,

bulky tweeds, bunched nylons and gap-toothed smile, bundled on through to the back workroom and settled herself down.

"Talking about me?" she gasped breathlessly. "Couldn't be good because you've set the angels crying, just started raining as I came in. So what was it you were saying?" And, more because she could think of nothing else than out of vindictiveness, Jean told the truth.

"I was saying to Melissa that maybe you could do with some help."

Her words had an immediate and disturbing effect on Mavis. The woman clapped her hands, then clapped Melissa's back, exclaimed that she was delighted that some young person was finally showing an interest in the parish and the poor, that it wasn't often she came across a child as good as Melissa, that of course she needed the help, that there was always so much to be done, that the angels must be crying with joy.

"Take this Sunday now, just for example, and the cake sale, which is what I was popping in to see you about." And she turned to stare directly at Jean. "You'll be there anyway won't you?" Jean nodded. "Good, it's bound to be a great old bash but the work involved! I'm tired just thinking about it. I have to set up the stall, and decorate the sponges, and manage to transport everything carefully while keeping it all fresh, and serve everyone while restocking from the fridge, and don't talk to me about hundreds and thousands and the cream piping."

"I'll be studying this weekend," Melissa said firmly and Jean, who was already sorry to have taken her taunt so far, backed her up.

"That's right," she said to Mavis. "Melissa won't have much time now that her exams are coming up."

"Oh, I won't take up much of her time," Mavis said

brightly, staring down at Jean, determination widening her eyes and pulling her mouth taut.

"Well, maybe best leave it for the time being," Jean said and Mavis, still smiling, agreed.

"For the time being then," she said. "Sure there's always plenty to do to get the doing done, so whenever you're ready to do it it'll be there waiting to be done," she said giggling at Melissa, nudging at her to join in the joke. Melissa politely smiled and Mavis happily took that as a signed and sealed contract and then, after smiling once more around the room and after declining Jean's half-hearted offer of tea, she left.

"Study indeed!" she muttered to herself as she let herself out onto the street. "Offer your services, get the thanks and then back out more like! But then, I suppose, as they say, a spit in your whistle is better than a spit in the wind." She said that out loud to a passing child as she unlocked her bicycle and settled herself astride it.

She took the time to cycle slowly past the long plate window of The Continental and, although she saw that there were few people in there, she saw no sign of Tracy and knew better than to disturb her when she was in her kitchen. Tracy's involvement in Sunday's cake sale would have to be organised at some later stage.

CHAPTER 6

After his second cup of coffee in The Continental Tom lost the urge to leave; instead he sat back in his chair and abandoned himself to the comfort of his surroundings.

It was still bright outside but the evening was coming, drawing the night down with it. You could feel it in the movement of the wind, in the way the birds circled and cried, in the way the breeze lay heavy on the remains of the day, dragging scraps of paper through the streets, listlessly rattling the looser shutters and gates. And Tom felt that same wind lay him low. He was tired, and warm, and far too easy to move, so he just stayed still, leaning back in his chair, smiling.

The Continental seemed to soften with the dying light;something about its thick red walls licked through with pink reminded Tom of flames. He watched them, tilted back in his chair, through half-closed, heavy lids; he watched those licks of pink play along the length of the wall in front of him. Shooting up from the honey-varnished floor, lapping over the clean green woodwork, it seemed to Tom as if those flames were cooking the very air he was breathing.

And every breath he took warmed him. The air in the

café seemed to first settle on his memories before spreading from his lungs to settle on his hunger. He was slowly getting hungry, but in a very enjoyable way. For the time being all he wanted to do was anticipate his dinner and remember past meals but the two elderly men, who had, up until now, sat in complete silence, had tired of their game of chess and so Tom's moment was interrupted.

"On holidays then?" one of them called over, reaching around his opponent's head to aim his words directly at Tom.

"No," Tom answered. "No, not really." It was the wrong answer. A simple yes would have explained his presence, but his "no" just invited more curiosity, and Joe Hardy was a curious man. Not a gossip, he left that to the women, but he did admit to being curious.

"You're not from here though, are you?" he asked and Tom shook his head.

"No, no I'm not," he said and then, because he knew something more was expected of him, he added. "But I plan on staying around for a while."

"Staying around for a while, eh?" Joe repeated and Tom uneasily heard the twang of his own, relatively recent accent brush against the words. But the man was smiling and so Tom smiled back and nodded.

"Mind if I join you?" Joe asked and then, without waiting for an answer, he stood up, abandoning the tedium of a game that, after twenty years of playing the same man, always ended in stalemate, and walked over to Tom.

"No, not at all," Tom said shifting forward in his seat.

"Joe Hardy." The old man introduced himself holding out a large, flat hand that squeezed Tom's and dropped it without shaking it. Then he smiled broadly showing a patchy arrangement of teeth.

"Tom," Tom said and smiled back, but uncomfortably.

He was still young enough to feel constrained by his elders and this balding, wizened little man was certainly that.

"And that there," Joe turned and pointed at his friend who was clearing away the chess pieces, "that bald old coot's Dean Kelly. Romeo to his friends."

"Less of the bald," Dean muttered without raising his head.

"Lost his hair when he was no older than you," Joe continued. "Lost it in a card game."

"How did he do that?" Tom asked politely, as Joe obviously expected him to.

"You want to tell your story?" Joe called out, but Dean didn't answer and so Joe continued.

"It all happened way back when we were lads so it must have been – when was it Romeo?"

"Fifty-four" Dean answered, finally raising and turning his head. Tom nodded to him and smiled but got no response. The man wasn't bald, Tom thought, not too bald anyway, not considering his age. Quite thick tufts of white hair still sprouted from above his ears and a smattering covered the dome of his head.

"Ah yes, fifty-four, the summer ..." Joe continued.

"Spring," Dean corrected.

"... Spring of fifty-four. We were both thick-haired youths back then."

"Lovely thick hair I had with a grand, high quiff," Dean elaborated dreamily, a simple smile spreading over his small, wrinkled face.

"Oh, you should have seen it," Joe said, rolling his eyes to heaven. "The pride of the town it was." And Dean, sitting behind his friend, twinkled at the compliment.

"Oh yes, it was a grand quiff," he sighed in happy agreement.

"But ..." Joe said in a suddenly serious voice.

"... I lost it in a card game," Dean continued in exactly the same tone.

It was only then that Tom realised he was being treated to a set piece. He sat back happily, ready to be entertained, and he was. It was a good story.

"It all happened here, at this very table," Joe said, hitting the table in front of Tom slam down with the full force of his spread palm. Tom jumped back a little. "There were four of us there that night: me, Romeo there, old Rose Taylor – she'd sneak into The Continental without her daughter knowing, a few notes stuffed down her chest and a bottle of whiskey stuffed into her bag – oh yes, and of course Bob Sheehy."

"And Bill Last."

"He left early that night."

"It was a weekly game," Dean said as he crossed the room to join his friend at Tom's table. He sat himself down beside Joe, ignoring him, keeping his eyes fixed on Tom. And that was how the men told their story, taking turns to move it along, focusing all their attention on their audience.

"Every Thursday low stakes but serious poker. But low stakes to that lot meant something other to us two. Sure all we had to play with was a taste for the game."

"But usually, between the two of us, we'd win enough to keep afloat."

"We made sure of that all right," and the two men coughed out the same crackled laugh.

"Oh yes indeed boy, we made certain sure of that, and we'd have kept on making sure of it if it weren't for that old hen."

"Old Sheehy's best laying hen she was, with an arse full of eggs on her."

"But she wasn't laying for no breakfast special though, you could tell that by her. That old hen was laying for a family and my but she took it bad when none came her way."

"Like this she was," Joe said standing up suddenly, cocking his elbows behind him and thrusting his head out straight from his shoulders. Dean looked at Tom, and Tom looked at Joe, and Joe started strutting up and down the length of the café. His pale blue eyes were fixed ahead, rounded, small and unblinking, the sinews in his neck were stretched taut and his rough brown skin looked raw and plucked. He was so like an angry hen that Tom thought it would be rude to laugh, and so he didn't, he just listened to what Dean was telling him and watched as Joe acted out the scene.

"I used to wear my hair high and combed forward, a thick golden quiff it was, something to be proud of, and something that had its uses too." And he winked. "Every seasoned card player knows where to look for double dealings but none of those old lads thought to check my hair."

Joe squawked and Tom asked, "Your hair?"

"My hair. Thick enough to hide a few aces and a few kings too. Though I only ever kept the ace of hearts up there. It would be all greased up and ready to fall into my hand at the slightest brush." And Dean demonstrated what he meant by sweeping his hand high over his head. "One flick of the wrist and my hand would be transformed and no one was any the wiser until one night ..." And behind him Joe squawked, cocked his head and fixed his beady eyes on a spot three inches over Dean's head. "... One night old Bob Sheehy's hen found her way into The Continental. Dragging her fat arse behind her she came right up behind me." And Joe, with a little shimmy shuffled that little bit closer. "She had her eye and her heart fixed on my quiff thinking, I suppose, that she had just found herself the world's finest rooster." And behind Dean's chair Joe lowered his eyelashes in a soulful portrayal of chicken love. It was then that Tom started laughing.

"Before I knew anything about it she was on me." Joe fastened his old hand claw-like on Dean's shoulder and Dean leapt to his feet. "I tried battling her off," he said and the two old men started flailing at each other. "But it was no use. She kept close to my head, picking and cooing at my hair." Which was exactly what Joe was doing, nuzzling and nudging at the air over his friend's head. "Until of course she finally pecked out the ace of hearts."

The two men sat down again then, both straight faced, barely breathless from their performance. Tom, still laughing, was about to applaud them but they didn't give him a chance: they weren't finished yet.

"Bob Sheehy renamed her Juliet that very night. And the rest of us renamed lover boy here." Joe said.

"It was a terrible thing," Dean said shaking his head sadly, so sadly that Tom stopped laughing and lowered his hands.

"A terrible thing," Joe agreed.

"It was that Rose Taylor made a tragedy of it all. The men would have taken the ace of hearts in good faith."

"Aye, that they would. They'd have seen the ingenuity in it."

"Aye, but not Rose Taylor, all she saw was the opportunity lost. I never saw that woman without some kind of fabulous hat on her head, and the smallest one she ever wore would have been big enough to hide a whole pack in. But of course she wouldn't admit to that, she had to take the high moral ground," Dean said and Joe nodded, and then there was a short pause before Joe suddenly shrieked in a shrill pantomime voice,

"Have you no pride, man!" Dean didn't even look around at his friend. Still staring at Tom he answered, "Of course I do, woman."

"Well you've lost it tonight," Joe squealed and then ducked under the table.

"Old Rose was a dressmaker," Dean said as if offering some kind of explanation. "She took her trade to heart and carried it about with her. She was never without that big bag of hers and, until that night, I never knew what she had in it besides her whiskey. Well she disappeared under the table for a bit and we all thought she'd maybe fallen asleep – she was a fine drinker but whiskey affects even the best of us – but then she jumped up." And so did Joe. "With a pair of scissors in her hand." Dean cowered back and Joe, miming the action of a shears, descended on him.

"Pride!" he squealed in his pantomime voice. "You'll have none of it after this night."

"And she cut off my quiff."

"And wouldn't give it back," Joe said in his normal voice. "She said a thing lost at cards must be won back at cards."

"And I spent the rest of her life trying to win it back. But sure how could I beat that ol' witch with nowhere to hide my ace?"

"No how," Joe answered definitely and both men sat back in their places. They were both quiet now, both looking at Tom. And then, because he didn't quite know what else to do, Tom laughed. It was the wrong thing to do.

"It was a very sad story," Joe said sternly,

"A man's pride is a serious thing," Dean said and so Tom stopped laughing. "Life doesn't happen so well to a man with no pride. My hair never grew again and so I just watched other men live out what should have been mine. Another man married my wife, lived in my home, worked my job ..."

"Had your children," Joe prompted and Dean nodded and then the chrome door that separated the café from the kitchen thudded closed and the mood was shattered.

"Telling you their story of cock and bull are they?" Tracy

called down the length of The Continental and Tom smiled at the two men facing him and called back. "They're keeping me well entertained."

"As long as they're helping you work up an appetite. I take it you've decided to stay on to be fed," Tracy said. She was closer now.

"Oh yes," Tom said nodding enthusiastically. "Oh yes." Suddenly the air in the room was dense with smells. "For some reason I'm dreaming of roast chicken." And young Tom was delighted when the two older men laughed. His answering smile ran wild over his face, lighting his eyes and flushing his cheeks.

"I've been thinking," Tracy said, low now – she was standing just beside him. "I've been thinking if you haven't made any other arrangements I've got some rooms upstairs."

Tom nodded again. That feeling that had been with him since he had stepped off the train that afternoon settled down and named itself. It was a feeling of warmth, a feeling of home.

CHAPTER 7

"Home" hovered over every meal in The Continental and over every casual conversation overheard. "Home" was just what described Tom's room: plain with cheap pine furnishings, a little bed, clean white sheets, one small window, curtains and coverings and lamps that all almost clashed – just like the bedroom he had left behind in his parents' house. And Tom was still young enough to appreciate the comfort in that. It was a homely, warm little room filled with smells and noises. And it was his. It looked out on the clutter of a busy main street and, downstairs, Tracy cooked, friends met, low music hummed up through the floorboards and Tom watched town's life pass by.

The first night Tom stayed at The Continental Tracy kept close by him. He thought she was just being friendly, easing him into the social life of the place, but everyone else saw that she was marking him. She still served everyone, still cooked and cleaned, cleared tables and generally kept the night moving along, but she managed to do most of this while keeping an eye and an ear on Tom.

The Continental never really worked to a menu. Tracy decided what dishes to cook and then, for the most part, she decided what dishes to serve you. She knew her regulars well enough to do this, and they trusted her enough to let her. So it was only the tourists who were allowed choose what they wanted from Tracy's limited selection, the tourists and the locals she didn't like. It was a great sign of acceptance to be just handed your meal by Tracy and most people had to prove themselves before they would be granted that privilege. But not Tom. That first night the people of Seeforge watched the young stranger being presented with a plate of colours and steam, and nudged each other. They started whispering when they noticed that he had been served a separate dinner to everyone else. That certainly proved something, they said to each other. That and the fact that Jason Last was nowhere to be seen.

Earlier Tracy had shown Tom his room. He had hitched his bag over his shoulder and followed her broad back up the narrow staircase by the café toilets. The stairwell was dark and dusty; it matched the click of his boots perfectly, as did the heavy swing of Tracy's hips. Tom watched Tracy flat-foot herself up the stairs and shook his head. He was a man who favoured style and elegance over the boredom of beauty and so, in aesthetic terms, he was quite difficult to please. He believed that natural beauty just exists and so can't really be respected, but that elegance demands effort and so it earns admiration.

"There's just the one bathroom," Tracy said turning and winking at him. "But it's got a lock so it should do the two of us fine. You're the only one staying at the moment so you got your choice of rooms: you want a big dark back one or a small bright front one?"

Tom took the front one. He took the one overlooking the town, and stood looking down on it while Tracy talked on about towels and laundry.

Tom wasn't listening. He was watching the last glow of the sun glint off the metal shutters opposite, and he was watching a young girl in a red jumper run the length of

Hephaition Way. He had found the vehicle for his one great truth. He would record a town, document a moment in history. It didn't matter how small a moment or how large – what mattered was how honestly he did it. A girl running could be a lifetime's work; this town would be his and he already had his opening story.

"Are you with me at all?" Tracy asked and Tom turned to her.

"You know those two men," he asked. "Joe and Romeo?"

"No one calls Dean Romeo except Joe and, yes, I do know them, a right pair they are too."

"And do you know the story of Dean's hair?"

"Oh yes, we've all been told that story."

"Is it true?"

"Of course. That old Rose Taylor cut the quiff off the poor boy and then kept it. Kept it for the company I'd say."

"For company!"

"Oh yes," Tracy answered. "Once Rose had that quiff she had a card partner every night 'till she died and God love her she needed that much. Her daughter was a mean-minded woman, 'not given to drink'," Tracy mimicked. "'Not given to gambling or smoking or anything that causes the blessed baby Jesus to cry'." And then she laughed, shaking her head, quietly lost in memories. "That Barbara Taylor! Every bit as narrow as the daughter she left across the road. It's a wonder to me how she got herself in trouble in the first place, but I tell you I bet it was a joy to old Rose.

"My, but Rose used to make clothes just for the purpose of inciting that kind of trouble. Trousers that rubbed the men's flesh up fine and shirts that bulged out their muscles. And as for the girls, for years every woman in town had a neck line that dropped almost as low as their nipples. They were fine years." And she laughed again. "Before my time but fine years all the same."

"But the quiff?" Tom asked.

"Ah yes, the quiff. I don't think Rose meant any harm by it. I'm sure she thought Dean would grow another – he was young enough to – but he never did. He had all his pride wrapped up in that hair, you know. It was the only thing he had ever done right and she took it off him. Of course he had no hope in winning it back. Rose never let anyone beat her in cards who wasn't cheating better than her and without his hair Dean had no way of outwitting her. They were still playing poker the day she died. And then that Barbara turned Dean out of the house and wouldn't open the door to him after. Poor Dean, I think he missed old Rose almost as much as his hair. You know Barbara's daughter Jean lives across the road now. I bet she still has that gold quiff hid away somewhere, but she's a sight meaner than her mother ever was. Wouldn't give you the hair off her back that one."

And for some reason Tracy found this so funny she had to sit down heavily on the bed to concentrate more fully on her laughing. Because he couldn't help himself Tom laughed as well.

"I'll tell you what you're laughing at later," Tracy promised before she left. "Come down when you're hollowed out with the hunger. I don't see the point in feeding people who don't need feeding." And she pulled the door closed.

It took about an hour but by then Tom knew he needed feeding. Sitting by his window, looking out over the chest of drawers that would double up as a desk, he had started by trying to capture the movement of the town's people in words, but had ended in just listing adjectives that were related to food.

"Evening bustle", he wrote on the first page of his new pad. "Shuffling gait", "loping strides", "easy stroll, crispy roll", "urgent run, cinnamon bun". He put down his pen and laughed. His room was filled with the sweet breath of newly ripped herbs: basil, lemon balm, sage, garlic, chives. Tom sat back, breathing deeply, feeling his lungs rise to meet each new breath, and below him the people of Seeforge settled into their evening.

Melissa crossed the road awkwardly, a carton of milk in one hand, a too-full bag in the other; her mother, waiting at the door of their house, was calling to her to hurry. Jason Last strode past The Continental looking straight across the road, catching Jean's eye by mistake and then ducking his head. He was going for a drink. Joe and Dean waved over to him from the porch of Hardy's pub, and Tom went down to dinner.

Tom was surprised by how many people were already in The Continental. It was still early and it was only a Wednesday, but then he was too new to the town to really understand what The Continental was. It was said that it marked the exact centre of Seeforge, and maybe it did. In geographic terms maybe "centre" is as good a word for "heart" as any.

"Sit yourself down there," Tracy called over to Tom, nodding at the table he had sat at earlier. The only table that was still free in the place, the only table that offered a view of the whole café and the full length of Hephaition Way. Tom could feel the people looking as he picked his way through them; only a few smiled, the others just watched. They had all seen people being turned away while that one table stayed empty, and here was the reason why. They couldn't understand it, eyes too close to a nose that was too large. They just couldn't understand it. But, from her bedroom window across the road where she was sitting, dreaming over her homework, Melissa understood only too well.

She also understood what Tracy was doing, why she spent the evening circling close to her new guest, why she continually dipped her mouth or ear to his. She was feeding him bits of herself and feeding off whatever he offered her in return.

"You said you were in the mood for a bit of roast chicken," Tracy said as she slid a plate in front of Tom. He had just sat down and was waiting to be given a menu and so he looked up, a bit surprised. Tracy was looking down at him and then, as if to guide him, she slowly lowered her eyes to the plate she had set in front of him. Tom's eyes followed obediently,

"It's exactly what I wanted," he agreed, and it was. It was a plain dinner. A rich, warm roast to welcome him home. Crisp, golden skin and moist, white flesh; bright white potatoes steaming under a garnish of thick yellow butter; deep green vegetables still smelling garden fresh.

"It's the breast," Tracy said. And, although Tom barely acknowledged the fact that she was talking, the people at the neighbouring tables listened carefully. Tracy had never been known to explain her meals to anyone before.

"It's the breast of one of my own birds so I know its worth," she continued. "My birds are here to work and die for me but I never let them know that and so you can always trust my chickens and eggs. It stands to reason, doesn't it, that the flesh that grows around the heart of a happy animal will have to taste good? The gravy is made from the same bird's heart and so that should taste as sweet as a satisfactory life and a meaningful death."

Tom nodded, and because he had started eating, Tracy didn't wait for any answering comment. She left him alone until he had finished but once he had wiped his plate clean she focused all her attention on him. She fed him tastes of various cakes, served him a brandy with his coffee and kept him amused and interested for the full length of the night. She worked around him, stopped by his table whenever she could, winked at him when she was too far from him to talk. She gestured at various customers, grimaced or smiled in their direction purely for Tom's benefit. She was letting him know who to avoid and who to encourage and, whenever she got the chance, she slipped into the chair opposite him, bent her head forward and whispered some detail.

Tom was still sitting at his table when the last people left The Continental that night. He felt warmed, and relaxed, and happy in the knowledge that, no matter how enjoyable his evening had been, it had been productive as well. Tracy had furnished him with all sorts of material for his book.

She had pointed out two affairs, one alcoholic and had told him how one old woman, wrapped in a black shawl, sitting by herself, was still mourning her daughter who had drowned thirty years earlier. She had drowned herself while trying to drown her unborn baby.

She had pointed out various outfits and had explained to Tom how it was easy to date them. The older dresses were made by a young Jean Taylor; the newer ones were made by either Jean or her daughter Melissa. She had told him how most people in Seeforge got their clothes made because the quality of the Taylors' work was so good and their prices were so low, and then she had laughed.

"What I told you before, about the hair off their back?" Tom nodded. "Well people say that those Taylors add a new meaning to 'manmade fibres'." Tom shook his head. "It's said," and Tracy shifted a little further forward in her chair, "that they're covered in hair, that they grow their own shrouds. My grandfather swore that he once saw old Rose Taylor stepping out of her bath – my granddad was a dirty old soul and proud of it – but anyway he said that she looked more like a monkey than a woman."

"Really?" Tom asked and Tracy laughed.

"As real as you want it to be – my granddad was a great man for the stories."

"And Jason Last?" Tom asked "That man who was here earlier."

"A good man from an old Seeforge family. He lived with his father, Bill Last, up until five years ago when the old man died. Bill was a great man but I think Jason was always a bit too ashamed of him to notice. Sometimes I think that Jason's not too smart." And she got up before Tom could ask her to explain herself.

Later that evening, once she had settled him into the habit of talking to her, and after she had poured him his second brandy, Tracy asked Tom all about himself and then listened to everything he had to tell her. The café was empty by then; all of the tables, except for Tom's, were in darkness, and the row of shops that spread either side of The Continental was dark and shuttered. Melissa, sitting by her window, ready to go to bed, sat watching that one pool of light and those two heads bent together, mouth over ear, the one feeding the other. Melissa knew only too well what Tracy was doing.

"A writer!" Tracy breathed and then was silent again.

"Not just a writer though!" Tom said, sitting forward in his chair, punctuating his thesis by rhythmically slapping his hand palm down on the table. "Something more than that, something as large as the very power of language. The novel has been forced down to the level of mere storytelling and isn't that such a travesty when its potential is so much greater? It has to be dragged into the realm of human experience. It has to describe and document and not doctor reality just to satisfy the paltry medium of fiction. Fiction is child's play and nothing more – it's no starting point for adult dialogue. And isn't that the reason for art? Isn't that why we bother to express ourselves at all?" Tracy nodded emphatically and opened her mouth but Tom didn't allow her the time to say anything: he just continued on. "To push ourselves forward, to explore our condition and now, in these days of mass literacy, isn't the most powerful medium the written word? The visual arts will always be limited by the decorative – they only appeal to the one sense – but words, words can trigger every sense, every tense, every truth."

And still Tracy listened on, and that night formed the mould for all the nights that followed. From Tom's second night at The Continental he had his own table, he knew not to ask for a choice when it came to his dinner and whoever else was in the café knew not to sit with him or engage him in conversation when Tracy was around. And Tracy was always around.

Tom stayed on at The Continental. He ate there and slept there, did his washing there, made his phone calls from there and assumed that Tracy was keeping some mental tally of his account. Sometimes he panicked, thinking that the food had to be beyond his means; the warmth of his room, the continuous hot water, the cups of coffee and nightcaps all had to be extra and would all add up to something more than he had. But whenever he broached the subject it was just ignored. Whenever he asked the cost of anything Tracy would just laugh, so soon he stopped asking, and then he started helping. He did a bit of painting, fixed a few hinges, carried some boxes, chopped some wood, listened to Tracy's stories and was made feel that she was the one taking advantage.

For weeks Tom stayed close to The Continental and close to Tracy. He avoided Jason Last and stayed on nodding terms with Joe and Dean and they nodded back. Every now and again they did a little more than that but they never treated him to another performance.

Once Tom went drinking with them, thinking that

perhaps he was expected to pay for his entertainment, but the two older men insisted on standing their rounds and, although they still worked their one conversation out of their two mouths, they limited the content of that conversation to the trivial.

"Cold for this time of year," Joe said.

"Better that than wet," Dean said.

"Rain in spring brings sun in August ..." Joe said.

" No guarantees but it's what is said ..." Dean said.

"Many a man's bet his crop ..." Joe said.

"On less though it's never been proved true," Dean said.

Tom found the two men, sitting opposite him taking alternate sips of beer and turns with words, deeply disconcerting. He never went drinking with them again and he made very little contact with anyone else. There were very few people his age in Seeforge – nearly all of the young people moved away as soon as they left school – and so, for the most part, he was left with his own company. He didn't mind too much; he had expected that, as a writer, he would be forced to lead a solitary existence. He went walking. He walked up into the hills to the south of the town and he walked east and west along the river bank, and he wrote. He took notes of everything Tracy told him and he fleshed out these stories of scandals and gossip with clear, concise descriptions of the town.

"Grey stonework," he wrote. "Tall trees mostly deciduous." "A slight slant to the main street." "A lack of planning resulting in an unattractive urban hinterland."

But when he came to describing the older buildings he was forced to use more fanciful adjectives. The more he examined the wrought-ironwork they boasted, the more he saw to admire in it and the more his clichéd descriptions failed him.

"Delicate," he wrote, "dainty, elegant, fine, graceful,

fluent, fluted, proportioned ..." And still he knew he hadn't done justice to the fine spider's web of metal that spun Seeforge together. He asked Tracy about the reason for the amount of ironwork but she had no satisfactory answer. She just told him it was something that the locals had bred a taste for; she just told him all she knew. Because, although Tracy talked about her town and her people a lot, she gave them no context, no unified history – she didn't know of any.

Seeforge's oral history had first slipped into inaccuracy before sliding out of memory, and so all Tracy could tell were the stories she knew and the stories she had been told. She knew most of what her family wanted to remember, and she knew most everything about every scandal that had happened over the last thirty years. She knew very little.

For instance, she had never heard of Foxy John.

CHAPTER 8

When Foxy John first came to Seeforge, when he first crossed the See, three hundred years ago and more, when he first hauled his boat onto the mud bank that formed the curve of that otherwise nondescript stretch of the river, there was already an established settlement there. But Foxy John was bigger than a riverside settlement and, until he saw a passing girl whose beauty caused his eyes to water, he was headed for the wider world. It took Foxy John three years to win that girl over and by then he had won himself a good way of life. He was a gambler by trade. A large, red-haired man with eyes that pleaded for respect and fists that commanded it. A very good combination for a gambler.

By the time he reached Seeforge Foxy John was almost forty and had travelled a good distance on nothing more concrete than the deal of a hand. He played for his food, clothes and shelter but he also played for his destiny. He gambled his every decision on the cut of the cards and the cards had never let him down. At almost forty he still had the right to look his world straight in the eye and under his shabby leather coat he wore a finely embroidered silk shirt. He kept the shirt hidden from the people of

Seeforge until after he had won his first game of cards. He knew from experience that no one trusted a well-dressed winner straight off. He also knew that no one trusted a man who won too frequently and Foxy John always won: that was why he always had to keep moving. But then he saw Dell Hardy and decided that the time had come for him to stay put.

Dell Hardy had never loved anyone. She had a good family, a father and a mother who cared, two brothers who grew into charming men and a husband who was wealthier than youth and good looks usually allow for. But Dell Hardy had never loved any one of them, not one.

No one ever suspected that, though. No one saw past her sweet temperament, her good nature, her soft smile and easy laugh. She had such surface charm that no one thought to look deeper and so they never touched her, and perhaps that was why they never moved her. But Dell, left lonely in her heart, just blamed herself. She took to loving God instead of man and that did well enough for her until Foxy John strode into town and saw the way she lifted her skirt when crossing the road, and saw the way she tilted her head when listening, and saw the way she smiled at something sadder than he had ever known. Loving God was all well and good until Dell found herself face to face with a man who stared down deep into her eyes and loved her.

Foxy John loved Dell for three long years and for three years she avoided his eyes, avoided the sight of his broad, embroidered chest, avoided the sound of his deep bass voice. But her world was too small to allow her avoid such a quantity as Foxy John forever, and Foxy John wasn't going anywhere.

During his first year in Seeforge he won the old black-smith's forge from a very old, charred little man whose hair burned in isolated orange tufts on his otherwise bare scalp, whose eyes were yellowed by the flame of his trade and whose mind seemed to be wandering.

"Stoke the very devil's hearth I do," he would mutter to himself. You could hear him through the soot-blackened, broken panes that rattled in his rotten window frames. "A hole from here to Armageddon and the devil's speed to your horse. An egg boiled on the belly of brimstone, now who's to pay for that, sir? Be it a privilege or a curse, sir?"

Foxy John had no real qualms when it came to cards. He knew the first rule that governed the table, "give no quarter and expect none"; he lived by that rule. But he had some qualms when it came to age. He never liked to beat a man who had already been beaten by life. But that crumpled, charred man with orange hair and yellow eyes seemed hell-bent on losing. He folded on a hand that a moment earlier he had believed to be strong enough to bet his forge on. He swept the winnings across the table to Foxy John and flung his hand in with the discarded pack in front of him before his opponent could question him.

"May your luck deliver you onto Satan's own sweet merc, sir," he said, but he was smiling. The next morning he was gone and Foxy John found himself with a new home and a new trade.

At first he sneered at the hovel that the men of the town laughingly referred to as his castle, but soon he was seen to be hanging around it more and more. Then he was seen to be coming and going from it, and then, one day, he was seen to go in and weeks passed before he came out again. But during those weeks something was happening in the forge, something bright and clean was burning through the filth. You could hear the rumble and shudder of movement from deep inside the ramshackle building. Thick blasts of smoke belched from its one high chimney and rich, rolling ballads continually spilled out through its rotten, soft façade. Foxy John was busy. By the time he was finished, by the time he stepped out onto the street again, he was smiling broad enough to fill the air with delight. He told everyone that he had mastered his new trade, but he sent away the scraps of business that his predecessor had built up.

He stopped gambling and hung up his silk shirts. Instead he wrapped himself into a long leather apron, locked himself up with his furnace for the most part of every day and sang. It was another year before Foxy John showed his work, and when he did and saw the reactions it sparked, he knew that he had finally found the calling that would automatically earn him the respect that he had, up until now, had to fight for. He had found a way to weave strips of metal into a mesh of filigree work as delicate as any lace.

Soon Foxy John's work was the talk of the town and the area beyond. It was a thing to see, a wonder what this great red-haired man could do with hands, hands that looked too clumsy to even work a plough. Everyone went calling to the forge and, in time, Dell went too. John was ready for her. He was wearing his embroidered shirt under his apron and was singing one of his sweeter songs.

> "If I was to lose you, if you were to go,
> Tell me where would I find you, how would I know?
> How would I know which stars were your eyes,
> Which were the stars that looked down as I cried?
> And how would I know which corn grew your ears,
> Which field I could trouble with my whispered fears?"

And for the first time in her life Dell Hardy fell in love.

For a time Dell and John managed to court quite openly without anyone suspecting anything. He had never shown any interest in women before and, although she was married, Dell Hardy was always considered more of a nun than a woman. She had the look of a nun, that soft, pale skin, that other-worldly expression in her eyes, that modest dip of her head, that simple, straight way of walking, all those little signs that, as the months passed, slowly melted away.

It was Dell's husband, Joe, who first noticed this change in his wife and, once he realised that the change had nothing to do with him, he began to question it. Who, if not him, was causing her to lift her chin and swing her hips as she walked? Who was causing her breathing to flutter and her chest to swell? Who had flushed her usually white cheek pink?

Dell shrugged off her husband's questions but she knew that she couldn't continue to. She had only slept with him during their first months of marriage, when she still had had hopes that she could love him, but, once she had discovered that even his most intimate caresses left her cold, she had moved to another bed and had refused him any further contact. For a short while she did toy with the idea of slipping in beside him one night, of tricking him. But that seemed to her to be too great a sin, too great a betrayal of the honest emotion she felt for Foxy John.

Dell never told Foxy John that she was pregnant; she took full responsibility for her condition and for her sin. She reasoned that she was the only one who had sinned, that she was the only one who had knowingly betrayed her moral code. Foxy John hadn't. His moral code was wide enough to encompass whores and gamblers, adulterers and drinkers. But Dell's was only as broad as virtue itself, and that's no breadth at all.

From the moment she discovered she was pregnant Dell knew what she had to do, and she didn't mind. From the first moment she had seen Foxy John and had recognised the echo of her own fire in him, she had been afraid. She had always known that that kind of passion would ultimately lead to destruction. What she had to do now seemed to her to be the only possible conclusion to a series of events that had started one spring day, years ago, when she had stepped up onto the pavement and, feeling someone's eyes on her, had turned her head. It was such a simple gesture but she knew that it had been waiting for her all her life. That there was no way she could have escaped it.

One night, when she was almost four months pregnant, a few weeks away from showing, she went calling on Foxy John. It was late, past midnight, when she crept up to his bedroom window and tapped their own coded knock on the glass. She spent that whole night with him. It was the first night she had ever stayed with him and slept with him, curled up naked in his arms, the fire behind her licking her flesh pink and warm. John held onto her for as long as he could. He counted her lashes spread flat on her cheek, he traced the fall of her lips dragged down with sleep, he breathed over her ear little words of love, little words of fun, and he stroked the full length of her coal-black hair, from the crown of her head to the small of her back. Her breasts and belly were curled tight together, pressed close to his chest. He remembered afterwards how hard they had felt.

When Foxy John woke the next morning Dell was gone. The moment he felt the coldness beside him he knew where, and he ran. He ran through the pink morning, the start of that blue, pink day, but he was too late. From the moment he had arrived in Seeforge he had been too late. Dell was floating naked on the water, her hair spilled wide, smiling up at the pale blue and rosy pink sky. Madonna colours.

Foxy John never said a word about Dell's death, never went to her funeral, never cried for the tragedy. He allowed

Joe Hardy the dignity to mourn the memory of a good wife and the grieving husband returned the favour by never asking for details or satisfaction. Joe married again soon after, married a good fat girl who cursed in company, farted in bed and produced a child a year for almost fifteen years. Together they trod all over the memory of Dell's tight-lipped kisses, high collars and religious devotion.

And, to a certain extent, Foxy John did the same. He started looking at the women who came calling to his forge, and then he started smiling at them. After that it was easy. He always knew that he could charm most living creatures with the spark in his eye and the rumble in his voice but until he met Dell he had been waiting; now he knew there was nothing worth waiting for any more, and he still had a healthy man's appetite. Soon strawberry-blonde haired children were cropping up all over the countryside, and that's exactly the term their mothers used to explain the phenomenon.

"A fitting head for a farmer's son," they told their husbands and then sighed with impatience when they were questioned further. "Don't you know that talent shows in the hair?" they asked.

"A corn grower grows as yellow,
Black for the mining fellow.
And the man who works in town
Has hair of brushed cloth brown."

Later, when these children's hair darkened to red and the boys discovered within themselves an unlearned mastery of metalwork, their mothers added another line to their rhyme.

"And the copper haired sire
He works with fire."

Because the women, and their sayings, were trusted their reasoning wasn't ever questioned closely. A generation of copper-haired boys were sent to Foxy John as apprentices and a generation of women, ashamed to share their secrets with their daughters, took their one great deceit with them to their graves. For years afterwards their old wives' tale was believed. Generations of black-haired men found it hard to find a wife in Seeforge because there were no mines nearby and few women were prepared to leave their homes in search of one. The black-haired men usually left home alone.

One of the few women Foxy John didn't manage to father a son with was his wife Molly, a sensible, kind woman whom he had hired as a maid and married because of her cooking. She cooked for him, cleaned for him, washed for him and seethed under his treatment of her. She had never expected much from marriage – she would have settled for a pretence of fidelity – but Foxy John wasn't prepared to agree to even that much. And so, in retaliation, she took to leaving her bedroom window open and one night a travelling salesman climbed in. Foxy John's one legal heir, David, was a black-haired boy who had a great interest in fabrics and ribbons.

CHAPTER 9

Foxy John lived a long life, too long he said. "The trouble with me now is that I don't have the energy to die," he said. And he said it for years, sitting up in his bed trying to muster together enough strength to meet his maker. One morning he slammed his breakfast tray back at Molly and shouted at her that he had had enough, that if only she would stop talking, if only the men downstairs would stop working, if only the window was shut and the curtains pulled he would be able to rest. His good wife did everything he asked – she even deadened the noise of the road outside by keeping it covered with straw – and it worked. Foxy John slept for the most part of a week and, when he woke, he was strong enough to die

For a few years after his death nothing much changed in the forge. Molly John, as the town called his wife, kept the place running and found the time to clean, feed and generally mother the men who had been apprenticed under her husband. She was a generous woman who hadn't much patience with luxury. She could have been wealthy, she could have broadened the business, but instead she kept it local. She could have exploited the workers but instead she paid them fairly and, to ensure that they had work to do, she doctored the prices of their produce to suit the economics of the town, and the town thanked her by buying as much metalwork as the men could make. It was a happy arrangement until Molly John died leaving David John in charge.

Poor David John only saw the world in terms of colours and fabrics. He had no understanding of fire and metal, no understanding of economics and a terrible fear of those broad, red-haired men who bellowed with laughter and dripped sweat down their bare chests. He tried to hide his fear behind an imitation of his mother's brand of authority but of course he failed and, as the months wore on, he began to drag the business down with him. The men watched him botch orders and skimp on materials, insult customers and undermine their abilities and soon they began their grumbling.

Under Molly John these men had been allowed the privilege to just concentrate on perfection. Molly had taken care of their finances and very often of their wives and families as well. She had fed them, and provided for them, and delighted in whatever they produced in return. But now all of this was being taken away from them.

Now they had to struggle with overpriced misjudged orders, with wives who demanded more of their time than they were willing to spare and with materials that snapped when worked too fine. And so their work suffered, sales suffered, salaries fell and the questions started.

"What's the point?" they asked each other

"Why blind yourself with flames?"

"Why work in the kind of heat that burns the sweat straight off your back?"

"Why blacken your hands and clog your lungs with soot just to achieve mediocrity?"

They turned to David with their questions but all he

could do was shake his head; he had no answers to offer them. By the time the circus tumbled into town that spring Foxy John's forge was just days away from closure. But, from the moment he caught a glimpse of the circus parade, David forgot all about everything. For the first time since Molly John's death he was dragged clean out of himself and left floating in a world filled with colour and movement.

The circus parade was led by dancers. Four girls dressed in light white shirts and full red skirts. David had never seen such lavish cuts of fabric before and was mesmerised by hem lines that flared out over legs and then swept the ground before being caught and bunched up hip high. And then there were the acrobats with their thin bodies painted over in coloured costumes; reds, yellows, greens and blues. And the musicians who clashed cymbals that were tied up with ribbons and who tooted on horns that dripped with coloured banners. Even the animals were dressed up. The one sad elephant was covered in thick, red velvet and wore a head dress trimmed with glass beads and feathers, and the horses were draped in garlands of multi-coloured silk flowers.

The circus stayed in town for three nights, and David stayed with it. At first he was just drawn by the colour and flutter of glamour but, once he arrived at the site, he found a more concrete reason not to go home. Her name was Joy, she was just seventeen and she was the most beautiful creature David had ever seen.

He saw her first from behind. He was walking through the field towards the main tent and she was standing by one of the caravans, leaning against it, listlessly scratching one bare toe up and down the length of her shin. The first thing David noticed was the sheen of her hair, and then he dropped his eyes and stared, fascinated by the perfect fall of her skirt. He was still staring when she turned and, when he moved his gaze back up to her face, he was dazzled by the beauty of her eyes. He blinked and only then registered her long, black, silky eyebrows and her neat little goatee beard. He was the first man ever who had to blink past her beauty before seeing her deformity and Joy never forgot that.

David left with the circus three days later and his disappearance was so convenient for the men left behind in the forge it was assumed by everyone that they must have had something to do with it. A few questions were asked, but nothing was discovered and, after an extensive search failed to produce a body, the matter was dropped.

The front door to the forge was closed. A sign reading "closed for holidays" stayed pasted to its window for almost thirty years, but no one paid it any much heed. The men came and went through the back door as they always had done. They worked their business under the co-operative tenets that Molly John had laid down and, under their elected representative, Jim Last, they made and filled however many orders they needed to keep the business going. No one missed David John. He was almost totally forgotten when, thirty years after his disappearance, Wild Walt Sheehy and his family rode into town.

Wild Walt took that name because he lived on the road and he knew that, at times, the road was a dangerous place to be. But he also knew that a name was as good a protection from harm as a loaded gun. So he wore his hair long and tangled; he filed his front two teeth into sharp fang-like points; he called himself Wild and was left in peace. And so was his family.

The Sheehys, Wild Walt, his wife, his four sons, his three daughters and his sick mother, arrived in Seeforge piled high in the back of a small cart that was studded all around with nails and from every nail there hung a different pot, pan or kitchen utensil. It was early in the morning when they clattered loudly into town, bursting over every tiny pit in the road, leaving a tide of disturbed dreams in their wake. It was just before dawn, just before Jim Last arrived at Foxy John's to stoke the fire up high enough for that day's work.

The Sheehy's got there first though and, as soon as they pulled up outside, they slipped off their perches and into action. In an hour they were unpacked, they had hung curtains over the two ground-floor front windows and the women were just starting to cook. When Jim Last crossed the road that morning the first thing he noticed was that the yellowed card, the one he had stuck up thirty years previously, was gone: the holiday was over.

On that very first morning Wild Walt invited the whole of Seeforge to breakfast. Himself and his sons put up chairs and tables on the road outside the forge and his wife and daughters served anyone who sat down with eggs, bacon, sausages, beans, potato cakes, bread with sticky black jam, coffee and sweet green tea. It was a meal like no one had ever eaten before and by the end of it everyone was ready to welcome their new neighbours and, as it turned out, they had no option but to. Wild Walt produced the deeds to Foxy John's; he said that he had got them off a travelling minstrel.

"A little man all dressed up in red with ribbons tied around his hat."

"See! I never killed him!" Jim Last yelled out triumphantly, but his triumph only lasted as long as his cry. That morning, over that one meal, him and his men were done out of their livelihoods, done out of their art, and the worst was that no one seemed to care. Seeforge was already caged in with metalwork. The town was ripe for a change.

At first Wild Walt promised the red-haired men their fire back. He explained to them how he wasn't a man for staying still.

"The road's my home," he told them and years later,

when he was a white-haired old man, he was still telling them the same thing, still promising them the future they had wasted their lives waiting for.

"Give me the freedom of poverty and a quiet dirt track. Let me know I'm to work for my food and I'll work. But tell me to work for the privilege of sleeping in a bed and I'd just as soon down tools. There's men made for sticking and men made for moving – that's just how it goes, boys. I'll be moving along some day soon, that's what I'm made for."

But his mother took five long years to die and by that time his wife had grown too fond of her hearth to leave it without a fight, and Walt never was a man who had much fight about him. He saw his boys pack up and hit the road and, as the years passed, his girls slipped away too, and every time one of his children left they took a little of his heart with them. Soon he hadn't heart enough left to fight his wife any more; soon he hadn't heart enough left to remember the love he used feel for the road. As it turned out Wild Walt and his wife died of old age in Seeforge. They left behind them their only son who had been born and bred in a house.

The Sheehys had been travelling for generations before Wild Walt came to settle in Seeforge, and a family that lives off the road has to hone a skill to suit the road. They need a portable trade, one that doesn't need too much in the way of equipment and one that is always in demand. Most families on the road at the time took to mending pots or cobbling shoes but the Sheehys took to cooking. Wherever they stopped all they needed was a fire and they could earn themselves a welcome.

They knew how to maximise the smell of cooking so as to incite hunger and attract custom and they also knew how to minimise the overheads involved in feeding large crowds. They knew that the earth was covered in food, that all they ever needed was just lying about or running around them, and so they never wasted their money buying ingredients. They just ate what the seasons dictated, broadened the usual definitions of meat and vegetables and produced food that always smelled a little better than it tasted, but still tasted a little better for being exotic. Their talent for cooking was really little more than trickery but all that changed once they arrived in Seeforge. Once they settled the Sheehys could no longer just trust to the novelty of their cooking to carry them; they had to add substance to it, and they did. Within a very short time they had mastered the art of feeding the spirit along with the body.

By the time his parents died Jack Sheehy was left with a thriving business. He supplied jams, pickles and chutneys to the shops in the area as well as catering for most everyone in the town. He served the men his dish of the day through a hatch that opened straight into his kitchen. They came calling on their way to the fields, or on their way to the river, held out their wooden bowls and happily ate whatever they were given. Then, when they were gone, their wives lined up to collect their evening meals. For years that's how Seeforge fed itself and for three long generations that tradition was only threatened once.

Once, when Jack Sheehy was an old grandfather tending to his orchard and playing with herbs, the circus came to town. A wild, gaudy cavalcade of noise and music and foreign sights. All three generations of Sheehys ran to it not knowing that it was the dust of travel that attracted them and not the bright colours and strange acts. They had all grown so far from the road they could no longer recognise its draw, but that didn't stop them loving the taste of freedom that, for three whole days, turned their town up-side-down. And then the circus rumbled on, the wheels of its laden caravans cutting a wedge into the softer roads of the town. For days afterwards, before the rain washed those welts away, the Sheehy children used to run along those lines, following them out into the wider world, before reluctantly returning home to tea.

A week after the circus left town a man, who called himself John John, marched up to Sheehys front door and started making demands. He was a handsome man, slimly built with fine, silky black hair that trailed down his back. His eyes looked young and bright and he walked quickly and carried himself well but his facial hair made it difficult to put an age on him. His beard was long and thick and his eyebrows were so lavish they crawled up almost as high as his hairline.

"I wish to see the man of the house," he said as soon as the door was opened to him. He didn't smile and he offered no explanation for his presence. Old Jack Sheehy was fetched for him but he refused to step inside while he waited. He seemed to be angry about something but, as it turned out, it was all something of nothing.

"Tried to turn me out of me own home!" Jack told his family and his customers, laughing at the idea of it. "Some high flyin' fancy flutin' tale about his grandfather's father and my father and a night at the circus! These young chaps today! I tell you there's nothing wrong with that poor boy that a good haircut wouldn't fix. All that weight must pull the head down and all that hair must tickle the brain into believing all sorts."

And that's what most people believed, that poor little John John was a bit simple. No one, for a moment, believed his story about how his grandfather's father had lent a friend of his the use of his home so that that friend could nurse his dying mother in comfort.

"He gave him the deeds because he had no key to give

84

him," John John said. "My great-grandfather gave his friend the deeds because his friend was a wandering man and no one trusts them even when they do turn up with a key – I should know." He finished sadly and all the young women sighed a little and stroked his sweet, silky head. They still thought him mad, but he was also very charming. He was able to talk to them in a way their husbands never could.

John John stayed on in Seeforge. He said that Seeforge had always been his destination, that his road ended there, that he had nowhere else to go. He said that his family had been travelling back to their hometown since his grandfather's time, and that he owed it to his family name to stay put.

"But you have no family name," the people said. "John's no surname."

"It is in my family," John John said, but no one listened; they still thought him a little mad.

"I can work," he told them. "I can make clothes." And for a long time no one even believed that much of him,

It was old Mrs Browne, the oldest member of the wealthiest family in the area, who gave John John his chance to prove himself. Mrs Browne didn't hold with charity. She thought that it was God's will that the sick should die, that the poor will always be amongst us and that able-bodied young men should work. It galled her to see how John John was being petted by the weaker women of the town. How they fed him, and stroked him, and tucked him up all warm by their fires. Mrs Browne didn't think such actions were Christian at all, she thought them shocking, and so she went calling on John John.

She found him sitting outside the Lyons' farmhouse and called him over to her carriage. She gestured at some yards of material she had with her and said, "I hear that you can cut and sew."

"I can," the boy answered.

"Well, I need some clothes. Do you need a job?" The old woman meant it as a challenge but John John only appreciated it as an opportunity.

"Oh yes! Yes!" he said, his eyes filling up with tears. Tears that had to stay lodged where they were; his lashes were too dense to allow them to fall.

And that was that. Mrs Browne stopped shopping in Paris and London and soon she and every man, woman and child in Seeforge was dressed to a standard they could barely appreciate. John John the tailor made clothes that could cut through the shapeless bulk of bodies broken by labour just as easily as clothes that could skirt the charm of a young girl. He had an eye for colour and an intuition when it came to fabrics; he understood their failings and could work the cheapest cloth into successes. He could bring glamour to the mundane, and that's just what he did.

Within a year he had saved up enough money to buy a premises across the road from Sheehys, and after two years his workload was so great that he had to send for his sister Violet to help him.

Violet was a beauty, younger than her brother with a figure so light it bent in the breeze, and she had the most delicate fingers; deft enough to structure the finest of fabrics and sensitive enough to coax a tune out of any instrument. And she could sing.

She sang wild, low songs from the road, and she danced them out, stamping her feet deep into the ground and flinging her hair up to the sky, and she loved to laugh. She was used to laughter, for all her adult life the world had laughed at her, and she had laughed right back from behind the thick growth of her beard. She caused a sensation in Seeforge and she enjoyed every moment of it. If the town people thought her freakish she thought the exact same of them, common little people, tied to paltry concerns, unable to even sew a button on straight: they were a pathetic crew. And, just like her brother, she never forgot what they had stolen from her family.

They were the reasons she gave her brother for not marrying the nice neighbouring boy who had got her pregnant. She never admitted that he hadn't asked her.

"He's pathetic," she said. "He's part of this thieving town, he'll do us no good."

And that's what she told her daughter when her daughter came home in tears one night, and that's what she told her granddaughter when the girl came to her with the very same problem.

"He's pathetic, Rose," she said. "He's part of this thieving town, he'll do you no good."

And so, just like her mother and her grandmother before her, Rose didn't marry. Instead she watched Don Sheehy build himself a restaurant and she tried to feel that thrill of family pique that seemed to be keeping her grandmother alive and her mother thin.

It had no effect on Rose though. No matter how often she was told the story she confused the dates, and the names, and finally confused the insult itself. By the time Rose got around to telling her own daughter the story of their family's loss all she knew was that someone's grandfather had given a Sheehy the loan of a house and then years passed and everyone died before the favour could be returned. She was the first Taylor woman who didn't bear a grudge against the people of Seeforge and so, when her daughter arrived home one night in tears, she just asked her straight out,

"Will the lad marry you?"

"No!" Jean's mother, Barbara, wailed.

"I suppose he thinks it all right to grab a hold of your hairy back down a field in the dark and it's another thing altogether to put his arm around it in front of his people and his god."

Rose didn't mean to be cruel, she was only speaking her mind, but her daughter never forgave her. Barbara, who used to sew clothes as elegant and as simple as a young girl's expectations, started pulling her stitches in that little bit tighter. People used to say that she was trying to sew up the one rip in her virginity and, after Jean was born, they almost believed she had. They were all shocked on Barbara's behalf when Jean began to show.

CHAPTER 10

Jason Last always considered himself to be a proud man. He was proud of his achievements, proud of the fact that he had hauled his father's scrap trade up to the respectable level of a hardware shop. Proud that he had worked from the age of fourteen, that he had still managed to finish school, that he could keep his head clear in drink, that he was taller, broader, stronger than most of the men he knew, that he had always just loved the one woman and that he had always been honest and vocal about his love. But now, sitting waiting behind his counter for an apology he suspected wasn't coming, he starting wondering whether he was, after all, nothing but a fool.

Out back, in the yard, his father's collection of scrap was still heaped up in mounds. Five years after his father's death and Jason, for all his pride, hadn't the heart to clear away old Bill Last's life.

He had been a bent little man coloured up with drink and bowed down with age. Jason remembered him as a happy man, happily running his hand along the rusted end of an old bedstead or the point of some old bit of railing. Jason's father had never expected anything more from life than that. When Jason was a boy the sight of his father wrapped round in rags, sat up behind a cross, old, dirty pony, touring the town and the countryside beyond begging for scrap metal had filled him fit to burst with shame. He had always sworn to himself that he'd do better, that he'd aim higher. And so he had worked harder than he had wanted to, had sacrificed more than he should have done and had finally opened his shop.

And it was a fine shop. Clustered around the counter, at the front, was a very comprehensive collection of wires all coiled around fat, broad spools and a display case with shelves underneath filled with bits for drills. Behind the counter, in little square drawers, the washers, fuses, nails, nuts and bolts were all arranged strictly according to size. Then, stretching down to the back and to the scrap yard beyond, were two aisles both shelved from floor to ceiling, one stocked with all manner of tools, and the second filled with miscellaneous goods: pots and pans, metal tea pots, kettles, tin plates, baking trays, buckets, even an old high-nelly bicycle

Jason had always been proud of his shop; he liked the look of it, cluttered but still well organised, and he had an interest in what he sold. He liked the sleek look and the clean smell of metal. He liked the way the sun sometimes bounced off the copper wire in the evening, firing it up into the colour of a sunset. He liked the noise of metal hitting against metal, that solid slap that left a musical ring in the air. When he was in a good mood that ring would often start him singing.

But, despite all his pride in his achievements, every now and again Jason would doubt himself, and now was one of those times. Now he was thinking of his father's collection out back, of how the old man used to happily sift through a pile of rubbish for hours, always optimistic about finding a gem, and sometimes he did. Sometimes he found a fence or a fender or something that seemed to make every rainy evening, every heavy load, every hungry winter worthwhile for him. Jason could never understand that but he envied it. When he was growing up with just his father, after his mother had died, he would shout at the old man.

"Yeah, it's nice! Yeah, it'll polish up a treat, but even if we do sell it it won't even cover the gas bill, will it?"

"Sell it?" Bill would ask, shocked.

"You're not going to keep it are you? We can't afford it! Don't we have enough old junk?"

"But the workmanship, son! You can't even see how those leaves are welded on, can you son? They could be all the one piece."

Back then Jason would shout and insist but as soon as he grew up and started earning he allowed his father the luxury of his collection of scrap, and the old man did luxuriate in it. He hoarded all sorts of bits and pieces, polished them up and endlessly tried to explain their merits to his son. But Jason rarely listened; he found it impossible to see past the brilliance of his father's enthusiasm. Old Bill would hold out a filthy, rusty doorknob and exhaust himself trying to talk it up to an artefact, but all Jason ever registered was the light of pure passion in his father's eyes. That light absorbed all his concentration and, increasingly, as the years went by, the memory of that light was invalidating all his achievements.

After all, what was the point of an indoor job, a respectable business, a collar and tie, if it didn't excite you? What was the point of concentrating all your passion on the unobtainable? Jason had always known that his eyes burned bright whenever he was with Tracy and he had always trusted in the strength of his passion. Until now he had never really believed that that fire of his could go unanswered. Despite all of Tracy's evasions Jason had always assumed that one day she would call his home hers. Now he was beginning to question that, and that had always been his one great truth.

He started moving. He got off his perch behind the counter and picked up a brush; the floor needed sweeping, he told himself. But that one thought wasn't large enough to stop him thinking and so he tried cluttering his head with lists: the shelves needed tidying, the windows needed cleaning, the back wall needed painting, the books needed updating. But it didn't work. The one thought that he had been trying to fight for weeks still managed to surface, and now it was fully formed and clear bright. Too bright to overlook. So bright it seemed to blind his future.

"I'm a fool," Jason muttered to himself.

He stopped sweeping and stood leaning on his brush, looking straight out through the glass panel in his door. Across the street Jean Taylor was standing talking to Mavis Bradley.

"But I wasn't always," he said a little louder before bowing his head to his work again.

"Been there almost two months now," Mavis Bradley was saying. Working her lips so vigorously around her words that her lipstick was being rubbed clean away in patches. "Him young enough to be her son and her flaunting him around the town. As if she expects us to believe that the likes of him could be ..." But Mavis couldn't even voice what it was she was being led to believe, so she just let her words trail off and instead nodded her head violently to intimate at her meaning.

"I know," said Jean. "It's filthy is what it is."

"Filthy," Mavis agreed and the two women turned to look through the clear plate-glass façade of The Continental.

Inside, sitting at his usual seat, Tom was sifting through the spread of papers that covered the table in front of him.

Every afternoon between four and six, in return for as much coffee as he wanted and a slice of whatever type of cake Tracy thought he could use, Tom sat in The Continental, keeping an eye on things and working.

He had been doing that for almost two months now, keeping an eye on things and writing. Sometimes he sat up at his bedroom window watching the movement of the town below, trying to capture it in words. Sometimes he sat down by the river trying to paint its colours onto his page, or trying to write the flight of a dragon fly. Sometimes he loitered down Hephaition Way trying to filter through the mundane snatches of conversation he overheard, trying to hear the honesty behind the banal.

And then every afternoon in The Continental he read through that day's nonsense and discarded almost all of it.

Tom was no closer to the heart of his book but he was still enjoying the journey. He enjoyed the rhythm of his days. He enjoyed waking at cockcrow and getting dressed as quickly as he could, trying to beat the smell of frying bacon to the table. Tom loved those breakfasts with just him and Tracy, before the doors of the café were opened and the crowds came in. Just him and Tracy and those pink and blue spring mornings, and coffee whisked through with thick, creamy milk, and bacon fried in butter and fresh pineapple juice, and apple sausages grilled over cider and eggs newly laid and lightly boiled. Breakfast at The Continental was always a good way to start the day.

Afterwards Tom would help out around the place. There always seemed to be something to do, just enough to fill his time. There was always something to lift, or something to fix, or some trouble that Tracy needed to share as she came and went, serving and cleaning. Tom didn't know how it happened but somehow he had slipped into the habit of working his days around Tracy.

First he found himself waiting until after the breakfast rush before heading out for his first walk of the day, and that was when Tracy headed out to do her messages. So, within days of his arrival, Tom was to be seen strolling beside Tracy stopping here and there, carrying whatever she passed to him, dipping his head to catch what she was whispering up at him, folding his arm over her elbow as she stepped on to the kerb, dropping his arm on to her shoulder as he steered her clear of traffic.

Then, back in The Continental, Tom would work in his room for a bit while Tracy prepared lunch and then after lunch, and after his one solitary walk, Tom would return to sit in the café and keep an eye on things. At six Tracy would serve him whatever she felt he should eat and at midnight he would still be there, sitting at his table, his head bent towards Tracy's while all around them the town slipped into that day's dark end.

On Sundays Tracy closed the café.

"Tradition," she said when he asked her why. "Sure what's religion if not tradition?"

But Tracy never did anything religious on her day off; instead she seemed to have slipped into the habit of working it around Tom. Whatever time he got up she would always be there, ready with something special for breakfast: a cheese soufflé or maybe a herb omelette. And then, as he ate, she would plan her day aloud and whatever she proposed doing always seemed to just suit Tom perfectly. And so Tracy and Tom spent some fine spring afternoons and some bright summer days together rowing down the river, fishing and then rolling their catch up in the mud of the riverbank before baking it over a slow evening fire. Or walking through the bluebell woods that covered the surrounding hills, picking herbs and flowers and working up a great thirst for beer.

After two months of this Tom had produced very little in the way of work. He had filled one notebook with descriptions of food, but that was all. When it came to food he just couldn't stop the words: they piled up on each other, spilled over each other, leaked into the margins of his pages, and they read like pure, sensual poetry. As far as descriptions of food went Tom was well pleased, and so was Tracy. She took a flatteringly active interest in his work; she was always willing to listen and proved herself to be a very educated critic. She likened Tom's work to Balzac and Dickens and Tom nodded but accused those authors of creating caricatures rather than characters.

"And that's too easy," he said. "It merely cheapens the dramatic to continually heighten it to the level of farce. True art deserves a greater respect for realism." And, as always, Tracy would listen.

One night though, about two months after Tom's arrival, Tracy poured herself and her guest a third measure of brandy before stopping Tom mid flow.

"Yes, but," she said and Tom thought she sounded a little abrupt, "you need to really experience the different traits of your characters if you want to capture them properly, don't you?"

"Of course, of course," Tom answered emphatically. "Of course all good art comes directly from an honest and realistic appraisal of the human condition."

"So you do have to meet the people who will people your book before you write it?"

"Yes," Tom answered, shocked by the blatant simplicity of the question. He was wondering if he had perhaps overestimated his landlady's intellect.

"So if you are going to use Seeforge as the setting for your work shouldn't you make it your business to get to know the people who are to inspire you?" Tracy asked, and then continued without giving Tom the chance to agree. "After two months who do you know in this town?"

"You," Tom said, dipping his voice to signify that he hadn't finished his answer, but then he stopped. He had intended to list off a few names and was shocked to realise that he couldn't think of any, "You," he repeated and then in a relieved rush added, "Joe Hardy and Dean."

"Three people and two of them you only know to nod to. No, something has to be done about this. I blame myself, you know, I should have introduced you around earlier. But better late than never."

And that was how Tracy got Tom to ask her to Betty Lynch's summer party. But Mavis Bradley wasn't to know that. "Unnatural filth!" is what she called it and Jean Taylor nodded.

"And brazen with it!" she said. The two women were still staring across the street at Tom's bent, earnest head. It was ten days until the Lynchs' party but already everyone knew that Tracy Sheehy was bringing a date.

The people of Seeforge took their summer parties very seriously. Seeforge had no industries, no third-level educational centres and, aside from the few family owned firms, no employment to offer its school leavers. So, every summer there was a tradition of throwing large, leaving-home parties for that year's graduates. These parties usually included the full quotient of Seeforge society and spanned all ages. It was thought that something as momentous as a child leaving home was a tragedy that forced the community to rally round and, before telephones and cheap travel, it had been. Now it was just traditional to mark the occasion with support and good wishes but, as Tracy would tell you, tradition is important in itself.

As Betty Lynch was going to spend the summer studying languages in Europe before going on to study them in university, her party was to be the first of the season and as such would set the tone for the rest. Rumour had it that it was to be very lavish, and the rumour seemed to be well founded because it appeared that just about everyone in the town was invited.

Mavis Bradley had been asked because she was so far steeped in charitable works it would be considered a sin to exclude her. Jean had been asked because she had made Betty Lynch's dress, and it had been proved that she sewed better when she didn't feel slighted. And, even though she was in Betty's class in school, and even though the party was, primarily, for her age group, Melissa knew that she had just been asked along with her mother because etiquette demanded it. Tracy had been asked because she was responsible for providing the food and, whenever she was invited to these functions, she would offer to do the cake as a gift. And Jason had been invited because the Lynchs, like most everyone else in Seeforge, were very fond of him.

Jason was still pushing his brush over and around the front area of his shop when Joe Hardy popped his head through.

"Hello there," he said, and Jason nodded. "Said I'd meet Dean at four, at The Continental, we're going to play a bit of chess," he said, and Jason nodded again.

"You should be off then," he agreed. "It's ten past now."

"So you walking as far as The Continental?" Joe squeaked in his effort to be casual and Jason smiled at the old man's attempt at tact.

"Not today, Joe," he said and so Joe turned to go without any further comment. It upset him to see his dead friend's son so sad, but he knew that there was nothing he could do about it, that it was none of his business. But all the same, just before he closed the door, he tried once more.

"So you going to the Lynchs' bash?" he asked.

"Think I'll give it a miss."

"Right you are, son," he said pulling the door to. Its little brass bell clanged as it fell back and the two women across the road turned towards the noise. Mavis waved at Joe, and Jean stared past him at the shadow behind the glass. Jason moved his brush a little deeper into his shop, a little further from the street, and Mavis Bradley took advantage of Jean's suddenly vacant look.

"Melissa in?" Mavis asked and Jean nodded. "Mind if I pop along in to have a wee wordy with her?" Jean nodded again.

CHAPTER 11

Mavis Bradley needed no further encouragement. She walked straight through the Taylors' reception area and, before Jean had registered her departure, she was standing over Melissa, smiling.

"How de do de," she said. She was fond of saying that; she thought it cute.

"Hello," Melissa said without looking up from her work. She had been sewing the word "patience" through the seam of a dress she was making for one of her old teachers, and could see the humour in her immediate rush of irritation. She was careful not to smile though; she knew how little encouragement Mavis needed.

"I just popped in to have a wee chatty. You know what we talked about before the holidays, about you giving me a bit of a hand?"

Melissa shook her head pretending to look confused, but Mavis just ignored her expression and didn't allow her the time to deny anything.

"The thing is I have a lot to be doing at the moment and so I've come to catch you. Finished your exams then?" She let Melissa time enough to answer that question, all right, but, "Yes," was all Melissa had a chance to say before Mavis took hold of the conversation again,

"Good, good, and I bet you've done a wonder at them, smart girl like you. Now, what I need you for is the annual old-folks jumble. My but there's such a lot to be done there," and she flopped herself down opposite Melissa on Jean's chair. "Collecting, sorting, pricing, arranging," she was ticking the jobs off on her fingers, "cleaning, selling, and then there's the administration, the phone calls, the post ..."

"I am busy already," Melissa said. "With my mother. I'm working here full time now." And she looked to Jean, who had just appeared behind Mavis, to back her up.

"Yes," Jean said, "Melissa is busy enough here these days."

"Well isn't that great!" Mavis said smiling about her at the two women. "Isn't that just wonderful!" And then, because she knew Jean so well, she knew exactly what to say. "It must be great now to have Melissa here all day long with you, just the two of you so cosy together and busy at your work. The business must be doing very well if it keeps you two ladies occupied full time. So is it then, Jean? Is it going that well?" And Jean, who had grown far too fond of pity to be able to admit to success, fell right into Mavis's trap.

"Not well enough."

"But if you're that busy ...?" Mavis pushed her point and Jean gave her the advantage.

"Ah, we could always do with being busier." And immediately Mavis smiled straight down at Melissa and Melissa knew she had lost.

"Well if you're not too busy here perhaps I can borrow your assistant for a little bit every now and again?" she asked Jean while she was still looking at Melissa. Melissa swallowed hard and, to her credit, Jean did try to think of some excuses but, between the two of them, neither Melissa nor her mother could come up with one large enough to fill the whole summer. Mavis pooh-poohed the few objections they set before her and settled herself back into listing the chores associated with her jumble sale. Thankfully she got up to go without giving Melissa anything specific to do but then she stopped at the door, as if she had forgotten something trivial.

"Now what was it?" she asked the room, tapping her finger off her yellowed, plastic front tooth. "There was something else, something I just remembered before – ah yes! Mrs Levine!"

Neither Jean nor Melissa responded to this revelation at all. Melissa had already buried her head in her work and, now that it looked as if Mavis was settling herself into another speech, Jean left the room muttering something about having to make a few calls.

"Yes, Mrs Levine," Mavis prompted again and then, as Melissa still didn't say anything, she started to explain herself. "The thing is I was just on to Father Leary there and he told me an awful sad story about Mrs Levine. You know Mrs Levine don't you?"

"No," Melissa said.

"Old lady, walks with a stick, one of the Brownes, very well to do, lives up in Elm House."

"I know the house."

"Well, Mrs Levine is the woman who lives there."

"I always thought it was empty."

"Sometimes it is. She's away a lot; her daughter lives in Canada, I think she visits her there quite a bit."

"And does her daughter visit her here at all?"

Melissa was just being cheeky now. Of course she knew Mrs Levine to see and she had heard all the gossip about the successful daughter in Canada; she was just seeing how far she could pull Mavis Bradley away from her question. She was wondering whether it would be possible to confuse the woman in trivia and then get away before she could ask her favour. It wasn't.

"Sometimes. But the issue at the moment is that poor Mrs Levine has had a nasty fall," Mavis continued in a much brisker tone. "She fell a couple of months ago and damaged her hip quite badly. She's well into her eighties and has, very foolishly, insisted on checking herself out of hospital and returning home. Of course, all things considered, she's in no shape to look after herself but she comes from the type of family that just can't accept help. All pride and britches and no thread to mend the family seat as they say." She paused but Melissa didn't laugh and so she continued on in an even brisker tone. "Needless to say her daughter has been alerted but she can't make it over for another while. Things to tie up, she says, though what can be more important than your own mother is beyond me. So there you have it, the long and short of it. What do you think?"

"What?" Melissa asked vaguely. She didn't know what part of Mavis's speech she was questioning. She had barely followed any of it.

"Mrs Levine is left all alone up in that big house with God knows what damage done to her hip, so would you pop along up to her? You know, check if she's doing all right, see if she needs anything done for her."

Melissa took a deep breath. "I don't think I'll have the time." She said, shaking her head slowly as if she was seriously considering the option. "So I think it's best if I say no."

"No?" Mavis asked calmly. She wasn't in the least bit offended, or deterred. She was used to rejection and was very adept at turning it around. "Right you are then, so could you do the Riverview estate with me instead? I'll call for you tomorrow evening and we'll go door to door asking what they have for the jumble. That shouldn't take too long, not more than an hour or so." And she smiled, nodded and turned to go.

A good majority of Melissa's classmates lived either in or near the Riverview estate and, although Melissa couldn't be sure if Mavis was aware of that, she suspected that she was. Either way Melissa knew that she had been left without a choice.

"Well maybe I could just call on Mrs Levine then and see if she needs some help. If she needs a lot though ..." But Mavis wasn't the sort of woman who waited for qualifying statements.

"Good so. That's settled so," she said definitely and then talked her way out of the room. "It'll only be for the odd hour or two twice or three times a week, maybe, and probably not even that much, and just think of all the good you'll be doing for that little effort. Do you know how much your visits will mean to Mrs Levine? Well you wouldn't, still being young, all it'll mean to you is a breath of fresh air, a bit of a walk and a chat at the end of it. But to her it will mean something maybe as crucial as a hot dinner. I'd do it myself but, well, I have the old folks' outing to organise as well as the jumble, and I'm running the tea dance in aid of the missions, the South American missions, and of course there's the school-gym raffle, and the parish-roof collection." And then from the street door she shouted, "So perhaps you could look in on her today or tomorrow, just say that I sent you, or maybe Father Leary, whichever, whoever."

It was only after Mavis had left that Melissa started to wonder why she was so eager to foist Mrs Levine on her. The name Levine still held some sway in Seeforge: in the recent past they had been quite a wealthy family, and Elm House was still quite a substantial property. Melissa would have thought that the likes of Mavis Bradley would jump at the chance of visiting it.

She wasn't to know that ever since Mrs Levine had first appeared in public leaning on a stick, all those years ago, Mavis Bradley had tried to help her. She had tried to bring her magazines, tried to interest her in local outings, tried to sit reading to her during those dark winter evenings that smelled of earth and decay, bad smells for the elderly. But every time Mavis had offered them, her services had been refused, and sometimes quite rudely too. Mrs Levine was a strange old lady, there was no denying that, but sometimes the old are strange and sometimes the rich are inbred and allowances should be made. Mavis knew that well enough. It was just that there was something about Mrs Levine's brand of strangeness that put her right on edge. If Father Leary hadn't directly involved himself in this situation she would have, quite happily, ignored it completely. But he had and so she couldn't. It was a great relief to her to be able to send Melissa up to Elm House.

"So did you get rid of her?" Jean asked, reappearing as soon as she heard the street door clang shut.

"I've to visit Mrs Levine," Melissa said tensely. Her mother's attitude to people, especially women, whom she pretended to be friendly with had always upset her. Her mother called it good business, but Mavis Bradley had never bought any clothes off them.

"Could you not have said no?" Jean asked crossly even though she knew that Mavis wouldn't have left without the promise of some help. She knew that Melissa's predicament was her fault and she did feel guilty, but she still hated the way Melissa slumped and she hated the way the girl minimised the beauty of her hair, wearing it full over her face and shapeless, and so she snapped, "For God's sake! What will you be doing up there giving bed baths and emptying chamber pots? Some work for a young girl!"

Melissa didn't answer and Jean sat down opposite her;

both women continued their work in silence. Since Melissa had left school everything was every bit as dull as Jean had anticipated. Melissa spent most of her days cooped up with Jean in their workroom, sitting sewing in silence. It was no life for a young girl, and no company for a young woman. Granted they could take on more work now and they were making more money than they ever had before, but sometimes Jean just didn't think it was worth it. And now was one of those times. Jean slammed her work down on the table in front of her and asked suddenly and too loudly, "So are you up to anything tonight?"

"Not much."

"Any films on? Anything on the telly?"

"Didn't look."

"What do you plan on doing do you think? Tonight? Tomorrow?" Melissa finally looked up from the shirt she was working on.

"I don't know," she said slowly.

"Don't know and don't care and for Christ's sake girl close your mouth, you look positively idiotic," Jean snarled and picked up her work. She left it a few moments before she spoke again. She had had an idea but she had enough tact to want to disguise her thought process.

"So Mavis is looking for jumble?" was how she broached her subject.

"Yeah," Melissa answered

"Well, I've just had an idea where you might get some for her." Melissa didn't react; she didn't care at all about jumble. "You know the little box room off the attic?" Jean asked and then waited for an answer.

"Yes," Melissa answered flatly.

"Well, I thought perhaps you could clear it out – it's full of junk."

"Yes, it is," Melissa said.

"I was thinking that perhaps it might make a good room for you to work in," Jean continued as indifferently as she could. "It's bright and would be big enough for a small table and ..." But Melissa didn't need convincing.

Up until now Jean had always insisted on supervising Melissa's work, and Melissa had always accepted that her mother thought her work need constant checking. She had never thought that Jean would allow her the freedom to work unattended. And working unattended meant so much more than just not having to offer up every seam for criticism. Working unattended meant that Melissa could play music as she sewed, that she could sing and keep that small, high window open, that she could work by a window, that she could watch the workings of the world and The Continental as she stitched and sang. That she could work without having to listen to her mother bury bitterness into every garment that passed through her fingers.

"... of course it will need work but a lot of that junk can go to the jumble ..." Jean was saying, but Melissa wasn't listening: she was just waiting for her mother to stop talking and then she would be able to excuse herself and start on clearing the way to her independence. "... And if you're willing to do the work then I'll be willing to trust you to ..." and still she talked on. Finally Melissa stood up anyway and talked over what her mother was saying.

"I'll go have a look at it now, will I?" she asked heading for the door, and then she was gone, leaving Jean to settle back into the boring comfort of her solitude.

The Taylors' house was small. The workroom and the front reception area filled the ground floor and so kitchen, bathroom and bedrooms all had to be fitted in upstairs. The kitchen and bathroom were close together and tightly squeezed onto a narrow return and the two bedrooms on the first floor were both tiny little rooms crammed full with beds and wardrobes. Just outside Melissa's bedroom an ornate iron ladder led up to the attic, and the box room, that Jean had been talking about, was just at the top of that ladder, built into the eaves. The attic itself had room only for a water tank and so the little box room constituted the only storage space in the house, and it was full. From floor to ceiling and door to window, it was full.

Melissa had always been disappointed by the contents of the box room. From as soon as she was able to negotiate the ladder that led up to it, she had searched it through looking for some reference to past personalities but, aside from a few bits and pieces suitable for dress-up games with Louise, all she ever found was rubbish. She was still too young to appreciate this as a proof of love; she still only saw it as a disappointment.

She was too young to appreciate that the lack of carefully stored mementoes meant that every mother's dress, every favoured accessory belonging to her, all her shoes, all her jewellery had been kept and worn by her daughter. That every book bought was still in use in the main house or had been read until it had fallen apart. That every ornament was still displayed downstairs or had been displayed until it broke. That every piece of furniture, every carpet, every bedspread or curtain or cushion was still in use or else had been worn out. That nothing of worth had ever been banished into storage because no daughter had ever thought to distance herself from her mother's possessions, not even Jean's mother Barbara. Even Rose Taylor's influence had been left scattered about after her death. Most of her romantic novels had been read by both Jean and Melissa, her cards were still kept in the box on the piano and her clothes had long since been cut into more respectable garments.

All that was left to fill the box room with was the debris

of generations of women's lives, just so much rubbish; ripped pieces of material, battered-down hats, shoes split at the seams, threadbare boas, coats worn green and shiny, pieces of papers, old magazines, newspapers pressed down into the grain of the wooden floor, bottles, broken twigs of furniture, old rusted tools, half-used tins of paint and everything in an advanced state of decay, everything all eaten through and rotten. Bits of indistinguishable matter disintegrated in Melissa's hands, flying up her nose, working age-old dirt in through her pores. It took Melissa three full days to clear the room and when she had she could only produce two bags of goods fit for a jumble sale.

Melissa waited until dinnertime before she dragged them over to the church hall. She was hoping to avoid Mavis who, she knew, usually ate at The Continental at six. Unfortunately for Melissa though, Mavis rated her jumble sale higher than her hunger and so was still hard at work pricing and sorting when Melissa bundled in through the metal porch doors of the hall.

"Well, how de do de!" Mavis called from the cool gloom of somewhere by the stage. "Been up to Elm House yet?"

"No," Melissa said and then, to clear herself, she added, "I've been collecting for you."

"Why Melissa Taylor, you star! And I was just going to pop over to you tonight to ask for a wee hand, but then I thought that you'd probably be busy with Mrs Levine. Either which way though it's a blessing to see you. Can you imagine, less than a week to go and just look!" She gestured around her and Melissa, who had dragged her bags up to the far end of the hall, groaned. The place was a mess; she would be stuck with piles of rubbish and Mavis Bradley for the rest of her evening and she had hoped to finish the top she was working on for herself – she had hoped to have it ready for the Lynchs' party.

"Would you be a love and mind continuing on here for a bit while I go have a bite to eat? I'll pop in on your mum on the way and let her know where you are. You know the drill don't you? White elephant, bric-à-brac," Mavis was pointing at the surrounding mounds of goods, "bottle stall, clothes, children's clothes, raffle, books and what do you have there?" She had just noticed Melissa's bags.

"Magazines, hats and bits of old trimmings," Melissa said. It was the briefest description she could give and it more or less summed up what she had retrieved from the box room. The hats must have survived because they were built to withstand weathering. The damp hadn't affected them quite so badly as it had the more delicate bits of material. The magazines were all brittle and yellow but Melissa had brought them along because of their age – they were interesting in a socio-historical way – and the pieces of trimming were just the scraps of lace or ribbon that she had managed to salvage.

"Wonderful!" Mavis said. "Wonderful, we can have a hat and trimmings stall and you can run it." And she left for her dinner in high hungry spirits.

"But I don't want to!" was Melissa's automatic response, but Mavis just ignored that. She didn't even hear it, her whole being concentrating on her dinner. She thought she would have the fish: Tracy always had tasty fish dish on her menu.

"There aren't enough hats," Melissa said. "I'm going to a party that day so I won't be around," she said a little louder. "No one will buy these hats anyway," she shouted as Mavis clanged the screen door closed behind her, and Melissa was sure she was right about that. The collection of hats she had brought were all terribly ugly. Most of them had belonged to her great-grandmother Rose and most of them had been flamboyant in their day, and flamboyance never dates very well.

CHAPTER 12

Tom was looking forward to the Lynchs' party with a
city sense of superiority. He was imagining a collection
of wise, wizened old men in tweeds, a few thick-set women
in floral suits and a bunch of youngsters driven wild and
drunk with boredom. He had no doubt that the whole
affair would be depressing but he agreed with Tracy that it
was important for him to experience all aspects of small-
town life if he was to portray it honestly. And if he was to
be honest he was quite surprised by how seriously Tracy
Sheehy was taking it all; he had always considered his landlady to be quite urbane. But from the moment she mentioned the party she hadn't stopped talking about it.

First she talked on and on about the cake she was going
to bring, ignoring Tom's obvious disinterest in the topic.

"These kind of cakes are very important you know," she
said on the first night after Tom had agreed to accompany
her to the party. The last customers had left The
Continental and Tracy was leaning over the one low candle
that lit her and Tom's table, staring straight at the boy, and
so Tom nodded his encouragement although he was
waiting to talk about his day's work. "Commemorative
cakes have to be memorable, they have to commemorate all

the best qualities of the person they're made for and, in cases like this, they have to create a taste of home as well. And that taste has to be strong enough to follow that traveller out into the world. For instance, Polly Ryan had a party last year and she has a big brown birthmark all down one side of her face, so that ruled out chocolate. But her mother was a cleaner so I added a zest of lemon freshness to her cake – you see what I mean?"

She paused, waiting for a response, and so Tom nodded his head in bewilderment. He was beginning to feel achingly bored, but Tracy didn't seem to notice – she just continued on.

"And that poor Melissa Taylor across the road, with her shape, and that skin, and those black little piggy eyes of hers! Well you couldn't send her out into the world with the memory of home all wrapped up in a currant cake, now could you?" And because Tracy was laughing Tom did. "But Betty Lynch, I think she'll be quite easy. Do you ever remember seeing her?" Tom shook his head and, hoping that that was the end of that conversation, slapped his notebook down on the table in front of him.

"Today I think I captured something of the spirit of summer ..." was as far as he got before Tracy glided straight over his interruption.

"She's blonde, strawberry blonde, and quite tall and slim. So that much is easy, a light sponge mixture. Say a three-tiered lemon cake with strawberry filling, but that's a little too obvious don't you think?" Tom nodded. His notebook was open in front of him and he kept glancing down at it. Tracy didn't even seem to notice that. She just talked on over his bobbing head.

"Maybe a butter cake would be better. It would still be the right colour and consistency and perhaps I could blend it with a cider base. The Lynchs' have a wonderful orchard, but June just isn't the right season for cider. I think I'll try a marble cake, lemon and strawberry with maybe a hint of mint. The Lynchs' wrought-iron is painted mint green."

And as if that wasn't enough Tracy brought the party up again the following morning,

"What are you going to wear?" She asked but, because Tom was lost in the trance of his breakfast, she had to repeat her question twice. Finally he looked up in complete bewilderment, a warm cheese scone just hovering in front of his mouth.

"Where? When?"

"On Sunday to the party."

"Clothes," Tom answered and bit down on his scone. Tracy left it at that for the time being – she had no choice but to: she knew how absorbing her scones were. But after breakfast, when herself and Tom were happily strolling down towards the cluster of shops that marked the centre of Seeforge, she asked again.

"So what are you going to wear?" And then, to pre-empt any repeat of his earlier wit, she added, "specifically."

"I don't know." Tom answered, still confused by the question. "Is it formal? I thought it was just something like a barbecue."

"Oh no!" Tracy said, slowing down so as to lend weight to her denial. "Oh no, no, no, it's nothing like a barbecue. It's a garden party."

"So it is formal."

"Well, not quite, but it is smart. It's shirt smart."

"Then I'll wear a shirt," Tom said happily and quickened his pace. Tracy followed thoughtfully. This was the tricky bit.

"Which shirt?" she asked.

After two months of doing her lodger's laundry Tracy knew all there was to know about Tom's wardrobe and she knew that his few shirts were fine, suitable to his age and requirements, but over the years the people of Seeforge had developed an overly critical eye when it came to clothes and Tracy, knowing that Tom would be the focus of everyone's eye that coming Sunday, didn't think it fair to start him off at a disadvantage.

"I don't know." Now it was Tom who slowed down. "Why? What's the problem?"

"Well, I was thinking," Tracy said, drawing out her words as if she was just forming her idea that very moment. "I was thinking that perhaps this is as good an opportunity as any for you to go and get yourself a shirt made."

"Made?"

"By the Taylors." And Tracy gestured across the street. "Remember I told you about them. They're very good and very, very cheap and really quite an interesting part of this town's life. You know, if you want to understand Seeforge."

But she didn't have to say anything more, Tom was convinced. He liked the idea of having his clothes made for him: it smacked of individualism and sophistication. It would be a fine thing in later years to be able to talk about his little woman in Seeforge who had his measurements and sent him up his shirts as he needed them.

"That's a wonderful idea," he said and Tracy sighed with relief.

Later that day Tom crossed the street to Taylors' and, after first peering through the ornate metal grid that covered both ground-floor windows and seeing that the room inside resembled nothing more than a pretty parlour, he knocked on the frosted glass of the front door. When no one answered he opened the door himself and bumped straight into a rather large, red, damp adolescent girl. Melissa swallowed hard and held out her hand.

"Sorry," she said. "I'm Melissa," she said and Tom took her hand briefly and smiled past her.

"Is your mum in?" he asked and then Melissa, knowing that she had obviously already failed, relaxed a little.

"She isn't but I'm sure that I can help you."

"I was looking for a shirt," Tom said but he still didn't look at Melissa. He was staring around the clean bright room, thickly carpeted and furnished with standard lamps, low, delicate coffee tables, two pretty floral couches and a well polished piano. There wasn't as much as a hint of retail about the place. "Have I come to the right place?" he asked.

"Of course," Melissa answered in her best customer voice. "If you don't mind I will have to measure you."

"Right you are then." Tom turned, stuck his arms straight out from his sides and stared up at the ceiling smiling. "How's about this then?"

"That will do very nicely," Melissa said, unhooking her tape from the back of the workroom door and swallowing hard again. Her face was burning; she could feel its heat creep up as high as her hairline, drawing drops of moisture out from behind her thick fringe. It helped that Tom wasn't looking, it helped that he was still smiling up at the ceiling, but she still had to touch him and that was no help at all.

She did it well, though; lightly and quickly, barely letting her fingers rest on his body, she wrapped her arms around and about him in silence. It only took a moment and, as soon as she was finished, she stepped away, picked up her order book and bowed her head over it.

"What kind of shirt were you looking for?" she asked and when Tom turned towards her to answer all he saw was the top of her sleek, black head.

"A nice one," he said but the girl didn't laugh, she just stood there head bent, pen hovering over paper. "It's for a party," he said.

"Well then I suggest linen," the girl said, noting down her choice beside his measurements. She quoted him a price and promised the shirt in time for the party and never once lifted her head to his. She couldn't: her eyes were too heavy with emotion; they were weighing her down.

"An odd girl they've got working over there," Tom said to Tracy that evening, jerking his head across the road.

"That would be Melissa," Tracy said nodding in agreement. "She's the one that I was telling you looks like a currant cake." And they both laughed.

Across the road Melissa sat watching from her bedroom. She had cut out Tom's shirt that afternoon and had taken it upstairs with her. Sitting by her window she was hand sewing the seam of one of the sleeves.

"Comfort, ease, sweet warmth, love," she wrote with her needle. She had nearly reached the cuff. There was only room for one more little word: "me" she stitched with deliberate care before folding her work away. Across the road Tracy leaned forward and blew the candle out.

CHAPTER 13

Melissa left it a couple more days before visiting Elm House. She spent most of that time sitting up in her new workroom reading, sewing or just staring down while below her Seeforge worked its way through two full days, starting with Tracy's rooster and finishing with Tracy's coffee. She loved the feel of her new room, light, airy and disconnected from the house, and she loved the view from her workroom window. It stretched her horizons further than her bedroom ever had. From it she could see the whole of Hephaition Way, and she loved to watch all the life that buzzed up and down there and circled around The Continental. That was as close as Melissa could ever get to The Continental without having to face her mother in an argument, and for the most part it was close enough, for the most part Melissa was happy.

Jean wasn't though. It was a beautiful day – granted there was work to be done. The Lynchs' party was coming up and most everyone wanted something tucked in, or let out, or taken up, or made from scratch, but still most of that work was done. It was a beautiful sunny summer's day and Melissa was sitting upstairs wrapped in fur and black, spreading her fat arse over the width of the house, just like she did every day, just like she was going to continue doing. Putting the girl out of sight hadn't helped as much as Jean had hoped it would.

"Melissa!" Jean yelled out, still sitting at her work – she just pulled her head back and yelled, "Melissa come down here." And eventually Melissa did.

Jean did try to be nice. She did try to keep the edge out of her voice, but still, whatever it was she said just caused Melissa to slump that little bit deeper into herself and retreat a little further behind her hair, and it was that reaction that finally triggered Jean's anger and drove her voice high and thin with exasperation.

"What?" Melissa had asked from the doorway. Not "hi", not "how are you", just "what?" but still Jean managed to answer sweetly.

"I was just thinking it's such a lovely day wouldn't you rather be out?"

"I've to finish doing that shirt."

"What shirt?"

"The one for the guy who's staying at The Continental."

"There can't be much more work needed on that, is there? You've been at it for days now. I'm going to head out this afternoon myself," and she tried a little laugh. "Maybe sun myself up for the party."

"I want to get it finished," Melissa said sulkily.

"But you'll be able to do that after a bit of a walk."

"It's too hot," Melissa muttered, folding her shoulders forward.

"Nonsense."

"I don't want to go." And what annoyed Jean most was that she knew Melissa didn't want to go but she also knew that she would. The child had no backbone.

"Oh, for God's sake!" Jean all but shouted. "Have you not one friend to call? Not one thing to do all day long except sit up there staring down on the world? When I think what I was doing at your age, oh, the fun me and the gang would be having. But sure what's the point talking to you: just get out of my sight!"

And Jean was disgusted to see that that was just what Melissa did. She closed the workroom door behind her and a moment later Jean heard the door to the street clang shut.

Melissa hated the heat, hated the way it heightened her colour and caused her palms and armpits to dampen. She felt swollen, heavy and leaden and she knew that people stared at her in her loose black dress. She loved looking at summer days, blue, white and gold days populated with swinging brown limbs and bright clean clothes, but she hated being included in them. She felt her bulk to be a blight on the landscape and so, keeping close to the shop fronts, she scuttled on up Hephaition Way and out into the wider countryside where she could at least be alone. It was just by chance that she ended up passing the gates of Elm House.

They were beautiful gates, or at least they had been. They were made from tall, imposing fluted iron columns worked through and bound together with an organic growth of leaves and berries. They were fairy-tale gates, loose on their hinges now and thinned out with rust but still pretty enough to charm Melissa, who was well used to the beauty of worked iron. She pushed them and they creaked open, dragging some gravel and weeds along with them. Melissa stepped onto the short, curved avenue that led up to Elm House.

Elm trees still lined that avenue. At one time they had done so regularly; sprouting out of a thick, shorn lawn, they had marched in pairs up to the gravel sweep that sur-rounded the house. Now they just struggled out of tangled undergrowth and stayed where they were.

Melissa started walking and overhead the trees reached up high enough to block the day. The old gravel was all overgrown and soft and nothing made a sound. The breath of the day lay suspended between Melissa's silent footsteps and the gentle wave that rustled through the upper leaves of the trees.

Elm House suited its surroundings perfectly. Melissa rounded the curve of the avenue and stopped: in front of her a grey-brown block of solid good taste loomed large and impressive, three tiers of blind eyes, heavy lidded with black iron lintels, stared quietly down on her. She was tempted to run but she knew it was too late: to escape now she would have to go back down that avenue and she knew only too well whose side the trees would be on.

So, instead, she sucked her stomach in, held her head high, crossed the open stretch of gravel that circled the house and climbed the three granite steps that led to the front door. She knocked firmly, lifting and dropping the stiff brass knocker, and was appalled by the noise it made. A dull, rounded noise rattled and echoed through the house and beyond, disturbing a flock of broad-winged crows that blackened the sky in a jagged, shrill cloud before swirling off into the day.

Melissa stayed rigid, waiting. She waited for what seemed like a very long time, and then she waited a little longer. She wanted to leave. She wanted to feel as if she had done her duty and could go home, but she knew she couldn't. She had been sent, and had agreed, to monitor the condition of a sick old lady and if that old lady was unable to come to the door it was her responsibility to try and discover why. She reached out a hand and pushed the hall door. It eased open a little and with pressure creaked open a little wider. Melissa expected a scared old face to appear demanding privacy or identification and so, to reassure, she introduced herself.

"I'm Melissa Taylor," she called. "Mrs Bradley sent me, and Father Leary."

There was no answer, but then perhaps she hadn't been heard: the door was making a lot of noise. It shuffled backwards and forwards, scraping over tiles, groaning on rusted hinges, opening only marginally wider at every manoeuvre.

Finally Melissa pushed with all her weight and stumbled a little as the door gave way.

"Hello," Melissa called out again. "Mrs Levine?" But she sensed she was questioning silence; it made her feel a little braver, gave her the courage to step into the hall.

The hall was a magnificent monument to form and order. It was two storeys high and lit by a long stained-glass window that was centred on the return of the sweeping, feminine staircase. A mottled red, green, blue and yellow light filled the space, colouring the air itself and reflecting warmly off the glazed terracotta flags on the floor. The only furniture in that broad high space was a long table that ran lengthways across it. Later Mrs Levine told Melissa that it was where she was to be laid out: she called it her coffin ship. Four doors opened off the hall but only two were unlocked. Later Mrs Levine explained that she had lived too long in the house to be fond of every room.

Melissa checked downstairs first, barely peeking in through the unlocked doors. She called as she went, hollowing out the air with her voice.

"Mrs Levine?" she asked.

"Are you home?"

"Anyone?"

As she stepped onto the stairs she was so confident of being alone she was shouting. Shouting loud enough to deaden the echo of silence that was following her – clustered up behind her, a tangible entity mocking her breezy attempts at cheeriness.

"Come out, come out wherever you are!"

An upstairs landing; one, two, three locked rooms and then a hand. Melissa didn't scream – there was nothing to be afraid up. Draped in the golden afternoon light, eyes blurred by sleep, a body wrapped in silk, Mrs Levine was not a creature to inspire fear. She was tiny, timeless, her face barely creased and her body straight and proud. But her hair was white and her eyes were ancient.

"How do you do?" She spoke beautifully, giving each word as a gift as she extended her hand. Melissa took it and it felt to her as if her own hand had closed in on itself, as if what she had grasped was negligible. Melissa had never felt so large.

"I was sleeping," Mrs Levine said as she pulled her bedroom door shut behind her. "I wasn't expecting a visitor." But she said this as a statement not a prompt and didn't allow Melissa the time to explain herself. It was a small gesture of politeness but still it was enough to make Melissa feel right at home. She relaxed right into the wonder of what she was hearing.

"Goodness you have fabulous bone structure!" Mrs Levine was exclaiming. "Of course it helps to have it covered with such beautiful skin. There is something I can't quite pinpoint about it, something about the texture of your skin that seems to trap light – my dear girl you seem to exist in a wrap of light. How wonderful for you."

Melissa, completely bewildered, just stared disbelievingly at the little lady and, luckily, the little lady expected no response.

"But, you won't mind me saying I'm sure," she continued, "that despite your wonderful attributes, or maybe because of them – men can be such brutes – you have the expression of one whose life to date has not been a delight."

She turned as she finished, walked the length of the landing and down the stairs. Melissa followed. She led Melissa across the hall, her feet bouncing noiselessly on the flagstones, soft slippers, cushioned noises. She crossed to the far left door and then stopped with her hand raised above the doorknob and turned, she was expecting some kind of response from Melissa. Apparently some sort of test was necessary before an unannounced visitor was allowed entry into the home. Melissa knew that Mrs Levine's hand could just as easily fall to her side as land on the doorknob.

"I'm only seventeen," Melissa said. "I've just left school and so I suppose I'm only really starting to live." Mrs Levine opened the door to her "friends parlour" and ushered Melissa in.

"Nonsense," she said. "At seventeen you haven't fulfilled your potential yet, you haven't accomplished all the things you will, you haven't loved enough, or drank enough, or met with enough valuable people. But you have definitely started living. You start that when you choose to take your first breath, you know, and ever after, with every other breath you take, you affirm your allegiance with life. At least you should do," she added seriously. "You should never even let the slightest breath be taken for granted or else where would you end up? You will take tea, won't you?"

Melissa nodded; she was only half listening. She had never been in a room like the friends parlour before and it made her feel curiously at home. It had originally been designed as a lady's morning room and so was delicately proportioned. Its two French doors, that opened on to what had once been the croquet lawn, filled the room with the all colour and light of the garden. The furniture was large, stretching up to the ceiling and across the wide girth of the room; sofas, chairs, footstools, sideboards, cabinets, book-shelves, occasional tables and a piano. The dimensions of the room could only be fully realised when all these pieces were mentally measured. Melissa found herself wondering at a side table swamped in magazines. It looked so inconsequential but was at least the size of the Taylors' worktable.

And everything in that room – all the clutter and all the furniture, the spacing of the windows and the distribution of light, the feeling of calm and the comfort of taste – everything seemed to answer to an order that included Melissa.

"Sit," Mrs Levine said. "Sit and I will fetch tea. Marvellous for the heat, and so surprising as one would expect a cooler drink to be more refreshing."

Obediently Melissa sat. She sank into the centre of one of the sofas and felt, underneath the initial softness of the cushions, the well placed springs support her back and upper thighs. The seat ended just at the bend of her knees; the sofa was made for her. Melissa felt supremely comfortable. She felt in proportion. Usually she dwarfed furniture. She towered over the delicate pieces favoured by her mother's generation. She had been brought up with tastes dictated by the ever-decreasing semi-d but here she was surrounded by furniture that had been designed with wealth and space in mind. Majestic furniture made for majestic women; wealthy, powerful women who stood tall and broad, commanding respect and flaunting femininity.

Melissa didn't allow herself get too comfortable, though. As soon as she heard clattering from the adjoining kitchen she got up. After all she had been sent to help not to create more work for Mrs Levine. The kitchen was obviously makeshift, an ante-room roughly furnished with the bare necessities: cooker, sink, a couple of cupboards. Mrs Levine was busy with a large pot, a tray and a kettle. It all looked to be a little too much for her and she was delighted by Melissa's offer of help.

"How lovely of you!" she exclaimed as if totally taken unawares by such a generous gesture. "Too, too lovely of you. If perhaps you would add a few leaves to the pot there, and a drop more water that would be perfect. We will of course take tea in the friends parlour. We will need a couple of cups, these will do. And if you would be a dear and carry the tray I will open the door."

They sat opposite each other and drank strong, black tea from thick mugs that Melissa found surprisingly crude, but Mrs Levine had been right: the tea was refreshing. As soon as she had finished it Melissa tried to broach the reason for her visit, but she couldn't make Mrs Levine understand that she was there to offer her services.

"Would you like me to do some cleaning ?" she asked and Mrs Levine stared back at her, round eyed and worried.

"Cleaning, dear?" She looked about her in consternation. "I dare say the place might be a little untidy but ..."

"No, no, of course it's fine. I didn't mean that – it's just with your hip, I thought you might not be able to ... well there might be some things like shopping, for instance. Do you need any shopping brought?"

"I don't think so. I haven't thought really – in a house this size one feels that one owns too much already."

"Well is there anything at all that you would like me to do?"

"My but you are a lovely young lady. I would of course love you to stay to lunch but I'm sure you must have a beau in the wings you're waiting to meet."

"No, not at all. I mean, yes I would love to stay to lunch and no I have no beau. But I must insist on making the lunch."

"Lovely. Lunch it is then. We will rustle up something

between us. Though of course as a guest you shouldn't be helping but seeing as you're so insistent ..."

"Well that's what I'm here for, to help. Mrs Bradley sent me."

"Oh I know her, a good woman," and here Mrs Levine shuffled forward in her seat and, after first glancing slyly to the right and left, whispered. "But don't you find all that organised do-gooding a touch bluestocking? When I was your age I tried the temperance league and the mission patrol and never once met with a gentlemen. All plain girls together we were. If I were you I would spend maybe a little less time with Mavis Bradley and a little more time dancing. Goodness!" And suddenly she sat bolt upright, splashing her knees with cold tea. "I've not introduced myself properly yet. Do please forgive my manners." She placed her cup carefully on the arm of her chair and rose; for a second time she extended her hand.

"Mrs Emily Levine at your service," she said perfectly, touching on every syllable.

Melissa stood then, without having to shuffle or sweatily negotiate her surroundings. All it took was one fluid motion and she was standing. She clasped Mrs Levine's tiny hand.

"Miss Melissa Taylor at yours," she said and she no longer felt large and awkward; now she just felt protective.

Melissa heated up a tin of soup for lunch. Plain tomato soup served in a silver soup tureen, balanced on an iron tripod shaped like three licks of flame. Mrs Levine half-heartedly cleared a space on one of her occasional tables and Melissa found two straight-back chairs. They sat opposite each other, drinking from transparently fine bowls, spreading margarine on stale sliced bread using bone-handled knives. Melissa had assembled all of this under very specific instructions from Mrs Levine.

"Forgive my being so particular, dear," she said apologetically as she followed Melissa from kitchen cupboard to parlour cabinet and back again. "But really, dear, this will aid our digestion. They say sauces are the thing to make bland food palatable but frankly I disagree – they merely give one heart burn. No I am absolutely certain that the only remedy for bland food is beautiful tableware. Luckily I was never taught to cook and I was left quite a selection of fine services – such a pretty coincidence, don't you think?" But she continued before Melissa could work her smile around an answer. "Do you know that the only thing I can make to perfection is tea, and I find that such a pity because I never get the chance to use my tea cups and some are quite wonderful."

She did sound sincerely sad and so Melissa didn't laugh; instead she said, "Never mind. I make horrible tea: I can use your cups."

"Oh you are so kind, thank you. Perhaps after lunch you will do me that favour. But you must forgive me, I think so much kind company must have gone to my head. I'm talking far too much, assuming that you have an interest in my conversation and that you are going to stay for the length of some tea after your soup. Please do disregard my presumption."

"Oh no," Melissa said, horrified at the thought of being politely dismissed. "Oh no, really I do like your conversation and would love to stay."

"Oh dear, you sound so sincere that I am forced to believe that you are either a most talented liar, or that you are being honest."

"I am being honest."

"And that is the better way to be. It helps the digestion, you know, cures insomnia and clears the complexion. But I am afraid that I usually find that it makes one happy as well, and that is why I am being led to think that you are a talented, albeit well intentioned, liar." Melissa looked blankly at her hostess and so Mrs Levine explained further. "I have no wish to accuse, and I appreciate your intentions, but I am afraid that I cannot believe you to be honest because you seem so sad."

"But I'm not sad," Melissa said and meant it. She couldn't remember enjoying an afternoon so much,

"I must disagree, you are sad and I am impertinent to press you with these personal questions, but then I am nearly dead and so must be excused the occasional lapse in manners. So tell me, dear, why are you sad?"

It was such a large question Melissa didn't quite know where to start looking for an answer to it. Now that she thought about it "sad" seemed to her to be her natural state of mind. A more apt question would be "what is there to be happy about?"

"I don't know of anything to be happy about," Melissa finally answered, causing Mrs Levine to sit bolt upright and suck her cheeks in tight with disapproval.

"Nothing to be happy about?" she said as if disbelieving what she heard. Melissa nodded her head. "But I can name a hundred reasons for you to be happy," Mrs Levine continued, still sounding shocked. "All the world and all its potential is open to you. You can choose to do anything, be anyone. And on a smaller scale, it is summer time, soup is always tasty, you can run home if you feel like it and listen to the air in your ears, and you are so beautiful. When I was your age I had cause enough to be miserable, such a scrawny child you never did see. I did try to eat milk and cheese and all the foods that rounded the other girls up, but nothing worked. I was well on my way to becoming a flat-chested spinster when I met Mr Levine, bless him." She misted over a little then, and paused before continuing.

"He was huge, you know, just like his photograph on

the piano." And she gestured over to the picture of a large man standing legs apart, arms akimbo and head held high. A big powerful man dressed well and well pleased with his world.

"He used to say he was big enough for two and when I was expecting he said he was big enough for three, and I believed him. I thought any child of his would have to be large but no: Vera is as scrawny a child as I ever was, no-where near as majestic as you."

Mrs Levine pushed away her soup and shook her head sadly. Melissa, although knowing that it was wrong to feel happy about another's disappointment, couldn't help feeling a glow of delight. The obvious inference was that Mrs Levine saw in Melissa some crucial attributes which her own daughter lacked.

"But there I go again," Mrs Levine said shaking herself back into good humour. "And there you go with your liar's manners allowing me to bore you. We were supposed to be talking about you and your sadness. Now, if your story to date has been sad there is nothing for it but we must change it."

"But what can I change?" Melissa asked

"Why everything. Just think of your life as an unwritten book and you will realise your potential. It is only the old who cannot change their stories but you can write any kind of story you want to. The only advice I can give you, dear, is that you must take care to write every word of every chapter yourself. I'm proud to say that I did; I suppose I still am but really, if I am to be honest, I know that I am just writing my epilogue. I do love epilogues, don't you? I've always found them so thoughtful." And then the telephone rang. It took Melissa a moment to realise what the sound was; it seemed so out of time and place.

"Would you get that for me, Miss Taylor?" Mrs Levine

asked. "Tell whoever it is that I am not to be disturbed. No one I like ever telephones – I must have given my number out to all the wrong people."

Melissa had to follow the noise of the phone to locate it; it was pushed half under an armchair covered over with some magazines. It was Mavis Bradley.

"Ah Melissa," she said. "So you have arrived at last? And how is our patient?"

"Well," was all Melissa answered. She didn't want to have to share any of her experience with Mrs Levine, especially not with Mavis Bradley.

"Well, well, well and who's to get the water? I need a bit more information than 'well'. For instance is the old lady up and about? Does she need any further care? Is she satisfied enough with you? Should I call by later?"

"There's no need."

"I think to be safe I'd better check myself. Put her on."

"She's out at the moment." Mrs Levine nodded her encouragement and Melissa mouthed, "Mavis Bradley." At that Mrs Levine shook her head violently, setting her cobweb of curls tumbling about her head and both she and Melissa began to silently laugh.

"Out? Where? When will she be back? Should she be out? When will I –" Melissa collected herself and interrupted with a firmness she hadn't known herself capable of.

"Mrs Levine didn't tell me where she was going or when she'd be back. I'm only here to help. Of course I can leave her a message."

"Well if you could just tell her I was asking for her and if there is anything she needs I will be all too willing to ..."

"Of course, of course," Melissa said kindly and that was that but the phone call did seem to break Mrs Levine's concentration. Under her direction Melissa helped her onto one of the sofas, propped her up with cushions and tucked the rug, which was folded there, around her. She looked so frail then: her head barely dented her pillow; her body was barely discernible under the weight of her blanket.

"You are quite a find, Miss Taylor," she whispered, fading into sleep. "And to think that I had to look no further than my doorstep. I am going to have an old lady's nap now so please do feel free to look around the house. But oh dear!" And she roused herself slightly, opened her eyes fully and struggled a little to sit up.

"What's wrong?" Melissa asked. "Can I get you anything?"

"Better manners, dear girl, better manners. I am just rudely presuming on your time again and you with your beau in the bushes," she said, settling herself back down to sleep. "Of course you must go to him," she whispered and then, softer and softer, she asked her favour, "but if you are in the area I would love you to visit again. I am so old now that I just live by reflection. If no one sees me for too long I almost doubt my existence. But then, this house is a constant source of reassurance for me. It is my home and that is what homes are, a reflection of oneself. I am lucky really," she sighed and she was asleep with a smile caught on her mouth

CHAPTER 14

After it was all over Mavis Bradley made it her business to tell everyone that that year's jumble was the best she had ever had the privilege to be involved with.

"And not just because of the amount of money we made, oh no," she would say shaking her head. "No, it was because of the atmosphere. A great atmosphere it was and a great day for the community."

And she was right. The community did turn up. During that long, showery, Sunday afternoon more or less everyone, at some stage, made an appearance in the church hall – no one seemed to have anything better to do. Melissa knew because she was counting; by the end of the afternoon she estimated that her presence behind the pitiful hat stall had been witnessed by almost everyone she knew. She had tried to get out of it. She had avoided Mavis's calls but she couldn't avoid the actuality of the woman herself, standing over her as she ate her breakfast on the Saturday before the sale.

"Well here we are!" Mavis had said happily, pouring herself a cup of tea and sitting in the chair Jean had just vacated. "Just popped by to fix up about tomorrow – you should get your phone looked at, Jean, it seems to be on the blink. So then are we all set?"

"Not really," Melissa said with far less conviction than was necessary to convince Mavis Bradley. "You see I am still quite busy, amn't I, Mum?"

"Oh yes, yes she is Mavis," Jean said from the doorway and then she left the room, leaving Melissa to continue her argument alone.

"Busy! Busy with work on a Sunday? So busy you can't spare an afternoon to spread a little charity about? And on a Sunday? I can't believe that …"

"Well actually …"

"And you going to have your own stall and all? Oh we'll have such fun, just you see. Dora Daily is beside you on the cake stall and she's an absolute hoot, never shy of a joke that one, keeps all the customers happy, she does, with a bit of a chat. But it's not all about fun – we have to remember that. If it was all about fun the good Lord would have given us a funday between Sunday and Monday, eh? Wouldn't he have?"

"Maybe. But really I …" Melissa tried again, but she had already lost and she knew it. Mavis was still talking.

"No it's not just about fun. We have to remember that it's about all the good we can do and I'm not just talking about the money we'll make, but it's a chance for everyone to get together, have a bit of a natter. You've no idea how the old folks love the trip and the hope of a bargain and we'll have the raffle and everything and then afterwards you'll have the satisfaction of knowing that all your hard work has maybe bought old Dan Jones a new pair of slippers for the winter, or Betty Hardy those magazines she loves, or May Harbisson a place on the south sea coach, or …" Over the years Mavis had developed the knack of being able to list where every pound she ever raised, for every charity she had ever been involved with, ended up. It was a speech that usually wore away any resistance she ever came up against, and Melissa was no match for it.

And so, the following afternoon, Melissa was forced to stand between May Hardy's white elephant stall and Dora Daily's cake stall, behind a table covered with a layer of old ugly hats and a heap of rotten scraps of rubbish, while right in front of her her peers ambled by in twos and threes, sometimes stopping to look at what she was selling, sometimes throwing some comment over to her, but more often than that they just laughed and walked on. And all the while Melissa kept praying that Tom wouldn't come in.

He came towards the end of the afternoon when the sun was dipping low, lashing the sky through with orange welts. Melissa looked up and there he was, standing in the doorway, silhouetted against the sky, his hair light around his head, his long legs heightened by the heel of his boots, and all around him the opened metal doors echoed with the colours of a dying summer evening.

"What you got here then?" It was Dean Kelly, suddenly up so close his small, brown, wrinkled face filled all of Melissa's world. Behind him Joe was picking up a few bits and pieces and letting them fall again.

"I'm looking for a shirt collar," Dean Kelly said.

"Can't get them these days," Joe said.

"Everything all comes stuck together these days and so I'm to throw out my old shirts? Or go about without a collar?" Dean asked indignantly, staring straight at Melissa, but he didn't expect an answer. Joe was already continuing their conversation.

"And though there's not much harm in that on a Monday when no one's looking, it matters on a Sunday when the Lord and all his flock are out to judge."

"It matters then all right," Dean said.

"It does," agreed Joe and then, as if he had only just noticed, he dropped what he was holding and stepped away from Melissa's stall. "This is all women's stuff," he said.

"What's that? Women's hats?" Dean asked turning away in disgust, as if Melissa had been trying to make a fool of him. "Wasting my time on women's hats," he muttered to himself.

"Sure what else have you to be doing with your time?" Joe asked and the two men nodded at each other and turned to go

"Wait," Melissa said loudly, calling both men back. "There are lots of other bits and bobs here. Let me just have a look." She was hoping that if the two men stayed in front of her stall she might be able to stay hidden from Tom. "I thought I saw something that looked like a collar earlier," she said, enthusiastically rummaging through her piled table.

It worked. Dean and Joe came back to her and together they sifted through Melissa's shoddy collection of hats. It took them a little while because her stock was still almost complete – she had barely sold a thing all day – and, by the time they were finished, Tom was long gone. He had found the whole affair horribly depressing and had barely stepped into the hall before hurrying home to the comfort of The Continental.

"See, nothing," Dean said finally.

"All ladieswear," Joe agreed sadly and walked away.

"I'm sorry," Melissa said politely and then stood waiting for Dean to move on, but he didn't follow his friend. He was staring at one of the more grotesque hats. A small, brown felt skull-cap, cut to fit quite a large head and trimmed with a red-gold weave of what looked like actual hair. At the front, and reaching back down the centre, this weave was coiled high, very heavily lacquered and shaped to resemble a rooster's comb but, in spite of its high gloss and unusual shape, it maintained the texture of human hair.

"What's this?" Dean asked roughly and his eyes, which were fixed on Melissa, suddenly flickered into life.

"I think it must have been part of a fancy-dress costume."

"Where did you get it?" he asked leaning in close as he spoke, and then, while still staring at Melissa, he picked the horrible object up. Beside him the activity around the white elephant and cake stalls settled in to a listening silence and behind him Joe stepped up close and whispered, "I think you've got it there."

"At home," Melissa said quietly, scared by the old man's intensity and the waiting crowd's attention.

"You're that Taylor girl aren't you?" Dean asked and, when Melissa nodded, he stepped back and, raising his voice, almost shouted, "Well then, girl, in the name of your great-grandmother I'll play you a game of whatever you know for this here hat."

"What?" Melissa asked.

"What do you know?" Dean repeated holding his hand out behind him. Joe slapped a pack of cards into it.

"Nothing, I don't play cards."

"No you wouldn't, would you, being your grand-mother's granddaughter, but you must know something." He was clearing a patch of table and, once he had created enough space for a game, he started shuffling his cards with a professional flourish, holding them high and then dropping them back down on each other, playing them like a squeeze box. "So what do you know?" he asked again, just as loudly as before. Melissa looked around her. Both the cake and the white-elephant stalls were suddenly very busy with quiet customers: everyone was waiting for her answer.

"Snap," Melissa murmured, with her head bent. She could feel tears of embarrassment getting tangled up in her eyelashes. "But I can't gamble for things, you have to pay for things."

"Well OK then, girlie, I'll pay. Look at me now. That's one of the most important rules of gambling: always look a

135

man in the face when he's talking about cards – that's the only way you'll ever have a chance of beating him." And so Melissa looked up at a taller, brighter Dean, still flicking his cards together and apart. "I'll cut you a deal," he said smiling at her. "We'll play us a hand of snap and if I lose I have to buy up your stall but if I win you give me this hat here for free and I'll just buy up everything else you have. You think that's fair?"

"No ..."

"OK then, let me rephrase the question: you think that you're getting a good deal?"

"Yes, of course, but ..."

"And that would be another pretty important rule when it comes to gambling: never question a good deal when it comes your way. They come along so rarely, chances are they're usually a gift from God himself."

"Well all right then." Melissa said and by now she was smiling too.

Dean dealt the cards quickly. Sliding them over and back, his hand moving piston-like in and out of his cuff, and all around him all pretence at jumble selling and jumble buying was forgotten. The few remaining shoppers and workers stopped what they were doing and shuffled forward to see what was happening. It only lasted a moment. Dean was too quick for Melissa's round white hand. Three times it slammed down on his thin brown veined one and it was over. Dean picked up his well-won cap, handed over enough cash to cover the price of everything left on the table and walked away without even as much as a look to Joe.

"But your hats!" Melissa called after him.

"Burn them," he shouted back at her.

CHAPTER 15

As it turned out Jason did go to the Lynch's party. He didn't want to, he had tried not to, but he couldn't think of a valid excuse and Roy Lynch was a good customer as well as a good friend. And so Jason turned up along with everyone else that Sunday evening. He was late. The party had started at eight and he didn't get there until after ten. He had planned that: he didn't think that anyone would appreciate his presence during the initial polite thaw when everyone would still be sober enough to focus on his recent, very public estrangement from Tracy Sheehy. And he knew that Tom was going to be there. Mavis Bradley had told him that.

The Lynchs' lived a short distance from town in an old farmhouse that, although stripped of most of its land, was still surrounded by substantial gardens. There was a good-sized orchard, a well-maintained vegetable patch, a hen run, a tennis court and, out back, quite a formal arrangement of terraces.

The night of the Lynchs' party was one of the first really warm summer nights. A soft night cushioned by the evaporating heat of the day, thick scented and sweet. Mrs Lynch had made sure that every other aspect of her party was perfect and so, now that the weather was exceeding her expectations, the whole event promised to be rather splendid. By ten o'clock it was proving itself a success.

Someone had hung some lights from the lower branches of the horse-chestnut by the side of the house and, underneath it, two young girls in whites were stretching themselves across the tennis court. Swinging their arms and running, their ponytails flying, their faces set in concentration and the game working like a dance around them, they were that good. Behind them there were more lights and the clatter and rumble of food and conversation. Because of the weather the party had spread itself across the terraced lawn; it all looked brighter and sounded louder when flung up against the great dark quiet of the night sky. Jason took a deep breath and stepped into the crowd.

Mrs Lynch, Cathy, discovered him ten minutes later, leaning into some conversation about fishing, a beer in one hand, the other raised in greeting to a passing acquaintance and an easy smile spread straight across his face. She tapped his shoulder and offered him some food. He didn't want any but seemed pleased enough to chat for a moment.

"Oh, it was such a relief to see him happy," she whispered later to Jill Daily. "And with Tracy almost right behind him! I could have died right there."

Jason had seen Tracy almost immediately. He could always do that; since they were children together he had always been able to pick her out in a crowd. She was with Dean Kelly and Joe Hardy, and she was laughing at something they were telling her but her eyes kept darting past them, down into the unlit depths of the garden. Young Tom was nowhere to be seen.

"And have you heard about today's pantomime?" It was Mavis Bradley. As soon as Cathy Lynch moved on she had popped up right in front of Jason, her thick bundle of hair obscuring his view of Tracy.

"Pantomime?" Jason answered automatically.

"At the jumble. Where Dean swore he found his hair?"

"His hair?"

"A moth-eaten old hat more like. He has it with him now, proud as anything showing it around. He won it in a game of snap and bought up the whole stall for the privilege! What do you think of that then? I'd say I wouldn't be the only one to say he must be going a bit in the old upstairs department."

"Well at least his head will be covered on the outside if it's to be empty in the inside," Jason said automatically.

"Oh, I laughed then," Mavis told Jean Taylor later, "but it broke my heart to see him just standing there staring at that, that ..."

"Trollop," Jean finished firmly.

"Trollop," Mavis agreed.

"And her pathetically trying to keep a hold on that young man of hers."

"Sure didn't she know that he'd be out after the girls his own age as soon as he got the chance?"

Jason had been staring at Tracy. He had been staring at her and laughing at himself. He had never, for as far back as he could remember, and he could remember almost all of his uncluttered past, been without Tracy for any length of time, let alone two months. He had never thought of her objectively, he had never seen her fresh, but now he did and now, for the first time, he understood what loving Tracy really meant.

For the first time he was beginning to realise that he didn't need anything from her, not her love, not her approval, not even her friendship. For the first time he was beginning to realise that he could love her as something independent of himself, and that he did. That that was how he always should have loved her. For the first time he admitted to himself that Tracy was never going to be his wife, that he didn't want her to be, that that wasn't how he loved her.

He loved all the traits in her that distanced her from domesticity. He loved all the things in her that he could never understand. He loved her distance from him. He loved the way she never needed him. He loved the way she stood so solid with one arm resting on her hip. He loved the way her blouses were always cut too low and her language was always a little out of place He loved that she had the strength to laugh at whatever Dean Kelly was telling her, and he hated that she was hurting. It no longer mattered who or what she was hurting for, it only mattered that she was hurting, and if easing her pain meant fetching her young boy back to her side then that's what Jason would do.

"Excuse me," he said to Mavis Bradley, resting one hand on her shoulder, gently pushing her to the side. "I think I'll go see this famous new hair." And he walked straight past her and, to her surprise, straight past Tracy, Joe and Dean before disappearing into the dark garden beyond.

Melissa and her mother had been one of the first to arrive at the Lynchs'. Melissa tried to hold back but Jean insisted.

"If the invitation says eight it's only polite to turn up at eight," she said. "All this stupidity about arriving late does no one any good, especially when they're serving food. Imagine poor Betty and Cathy left sitting waiting for an hour or more, scared out of their wits that no one will turn up, and the dips going off in the heat, and you call that being polite! Well, child, all I can say is I'd hate to see you being rude!" And she laughed.

Jean was in a good mood. She liked parties – she still believed that all it needed was the right invitation to the right party and her world would be turned around – and she thought that she was good at parties. She certainly looked good. She was wearing one of her own dresses, cut and stitched with just this sort of occasion in mind. A deep blue dress that was of no specific style but it clung and flowed where and when it was supposed to. She wore it with a plain double string of pearls and with a little more make-up than was necessary. She felt good. She was in a good mood and she was ready to start enjoying herself.

"Come along!" she called up the stairs to Melissa.

"Come along!" she hissed at her daughter as they set off down Hephaition Way. "Goodness, child, can you not put a bit of enthusiasm into it, we're going to a party not a funeral for Christ's sake. And did you have to wear black? It's June! Black in June! I don't know."

Melissa didn't answer; she wasn't expected to. Both she and Jean knew that she wasn't listening. She just continued walking a little behind her mother, slumped into her black clothes, sewn through with wishful, wistful words, dragging herself on towards what she knew would be just another proof of her inadequacy. She didn't want to go, she never had, but her mother had insisted.

"I don't know them," Melissa had wailed. "I don't like them. Myself and Betty have never ever been friends, not at all. They were all at that sale today and they were laughing at me."

"Nonsense," her mother had said. "They could have been laughing at anything – you're not all that important, you know. And anyway this is a party, this is how you get to know people. Anything could happen. They won't be the only people there. You can never know what treasure may lie hidden in the promise of the night. How are you to make friends if you won't even try? And how are we to sustain a business in this town if you won't involve yourself in it socially?"

And so Melissa was made go.

At first everything was just as bad as she had expected, and then everything got that little bit worse. Jean disappeared the minute they arrived in the Lynchs' garden. She nodded Melissa over to where Betty Lynch was standing leaning against an apple tree, surrounded by the pretty flurry of all her best friends, before tripping on down to the lower terrace where the men had gathered.

Melissa watched her mother join them. Watched how she raised her glass and laughed out some bright, sharp comment, how she swirled her skirt wide as she stepped down to their level and how she reached for Roy Lynch's arm to steady her. Her hand lay resting on his forearm long after she had regained her balance. Melissa looked away and walked towards the house to offer her services in the kitchen.

There wasn't anything to do there, though. Tracy had delivered the food earlier that day; it was all cold and only had to be arranged on plates. But Cathy Lynch was a nice woman and she found Melissa enough little jobs to occupy her for a while.

"You're an absolute treasure," she told her. "You put my Betty to shame." And Melissa smiled but she knew well enough where the shame lay.

It was still quite early when Cathy ran out of excuses for Melissa to stay inside, but the garden had filled up a good bit by then. The party was almost in full swing. Melissa recognised a few more of her peers scattered about. Louise was there and that was a relief; Melissa was still friendly enough with her to tag along beside her for the night. The evening colours lay heavy in the air, the outdoor lights hadn't been lit yet and there was a wonderful stillness hovering over even the more animated conversations. For a moment Melissa understood what her mother meant by "the promise of the night". And then some small sweet taste of magic came her way.

"Oy, Melissa!" She was being called. She looked around and there, waving her over, was Betty Lynch herself. "Hey, Melissa, we've been looking for you." And her surrounding flurry of girls and block of boys all nodded in agreement. Melissa smiled, waved back and almost ran to join them. They were all grouped together on the lower terrace, all carrying bundles: blankets, coolers, bottle-shaped brown bags, plates of sausages and burgers, a music system, one boy even had a guitar,

"We're going to build a bonfire," Betty explained as soon as Melissa was within hearing range. "Down the end of the garden, away from this lot." And she rolled her eyes and jerked her head in the direction of the adults.

"Yeah!" Samantha said gesturing over to the far left of the garden. "And the guys need a hand moving the stuff down."

Melissa looked over to where Samantha was pointing and saw "the stuff" piled high against the side of a shed. It was a big dirty heap of stuff: wood, crates, bits of rubbish, a murky black heap that no girl wanted near their clothes.

"Good job I'm wearing black," Melissa said cheerfully, but no one was listening.

"Well here he comes," sighed Louise, stepping down to join the gang, jerking her head behind her as she spoke.

"And there he goes," whistled Betty long and low, and strolling past them, one terrace up, was Tom, linked tight to Tracy's side. She was weaving him through introduction after introduction.

"Ooh, catch me I'm falling and I think it's in love," Sue said, laughing.

"He's got a huge nose," one of the boys said, pretending disinterest but sounding sulky. "I can't see what all the fuss is about." Betty turned to laugh straight in his face.

"You wouldn't, Mark Hardy!" she said and the girls all nodded their agreement.

"But he's not much to look at is he?" one of the other boys asked.

"No!" groaned Samantha. "But he's all we've got to look at around here."

"And I plan to look at him up close," Betty said and, because it was her party and because she was leaving the next day, the rest of the girls immediately backed out of the running.

"Go for it," Louise said.

"Yeah, you go get him," Sue said, and that was exactly what Betty did. She dropped what she was holding, wriggled her skirt straight and smooth, and cut straight across Tracy's path – poor Tracy had no option but to introduce her.

"This is Betty," she told Tom, smiling hard. "She's our hostess and, Betty, I knew you wouldn't mind if I brought a friend. This is Tom, he's staying at The Continental, with me."

"Oh, I know who this is," Betty said sweetly, stretching out her pale, smooth eighteen-year-old arm towards Tom. "You've been the talk of Seeforge for months." Tom smiled as he took her hand.

"I have?" he asked,

"Oh yes," Betty said stepping in a little closer, letting her hand rest where it was. She smiled her clear, bright eighteen-year-old smile and then laughed for no other reason other than she was happy. "We're building a fire down the back of the garden: that's where the real party will be. Come on, I'll get you fixed up with some beer and we can head on down. I suppose first, though, I should show you to my parents."

"OK," Tom said. It was as easy as that. He stepped clear of Tracy and followed Betty on into the house.

Tracy turned and marched straight up to Dean and Joe

and, still smiling hard, demanded that one of them get her a drink.

"So which one of you lads is going to prove yourself a gentleman and get this thirsty lady a gin?"

Both men laughed, more to encourage Tracy's bravery than to reward her comment. They had both seen, and understood, what had happened.

"Dean's the man for that now," Joe said.

"Yes, I'm the ladies man now with time to make up for."

"A lifetime to live in his twilight years."

"And maybe a drink to fetch for your old friend Tracy?" Tracy prompted, but neither man moved. They were both silent for a moment, looking to each other to take the lead. They were both twinkling with what they had to tell but their news was too recent. They hadn't fitted it into a story yet and so, eventually, Dean was forced to tell it straight.

"I got my hair back," he said and produced the old skull-cap from somewhere deep inside his jacket.

"You got your hair back," Tracy repeated. She couldn't think of anything else to say but Dean happily interpreted her tone as one of agreement.

"Got it off that young Taylor girl, he did ..." Joe said.

"So its authentic!" Dean said.

"It's Romeo's hair all right."

"Now what about I get you that drink?" Dean asked, balancing his hat on his head. Tracy thanked him and he walked off.

"What do you think?" Joe asked as they watched him cross the lawn with his stiff, gold quiff riding high over his head.

"He's finally lost it."

"Funny, he thinks he's finally found it."

"It?"

"Whatever it is that life never gave him. He's just

strutting about now waiting for it all to come his way and when he finds out it wasn't his hair stopping him it was his head, well, I don't know."

Both Tracy and Joe shook their heads in complete understanding and in front of them Tom and Betty crossed the lawn: Tom with an arm full of beer and Betty talking prettily by his side. As they passed Tracy, the lights that had been draped over the garden were turned on, throwing the gathering night into sharp relief. Tracy watched Tom step off the last terrace and on into the darkening shadows.

The bonfire was already lit. Melissa and two of the guys had moved almost all of "the stuff" down to the bottom of the garden. The others had piled some sticks of wood together, poured some gas over the bundle and struck a match. It looked beautiful, blue, green and red spilling into the soft warm night, shards of white heat sparking up almost as bright as the stars that were just beginning to appear. Melissa dropped her last load, a splintering old crate, beside the rest of the firewood and then dropped down herself.

All around her the girls and boys were doing the same, dropping their loads onto the ground around the fire and then dropping down themselves, but they were doing it in pairs. Laying down rugs, brushing up against each other, leaning close, laughing at quiet little jokes, whispering together, stretching out into the shadows. Melissa stayed close to the fire, staring at it. She was almost ready to leave, to go home, when Tom arrived. Betty was leading him by the hand.

"You sit yourself down," she was saying. "I'll be back in a second. I forgot the baked potatoes."

She turned and ran back towards the dim lights of the house and Tom sat down, right beside Melissa. Melissa knew that this was her chance. That she should comment on the night, on the party, on the fine shirt he was wearing, the same one that he had collected from her mother the day before, on life at The Continental, on anything at all, but she also knew that that would be impossible. Her throat, which was already constricting her breathing, wouldn't allow her to talk, and sitting there, beside him, in a damp, painful silence was more than she could bear. So she went to raise herself off the ground. She placed her two hands palm down about three inches from either side of her bottom and was about to lever herself up when she felt someone brush her fingers with their own.

Melissa froze. In front of her the night was tumbling on down and the fire was licking at its base. The air was thick with the smell of newly mown grass and loud with the call of nature settling to sleep, crickets, and birds, and far away dogs. And Tom was brushing Melissa's fingers with his own. To be sure she moved her fingers, and then she felt his ripple back into position. She turned her head slowly, not knowing what to expect. He could be laughing at her, or he could be waiting, with eyes ready to stare down into her very self before swooping for a kiss. But he was doing neither; he was just looking up at the stars.

Melissa felt this to be excruciatingly romantic. He obviously wanted to share the stars with her, to commune with her through the beauty of nature. She lifted her own head. He was right: what words could match the beauty of that soft, velvet night punctured through with polished beads of brilliance.

Melissa had never been happier. No one could know how happy she was, because the grass between herself and Tom was strewn with discarded jackets and coats. Someone's anorak covered Melissa and Tom's secret. Melissa slipped her hand closer, deeper under the anorak just to reassure Tom that she was interested. His fingers rippled again, settling over the length of her hand, keeping her safe, promising her ease, poise, beauty, love, all those words that she had sewn into the hem of her skirt.

Melissa turned to smile at Tom. She smiled at him with all her soul; she felt that she was smiling into their joint future, and that lit her up. Tom must have felt the heat of her emotion because he slowly began turning his head towards her, and then, from halfway down the garden, Jason called out.

"Tom! Tom, you there?"

"Yeah!" Tom answered whipping his head back around.

"Come on up to the house. Roy's cracking open his malt and you don't want to miss a taste of that."

It was the perfect invitation, masculine and mature. A reminder that grown men did not hang around bonfires with a bunch of kids when there were more adult amusements on offer.

"Coming!" Tom called out, then got up and walked away.

But his hand was still covering Melissa's. He had left his hand behind. Melissa screamed. She leapt to her feet, still clutching Tom's hand, screaming.

Tom turned and looked and then so did everyone else. They all stopped what they were doing and turned and looked. In the quiet of that silence Melissa slowly opened her hand on a fistful of frankfurters. She threw them down on the ground and ran, ran so fast she outstripped their laughter.

CHAPTER 16

The Lynchs' party was considered a general success, even though it was made up of a succession of private failures.

Betty's for a start. She spent her night laughing too loudly and drinking too much. She told everyone that she was having "just the best time" and no one argued with her. Her friends told her how that weird Melissa had scared Tom off by leaping up and screaming in his face and Betty accepted their story, although on her way back to the bonfire she had passed Tom chatting happily to Tracy and Jason, and he didn't look at all scared.

Tracy had happily welcomed Tom back. She saw Jason lead him on to the lawn and had beckoned him over to her.

"Got a bit already or got a bit bored?" she asked, but then she just laughed and continued on without waiting for his answer. If he was going to treat her like an older woman she could act the part – she was angry enough to want that much revenge – and so she directed her laughter and the rest of her speech at Jason, Dean and Joe, at the adults. "More like got a bit bored waiting, eh?" she said. "Can't blame the lad, I suppose, those girls aren't the fastest are they?"

And that was how Tracy treated Tom for the rest of the evening.

"Is that a whiskey you've got there?" she asked him, shouted over at him, right in front of Roy, Jason and a couple of others. "Better go easy with it: you were drinking beer earlier weren't you? Just be careful you don't throw up on my sheets."

"Tom here wants to write a book," she said introducing him to a rather glamorous-looking woman. "He's been working on it for two months now. How far into it are you anyway? He thinks it's going to be a bit like *Ulysses*, don't you?"

It wasn't that she was being hurtful, not even rude, but still Tom knew that something was wrong. They walked home together more or less in silence; they were turning on to Hephaition Way when Tom finally asked the obvious.

"Have I upset you?"

"No," Tracy said looking straight at him and smiling. "No, not at all." What hurt her the most was that he really, honestly had no idea of what he had done.

And then there was Jean's failure to attract any long-term attention from anyone. Towards the end of the evening she had even tried to charm Joe Hardy, but by then she had drunk so much that Joe had difficulty understanding her. At first everything was going fine for Jean. When she talked people listened and when she was laughing they laughed too. And then they began laughing when she was talking and that felt mighty fine. She remembered leaning against the full length of Jim Lyons and how good that felt, with her head nestled into his throat, and all around the men were laughing at something wonderful that she had just said. Then she remembered dancing. She was the only one dancing and that made her feel so sorry for Cathy. Imagine having a party and no one dancing at it? She said that out loud a few times.

"Imagine having a party and no one dancing at it?" But by now no one was listening or laughing. She thought they hadn't heard and so she shouted. She didn't really remember anything much more after that. She didn't remember how she got home but she knew that she had to negotiate the walk on her own, and she blamed Melissa for that.

Melissa had wanted to run home. She had wanted to run crying into the night, to end up flung cinematically across her bed, her shoulders shuddering from the force of her sobs, her hair crumpled on to the smooth white cotton of her pillow. But she couldn't. She hadn't the looks or the figure for drama. By the time she had reached the end of the Lynchs' driveway she was breathless and so she strolled on into town. She didn't even cry, she didn't see the point. It was still early when she got home, and she was still very far from sleep and so, on the way to her new workroom, she picked up the top she had been making for the party and had never had a chance to finish. It was made out of a light rayon material that was quite cheap but still hung well. Melissa had had high hopes for it. She unpicked the work she had done already and started again. "Fat", she stitched, "stupid", "ugly", "vain", "failure".

"It's best be honest," she told herself as she worked. "It's the spirit makes the clothes and you can't change your spirit. I've always been wearing the wrong clothes."

A few hours later, in the pale, white hours of Monday morning, Betty Lynch left Seeforge for Paris. Tracy, standing in her yard with her pyjama legs tucked into her boots and her chickens pecking at her feet, heard her go. She heard the purr of the Lynchs' car pass on up to the station and she breathed a little sigh of relief. The field was clear again but only just and not for long. She had lain awake for hours ploting and scheming, wishing and hoping and finally laughing at herself. If she was going to get this man, and she fully intended to, she wasn't going to be able to compete with the likes of Betty Lynch – she wasn't even going to try. Instead she would set her own standards and let those scraps of young girls try competing with her. "Let them just try," she snorted out loud as she emptied the remains of the feed in front of her favourite two layers.

Two miles south of town Mavis Bradley was just getting up and getting busy about her day.

"No rest for the wicked," she said to no one at all as she slopped a wet tea-bag out of her mug. "A good start is half the job done," she said as she sucked her stomach in to pin her thick tweed skirt closed. "Another day another dollar," she said as she hopped up on her bike and kicked off in the direction of town.

She was a busy woman: the jumble sale might be over but it still had to be put to bed. The prizes from the raffle had to be distributed, those people and businesses who made pledges of money had to be made pay up, the unsold stock had to be sorted and the rubbish disposed of and no one to help her at all.

That Melissa was more of a hindrance than anything with her awkwardness and her sulky face. No one knew the work involved, and not a blind bit of thanks for any of it at the end of the day. People think they're pulling the wool over your eyes! Passing off their rubbish for charity! Think of charity as a bin collection they do!

She was in fighting form by the time she reached town.

Back in The Continental Tom and Tracy were having a quiet breakfast. Tracy had cooked up something special to sweeten the atmosphere. Little round waffles, golden brown and all puffed up with their own scented air, dripped over with lemon juice and fresh strawberries, dusted down with fine white sugar.

"Some are cinnamon flavoured," she said as she set them

down in front of Tom. "I know you like cinnamon." And Tom smiled; he guessed that cinnamon waffles on a Monday morning was as good an apology as any.

"Yeah," he said. "I certainly like cinnamon." And that was that. Neither of them ever mentioned the Lynchs' party again.

After the breakfast rush, after Tracy had cleared the tables and closed over the doors of The Continental to dissuade passing trade, she disappeared into her kitchen leaving Tom waiting for their usual morning stroll. Ten minutes later he was still waiting and so he went looking for her.

"Tracy!" he called and though he heard some movement in the kitchen he got no answer. "Tracy!" he called again but this time he followed his words. For the first time he went in behind the bar of The Continental and headed on down towards Tracy's polished chrome door. "Tracy!" he called again, but softer now. "Are you ready?" And he was there, his open palm resting on the door, needing just the slightest pressure to push it open.

"Oh, hi," Tracy said and suddenly she was there before him, with the door swung shut behind her. "Listen I'm a bit busy so maybe you go on without me this morning. I don't think there's anything much that I need anyway."

"See you later then," Tom said.

"Yeah, see you later," Tracy answered but she had already disappeared back into her kitchen.

Later that morning she strolled the two-door distance down to Last's Hardware. Jason was waiting for her, sitting up on his stool, nonchalantly looking over his paper, looking a little too well groomed for a Monday.

"I'd like some nails," Tracy said.

"Certainly, we have nails all right." He stood up. "What type?"

"Metal ones."

"Yes ..." He prompted.

"Long ones."

"Yes ..."

"Some long metal nails. I'd like some long metal nails, please."

"And how many long, metal nails would you like?" Jason asked. He was leaning over the counter now, resting his hands on the far side of it, his body curved towards Tracy, staring her straight in the eye. And she was smiling, smiling so broad her answer spilled out into a laugh.

"Three hundred thousand and forty two." They both laughed then, reached their heads a little closer together and laughed. "I made you a cake," Tracy said, and she handed Jason over a bundle wrapped in blue cotton. He didn't unwrap it; he could smell it – it was a carrot cake.

"You didn't have to," he said. "I was coming in this afternoon for some anyway." And that was that. Neither of them ever mentioned the ape comment again.

"My but isn't it well for some who have all the time in the world to be standing around nattering?" Mavis Bradley shouted from the door, shouting over the clang of the bell. "Isn't it though, eh? Isn't it well for you? I saw your young lodger down the town there, Tracy, nice lad isn't he? Polite. I like to see that in a youngster but it's rare enough these days."

She was still standing in the doorway, her left foot on the pavement, her right spread as far as she could reach it into the shop. The door was balanced against her right foot and her bicycle was leaning up against her left leg.

"I'm just popping by to see if you have that pledge ready for me, you know for the blind boys' band's uniform. I'd come in but I don't want to leave the bike. I forgot my lock. I'm not naming names now and I would never be a one for doing that but some young lads these days ..."

Tracy winked up at Jason and Jason, still smiling down at her, was happy enough to say just what he was expected to say.

"Come on in, Mavis. You can leave your bike in the shop while I write you out a cheque."

"See you later," Tracy said to Jason and, still smiling, she manoeuvred herself past Mavis.

"Friendly as pie they were together," Mavis told Jean later that morning. "As if nothing had happened at all between them."

Across the road Jean Taylor was still sitting in her kitchen having breakfast. She was having a slow breakfast spread out over a slow morning, and across the table from her Melissa sat bug eyed and hairy. It was more than a woman in her condition could be expected to put up with.

"For God's sake, child, would you sit up!" And Melissa did a little but it didn't help.

Jean didn't know what to do. She was at her wits' end, just didn't know what to do about the child at all. She couldn't understand it. Why oh why had she been lumbered with such a lump when there were girls like Betty Lynch in the world? Light-limbed girls who ran with the boys and brought all sorts of chaotic joy home with them, as well as all sorts of nice-looking young people. Summer, when you're seventeen or eighteen, should be filled with dancing, and swimming, loud music and good fun. God knows Jean was no prude! She was all for fun, but her every good intention was wasted on Melissa.

"That was some party wasn't it?" she asked, already angry at the response she knew she was bound to get.

"It was OK," Melissa said.

"OK? Is that all? And after all the work Cathy put into it! Well I thought it was a great party. Good food, good people, good music, it'll be a hard one to beat."

"I suppose."

"That girl Louise is going to have one soon isn't she? You and her used to be friends usen't you? What was her nickname again?"

"Lou."

"Oh yes, Lou, well you're bound to be invited to her summer bash aren't you?" It was a mistake. Melissa knew that at the time, but she couldn't stop herself.

"I'll not be going," she said firmly.

"Don't be silly, of course —"

"I'll not be going to Louise's or anyone else's party."

"But if you're asked."

"No." And she started violently buttering a slice of toast. Jean looked on in silence for a moment and then started again.

"Are you sure you should be eating so much toast, not to mention the butter? Should you not be looking after your weight?" she asked. "And would you not wax your arms and brush your hair? And for God's sake why are you looking so glum? You're not the one who's hung over ... are you?"

"No," Melissa said.

"So are you heart-broken?" Jean asked coyly, though she knew that her question was more cruel than cute.

"No," Melissa said.

"But something is wrong. All this 'I'm never going anywhere again' and you did disappear off somewhere last night, come on you can tell me."

"Nothing to tell," Melissa said, and Jean nodded in agreement. The child was very likely right; there was probably nothing to tell, probably never would be. The sulky teenage lump couldn't even take to charitable works with enthusiasm and wasn't that what plain girls of her size were supposed to do? Find their identity in the need of others?

And then, just as if Jean had conjured her up, the street door clanged open.

"How de do de?" Mavis Bradley called out. "Anyone home? It's only me! It's Mavis! Jean! Jean! You there, Jean? Melissa! Is your mother in, Melissa? It's Mavis."

"Mavis!" Jean called back. "We're in the kitchen, come on up."

"I don't like to," Mavis shouted back. "Don't like leaving the bike. I forgot the lock and, you know me now, I don't like naming names but there are some lads about who ..." Jean had no option. She got up slowly, leaving her coffee behind, and went downstairs to greet her friend. Mavis was straddling the doorway, propping the door open with one foot, balancing her bike along the length of her other leg. "It's a nuisance with the bike," she prompted but Jean, who was in nowhere near as good a humour as Jason Last, just agreed that it must be. "If it wasn't for the bike here we could have a bit of a natter," Mavis said sweetly but still Jean didn't take the hint.

"I suppose it's a bit awkward all right. Would you be around tomorrow at all ?" she asked and so Mavis, who was dying to talk, was forced to play her trump card.

"I've just been into Last's," she said leaning in a little further through the door. "And you wouldn't guess who I saw there, chatting away to Jason?"

"Who?" Jean asked obediently.

"Tracy Sheehy," Mavis whispered.

"Why don't you bring your bike in for a minute, Mavis?" Jean asked brightly. "Put it through into the work-room and I'll put the kettle on."

As soon as Melissa had heard Mavis call out she had disappeared. She knew that she hadn't the strength necessary to argue with the woman if she came asking for any other favours, but she also knew that she just couldn't compromise herself amongst her peers any further. She just couldn't allow herself be seen begging for some parochial charity so soon after ... And there she stopped; her humiliation was still too fresh to fit into words. She climbed the iron ladder to her new-found freedom and sat curled in one corner of that tiny room.

Once it had been cleared it had turned into quite a pretty space, not big enough for a bed but plenty big for a table and chair. Melissa wanted to paint it blue: blue seemed to suit a room that was perched sky high over her house and, sitting on the floor by the door, blue was all she could see through the small recessed window. The window itself was wedged shut, sealed up with decades of dirt, but Melissa knew that it wouldn't take much to open it and then she would be able to polish up its pretty iron window box and plant it full of ... She paused here again. She didn't know the names of any plants but her concentration had been disturbed by something more sinister. The drone of her mother's conversation had grown louder and louder. Mavis was dragging it out of the kitchen and up the stairs towards Melissa's room.

"Did Melissa not tell you? Some moth-eaten old piece of horse's hair, honestly ..."

"Oh don't talk to me! She'd never tell me anything, but isn't that teenagers for you?"

"Well I'll just have a wee wordy with her and I'll be on my way." And already Mavis was at the bottom of Melissa's ladder and Jean, still in the kitchen, was doing nothing to stop her.

"I'll come down," Melissa said – she knew that she had no option but to.

"Well, Melissa, aren't you a fine girl!" Mavis laughed, watching Melissa negotiate the ladder bottom first. "A fine big healthy girl, eh?" There was no answer to that and so

Melissa offered none. She stepped off the ladder and stood facing her guest.

"Just popped by to say a big thank you. Wasn't that a wonder with the hat and the cards and all? Not that I condone gambling – no better ever bested his best bet and that's what keeps him betting, as my father used to say, eh?" But Melissa didn't laugh so Mavis continued on in a less friendly tone. "What I came by to say was that although the fun of the jumble is over the work is still to be done. We have to clear out the hall, dump the rubbish, send what we can to charities, collect pledges, sort out the raffle winners ..."

"I am visiting Elm House this afternoon," Melissa said firmly. "I think I am needed there on quite a regular basis and will not be available to help with any of your other projects." And she immediately disappeared back up her ladder, closed the door to her boxroom and turned on her music. Mavis looked for a moment at the steep climb and the shut door and even then thought about pressing her point home. It was the music that finally drove her away. She found young people's music terribly intimidating.

CHAPTER 17

Melissa did go back to Elm House that day. She thought that her excuse should hold some truth and that it would be unfair to use anyone as sweet as Mrs Levine as an alibi. She also really wanted to although she suspected that her first afternoon at Elm House had been a little too perfect to match and was afraid of disappointment. She worried that if she were to try and replicate her first day with Mrs Levine she would destroy the memory of it. But, faced with the need to hide herself in something less obvious than her manageable workload, she was happy to choose Elm House and Mrs Levine.

She waited until after lunch and then told her mother where she was going.

"Are you finished June Daily's skirt?" Jean asked and Melissa said that she was and that was all Jean could say. If her daughter chose to clutter up her life with old women there wasn't a blind thing she could do about it.

Melissa walked the two miles to Elm House very slowly. She felt a little awkward about calling without a specific invite, but she did trust that Mrs Levine would appreciate the company. However, at first, Mrs Levine was nowhere to be found and that was a great disappointment to Melissa.

Until she arrived at Elm House, and was left standing by the door, she hadn't realised how much she had been looking forward to her visit.

She stood by the door for a long few minutes and then she pushed it open. Just like before it grated slowly over the tiles in the hall.

"Mrs Levine!" Melissa called out and then, remembering the time before and how Mrs Levine had slept after her lunch, she stopped calling and, as quietly as she could, slid the door closed. She crept over to the friends parlour first but it was empty and then, as silently as she could, she climbed the stairs and peeped into Mrs Levine's bedroom. She was there, laying flat under the weight of a primrose quilt. Her hair, as thin as wrinkled cotton, was spread wide over her pillow and her face was turned towards the warmth of the window. Melissa pulled the bedroom door to and tiptoed away.

After that she spent two, very quiet, hours trailing around Elm House, moving softly from room to room, moving silently through a thick cushion of dust. She found generations of belongings well worn with the intimacy of the dead; toys, books, clothes, writing boxes, threadbare cushions, lumpy beds.

In one room she found an enormous wardrobe that must have been assembled where it stood. Inside it was filled with age-old finery. Linen blouses in yellowed white and cornflower blue, dresses and skirts cut from plain cotton and stiff serge hung from uniform wooden hangers and, on the shelves to the side of these, lace wraps, cashmere cardigans and finely knit jumpers were folded one on top of the other and scented through with sachets of lavender. The top shelf was filled with hats: berets, and bonnets, and plain old rain proofs. But there were a few creations as well, broad rimmed and trimmed with frivolities and gay, sweeping feathers. On the rung that ran along the bottom of the wardrobe was a collection of shoes that varied from ugly, worn walking boots to finely beaded pumps.

And then, on a second rail, behind the everyday clothes, Melissa found the formal dresses. Loose, floating silks with scooped necks and bold patterns. Thick, sculpted velvets dense with colour and weighted with dust. Melissa ran them through her fingers, pulled them out from the depths of the wardrobe and swirled them through the air. They flared wide and settled slowly, filling the room with the scent and sense of a long dead woman. Melissa put them back just where she found them but she knew that later, with Mrs Levine's permission, she would try on every outfit.

She went back down to the friends parlour then and ran her hands along its details: photographs framed in silver, faded ornaments, unwound clocks, some elaborate, dried-up writing implements and a selection of magazines, much like the ones Melissa had sent to the jumble. Old periodicals that mostly concerned themselves with gardening, cookery and points of etiquette. After flicking through a few of them Melissa let herself out into the garden. From the back Elm House didn't look so impressive. The windows there were crowned with lighter lintels than in the front and their symmetry was broken up by a mishmash of curtains and blinds, giving the whole façade a far less formal appearance.

The garden itself was very overgrown but its original design was still apparent. A wide lawn sloped away from the house and, to the left of that, through a wrought-iron arch, there was a rose garden. Then further on, fenced in by high, elaborate railings, was an orchard. To the right of the lawn, through another matching arch, were four outhouses with moss-covered roofs and broken windows behind metal grilles. On their doors were lists of dates and beside them strange names: 1-8-'52 Lady Lilly, 2-3-'02 Last Push, 11-1-'84 Morning Glory. When Melissa asked, Mrs Levine explained that that they were the names and birthdates of quite famous horses.

Just past the stables there was a romantic, well-planted wilderness. Soft ground, dense undergrowth and broad, hardwood trees surrounded a central clearing that housed a beautiful gazebo. Ivy covered most of it, but behind the bright, glossy leaves Melissa could make out a dense working of iron over iron, of metal leaves struggling through a metal mesh, of stem and thorns and tight black berries. She cleared some of the ivy away and then, following the pattern around, she found the door. After a little effort she forced the catch and pushed her way in to the green scented chill. Inside she found a selection of garden furniture. She couldn't move the wrought-iron pieces that were all jumbled together: tables, chairs, stools and the skeletal remains of umbrellas. But she found some pieces of wicker that still seemed to be strong enough for use, and she carried them to the house and set them up on the lawn outside the friends parlour, two chairs and one low table.

It was almost four o'clock by then and Mrs Levine was awake. Melissa could hear her moving around upstairs and so she called up to her.

"Mrs Levine," she shouted up from the hall and the great stone space rounded her words, giving them weight and throwing them back on her. "Mrs Levine, it's Melissa Taylor. I hope you don't mind but I let myself in."

"Miss Taylor," Mrs Levine answered quietly, her voice barely louder than the echo. "Miss Taylor," she repeated and was there at the top of the stairs, one hand on the banister the other stretched out in greeting. She glided down to Melissa smiling so sweetly.

"I am sorry to –" Melissa began but Mrs Levine hushed her up. "I'm too old to waste time either apologising or forgiving so stop that. Come," and she linked Melissa, "come tell me stories of the young outdoors."

And so, to Melissa's surprise, Melissa found herself telling Mrs Levine the whole story of the sausages, and she told it well. She told it like a funny anecdote and Mrs Levine accepted it as such.

"My dear Miss Taylor," she sighed wiping tears of laughter off her face. "You are such wonderful company. Would you do me the honour of staying to tea?"

They had passed through the friends parlour now and were stepping on out to the lawn where Melissa had set up the wicker furniture. Mrs Levine stopped speaking, stopped laughing, reached for Melissa's arm and gave it a light squeeze.

"Why how terribly sweet of you to have gone to all the trouble of retrieving the shell of my childhood summers. But," and she did look genuinely upset, "but what are we to eat? I doubt I have a thing that suits those chairs. No cucumber, no scones, no cakes, no muffins even, not that they are very nice." And Melissa smiled.

"Don't worry," she said. "I was rude enough to come calling at tea time, so of course I brought it with me. We have cake and salmon sandwiches."

"Why then, Miss Taylor dear, then we have a feast and cannot possibly use the good china."

"We can if I make the tea and the sandwiches. I'm bound to make a mess of them."

"Oh please do, Miss Taylor, the day, the garden, the company all demand the good china."

Melissa smiled and said she would make the food as badly as possible and then she left Mrs Levine in the garden and went back to the kitchen and the bag of groceries she had brought with her. It only took a few moments to slop some sandwiches together, slap a cake on a plate and pour some hot water into the pot, but it took a little while to present everything neatly on the best china and load it all onto one of the better silver trays.

Mrs Levine was waiting for Melissa as she wobbled out into the garden, laden down with the weight of the meal. She was standing perfectly still just by the wicker table, resting one pale brown hand on it. She was framed by the sharp blue of the sky and the pale blue shawl that she had wrapped loosely about her shoulders seemed to ease her perfectly into the setting.

"Dear Miss Taylor," she said. "I am so sorry, and possibly quite dotty, but I would like to ask you one last favour. Would you mind drawing up another chair and bringing out another cup?"

Melissa nodded and smiled but her heart sank. Mrs Levine was expecting company, some horrible old lady no doubt, bound to ruin everything. She brought another chair from the gazebo and another cup from the kitchen and by the time she did finally sit down her tea was cold and the sandwiches had turned slightly in the heat. Melissa didn't mind, though – she was too hungry and thirsty to even taste them – but Mrs Levine, who had been politely waiting for company before eating, pushed her food away and didn't touch her tea.

"I feel too full of conversation to eat," she said sweetly by way of apology but then laid her hand on Melissa's arm and apologised sincerely. "I am so sorry to have sent you away on an errand. I am aware of how rude it was but it is just that ever since his death I have always made a point of taking afternoon tea with Mr Levine." She nodded at the empty chair facing her and Melissa, catching something of Mrs Levine's need, smiled at the space on the chair and said, "I am very pleased to make your acquaintance, sir," before tactfully withdrawing to allow Mrs Levine some time alone with the ghost of her memories.

Back in the friends parlour Melissa ran her fingers over the piano. It seemed playable although it was out of tune. The cushion of the piano stool lifted and, underneath it, Melissa found a muddle of loose music sheets. She took out a few and, after a few false starts, launched into a foot-tapping ditty from the twenties. The piano belted out a tinkle of notes and Melissa sang:

> Goodness gracious
> My man's at the races,
> He got paid on Friday
> Won't have time for me.

Behind her she heard the creak of floorboards and when she hit the chorus Mrs Levine joined in enthusiastically:

> Got me a red gown
> Got me some red shoes,
> Goin' to go down town
> Goin' to sing the blues.

And then she applauded and over the noise of her appreciation and Melissa's laughter said, "Such talent Miss Taylor! Such a voice and you sad! Is this what you want to do with your life?"

"Oh no," Melissa answered and, for the first time in years, she remembered how she enjoyed playing the piano. "I only do this for fun," she said remembering long after-noons with Louise practising scales and simple duets together. "Although I suppose I could do worse."

"Oh, but please don't," Mrs Levine said reaching out and grasping Melissa's hand. "There are so many things worse than pretty tunes; promise me that you will try not to involve yourself in them too deeply."

"I promise," Melissa said quite seriously. "And I already know what I am going to do with my life: I'm a dressmaker."

"A dressmaker? And you sound so definite – that is marvellous. It is very important to know what one wants to be in life, and who, and with whom, but what is a good start." And then she shot a hand to her mouth and rounded her eyes. "A dressmaker! Why of course your name is Taylor, how wonderful. Please forgive an old woman's mind. I had not placed you until this very moment. You a Taylor! You know my house is filled with your family's creations. But dear," and here Mrs Levine paused and sighed quite heavily. "Oh dear," she said shaking her head, "I know this will sound rude and I did so want us to be friends but ..."

"But?" Melissa prompted. Mrs Levine's grasp on her hand tightened a little before she continued.

"But dear Miss Taylor did you make the costume you are wearing now?" Melissa looked down on the broad, black smock that she had hoped would make her look waif like, and nodded.

"Well it is beautiful, dear, very well made I am sure. But I have to ask, when you say you are to be a dressmaker are you answering a call deep inside yourself or are you answering the expectations of those around you?"

Melissa thought for a moment before answering. Surprisingly she had never asked herself this before but after only a moment she knew why she had never questioned her career. It was because it was the only thing in her life she loved, the only thing she had any control over, the only thing she was good at.

"I am a dressmaker," Melissa finally answered. "There is no question about it."

"Well then," and Mrs Levine paused a little awkwardly. "Well then I feel I have to say this. The costume you are wearing, do you feel that it quite suits you? And I am only asking as a friend who has every confidence in your talent. Please do not be angry."

"Of course I'm not," Melissa said brightly. "And yes, you're quite right this doesn't suit me, none of the clothes I make seem to. They suit other people all right but not me."

"Hmmm, " Mrs Levine replied, wrinkling her forehead, obviously searching for some suitable piece of wisdom. "Hmmm," and then it came. "Do you know how the Bible asks us to do onto others what we would have them do onto us?" she asked. Melissa nodded, confidently waiting for some connection to be made with her problem. "And don't you think that perhaps the converse is also true? That we should do onto ourselves as we would have others do onto us?" After a moment's thought Melissa nodded again and smiled. "You see, it is probably that simple. You should just treat yourself with the same respect as you do others and all will be well. Now are we still friends?"

"Oh yes," Melissa said. "But I really must go home now."

"Really?" Mrs Levine asked and because she sounded sincerely sad Melissa added bravely.

"But I can call again if you would like."

"Please do," Mrs Levine said and Melissa knew she meant it. "I will live for your visit."

CHAPTER 18

Tracy was already serving dinner by the time Melissa strolled back down Hephaition Way. The Continental was bustling with the noise of eating, the ring of glass and metal and the deep quiet of appreciation. Melissa walked the length of its plate-glass window and, through clouds of condensation and patches of shadowy reflection, could make out table after table of hunched diners. She didn't see Tom though and he didn't see her. Sitting at his usual table, bent over his plate, he saw nothing except the colours of his dinner: black green and berry red, liquid gold and weathered pink. He was eating salmon baked in spinach leaves, garnished with redcurrants and glazed with butter sauce. Across from him, one table down, Jason Last was eating port-wine stew: a rich red soup of tender vegetables and firm flesh that tasted every bit as good as it looked but, Jason couldn't help thinking, didn't look quite as good as baked salmon in butter sauce. He wiped his bowl clean, smiled over at Tom, picked up his jacket and left.

"See you tomorrow," he called out to Tracy and Tracy, from behind her bar, tossed him over a cheese bread roll and called back, "See you tomorrow."

For the past few days Jason had been spending his afternoons in The Continental and for all the world it looked like everything was back to normal. Tracy was in her kitchen cooking, Tom was in his bedroom writing, Joe and Dean were at their table playing chess, Jason was at the window eating cake and all was well with everyone. But everything had changed and everyone knew it.

For instance Tracy didn't seem to be trying so hard with Tom. After Lynchs' party she had given herself a talking to.

"A girl's got to know her limitations," she told her aged, plain reflection in the bathroom mirror. "And a girl's got to know how to flaunt her assets," she told the sharp fragmented image of herself that echoed around the polished surfaces of her kitchen.

From the day after Lynchs' party she started spending her mornings cooking and stopped strolling through her daily shopping on Tom's arm. She didn't propose any more Sunday outings and she took to going to bed that bit earlier – she only stayed talking for the length of one brandy. But Tom never noticed; he was too busy writing. He was working on his first chapter and had already structured the whole book. He had tried explaining the concept governing the whole to Tracy but he mistook her lack of enthusiasm for lack of understanding and never made that mistake again. It was the night after the Lynchs' party and they were sitting together over their one candle, sipping brandies that had been brightened and warmed by the flame, when Tom, pushed forward by the force of his idea, started talking.

"It's a game, the whole thing is a game."

"What is?"

"This," and he swept his arm wide. "All of this, this life, and that's just what my book is going to be. But it won't be a game of chance, oh no, because that's not what life is."

"No!" Tracy said because she sensed that he expected some response.

"No, and not because of God or destiny, nothing like

that, but because I think that the absolute in chaos must be order, think about it."

But Tracy didn't think about that. Instead she just sat back and watched Tom through the soft amber glow of her drink. She thought about his bright eyes, twinkling at her but lit up by his idea. And she thought about the fall of his hair, and the flush on his cheek, and the way his voice broke on some words pulling them low, touching her spine with them. Like when he said "morning" and she immediately thought of sunrise and death.

"Do you get it?" Tom asked but didn't wait for an answer; he didn't expect one. "Isn't it inconceivable that this whole universe, spinning through dimensions we cannot comprehend, has stumbled on a sense of order that controls our movements? But yet it does, gravity alone is proof of that, but there's so much more, spatial relations, our construct of time, and so why not expand that hypothesis? Why not equate my choice in shoes with the theory of relativity, or with the physical force of gravity? They are all of them as negligible as each other in the scheme of things and so they must both be of equal importance." He sat back, triumphant, and Tracy, still staring, smiled at him.

"I see," she said and then laughed because she knew how inadequate that response was. "I'm sorry, I think I may have lost you. Your book is going to be based on a game, isn't that right? I've got that much right haven't I?"

"Yes," Tom said, feeling a little foolish and a little annoyed at being made feel that way. "A game of chess." And that was the end of that conversation. Tracy drained her glass and stood up.

"My but I'm tired," she said although it wasn't long past eleven. "I think I'll go to bed. You can lock up can't you?" she asked and Tom nodded although he had never been trusted to do that before. "See you in the morning," she said and Tom nodded again.

"See you in the morning," he said and Tracy, walking away from him, wriggled her shoulders. He watched her go with an almost enjoyable ripple of disgust, watched the heavy fall of her feet and the swing of her skirt, and then she turned quickly and caught him. It was her expression that first caused him to blush but, once he had started, he couldn't stop. He flushed deeply red and Tracy watched from the distance of her bar. After a long, quiet moment during which she just looked him straight in the eye she tossed him over a large biscuit.

"I forgot these," she said. "Baked specially to aid a good night's sleep." To hide his continuing embarrassment Tom bit down hard and didn't notice anything more. Tracy must have left and he must have locked up before going to bed but all he remembered in the morning was the taste of warm honey and pale chocolate, the smell of bog fires and the sound of wild wet evenings.

That day he started writing in earnest. He appeared for breakfast but was too excited to focus on anything. He momentarily lost himself in the colour and comfort of pancakes, but he had no time to spare for Tracy sitting quietly behind her big blue teapot.

That morning Tom was planning on starting his first chapter and he knew exactly how it was going to go. He was going to bring the whole swirling mass of matter down to the level of two old men hunched over a chess board, spread open on a café table, playing a game that they both knew would end in stalemate. Joe and Dean were to be Tom's heroes stuck forever in the struggle of the game, gods to a certain extent but themselves victims of the wider game. It was perfect.

Later that morning Tom typed "Chapter 1" across the

top of a page and by that afternoon he had finished his opening paragraph

"The two men old men bent over with age bend over the game of their ancestors, the true game of kings, and queens, and knights, a courtly game. They play every day and they play well but are too well matched. Neither ever loses nor neither ever wins and so everything is equal."

Tom sat back well pleased and tired. He liked it so far but he knew that the hard bit was going to be connecting Dean and Joe with the greater workings of life itself; still he felt confident that it could be done.

"An even way to play the fates. To leave the game with nothing owing is a very good way to leave the game of life and, because both of these men are very old, that is what they will soon be doing, leaving this game of life and leaving everything equal behind them. The white-haired man moves his pawn forward and somewhere a child is born."

And there it was done.

Downstairs Jason pushed the door of The Continental open. It was ten to four and the place was empty except for Dean and Joe and the clatter of activity coming from the kitchen.

"That you?" Tracy called out from behind her chrome door, and Jason shouted back that it was. Dean and Joe didn't say a word but they looked up at each other in acknowledgement. They were both pleased – life in The Continental hadn't been the same without Jason – but they knew better than to comment on anything directly. So they waited until Jason had been served with his coffee and mint strawberry flan before they said anything at all.

"You hear Romeo's good news?" Joe asked barely raising his head from the game in front of him.

"I did," Jason answered without looking up from his paper. "Why aren't you wearing it?"

"Ah I don't want to bring it out here, not with Juliet's offspring about," Dean said without turning his head and that was enough. Dean and Joe had done their duty,

Jason had been welcomed back, but still everything had changed and everyone knew it.

Jason went back to spending as much time as ever in The Continental. He ate his dinner there, sometimes his breakfast and he spent two hours every afternoon sitting by the window eating cake and half-heartedly reading his paper. But he never forgot what he had discovered at the Lynchs' party. He no longer wanted anything from Tracy Sheehy except the privilege of being able to view her from a distance. And so he smiled and joked with her as he had always done but now he looked away as soon as she did; he kept his distance. And the more he distanced himself the more he realised how much there was in his life to distance himself from.

Jason's whole life to date had been based on the assumption that some day Tracy Sheehy would return his love. He had made himself continually available to her, had built up a business for her, had furnished a home, had worked out a social life, a certain status, had thought about children's names and children's schools. He had created a married world all for her, for himself and Tracy, and had always assumed that, when everything was in place, she would just come home. He had always thought that it was that simple. But now he knew different. Now he knew that he didn't want her. The Tracy he loved stood solid and separate, one hand on her hip the other holding a glass. That woman had no place in Jason's life, bearing his children and nursing his business, and that realisation kept Jason up at night.

He took to drinking. He took to sitting wide awake and dry eyed staring down the barrel of his future, and nothing meant anything any more, not his shop, not his neat upstairs apartment, not his hard-earned position and not his well-maintained respectability. It took only a few short days and he was spending his evenings in Hardy's with his father's friends, with all those men whom he had, up until now, thought that he was superior to.

Last's Hardware began to look a little shabby. Its corners were blurred by dust and its stock looked dull and tarnished; nothing sparkled there any more but Jason was still fond of it. He still opened up most days, he still liked to hear the ring of metal and sometimes he was still even moved to sing but, once he realised that all he had achieved was an elaborate failure, he lost his pride, and the loss cut deep. Except for Tracy no one noticed, though; all they saw was that Jason Last was coming out of himself a bit.

"Good to see the lad enjoying himself," Joe said.

"About time he learned to relax over his pint," Dean said and all the lads in Hardy's agreed and then Joe said, "Sure he had me thinking he was a woman, with all his hoovering and his dusting and his afternoon singing. It's a relief to me to see the lad grow a bit of stubble." They all laughed, and for the most part Jason laughed too.

Once or twice, though, after one or two too many pints, he stopped laughing long enough to think. He remembered once asking his father if he ever regretted anything but Bill had just shaken his head.

"No point, son," he had answered firmly. "What could I have done different?"

And Jason couldn't answer that. His father, wrapped up in some old, battered suit, with a complexion flushed bright red from drink and a body twisted by the elements. His small, wiry, strong, balding father spitting tobacco-stained phlegm from broken yellow teeth could never have been anything other than a scrap collector. But Jason knew

175

that the same didn't apply to him. His father had been true to his calling, and so he had been suited to his world. But Jason had been true to his idea of someone else's needs, and no good could come from that.

"Where does a man find his pride?" he asked Joe Hardy late one evening and Joe thought long and hard before answering.

"In his courage," he said finally and they both looked over to Dean who was standing up by the bar, one hand tucked into the breast pocket of his suit Napoleon-style.

"Still carrying it around with him then?" Jason asked.

"Yes, still waiting for it all to begin."

"He'll be waiting."

"Ah, he's used to that, sure isn't that all he's ever done?" The two men drank on then in silence for a while, lifting and lowering their pints in unison. It was Jason who broke the silence.

"Do you think maybe we could start the ball rolling for him?"

"How would we go about that then?"

"Well ... there are the classifieds for starters."

Two weeks later Dean Kelly strolled down Hephaition Way with his rooster skull-cap pinned tight to his head. Tom, tightening the hinges on the metal shutters of The Continental's side window, saw him from a distance and immediately rushed upstairs to his bedroom and his pen and notebook.

"Strutting by," he wrote. "Chin up and cock's comb bouncing, a proud call to cuckolds everywhere or a single man's warning to married men?" And then hurried back downstairs just in time to see him step up to The Continental.

Dean Kelly swung into the café, stared around at the breakfast crowd and silenced them. Then, instead of just heading straight for his usual table, he stood by the door waiting to be seated. He should have known better. He should have known that Tracy Sheehy was not the sort of woman who allowed herself be forced into a role. She passed him by twice saying nothing then, the third time round, she stopped in front of him and, as if she had just seen him, stepped back a pace, looked him up and down and finally said,

"Nice tie, Mr Kelly." There was some laughter at that and the nervous tension that Dean's appearance had instigated amongst the tourists dissipated.

"Wearing it new today," he answered proudly, and he was. New tie, clean shirt, polished shoes and his old quiff pinned tight to the tufts of white hair that still circled around his head.

"You want some breakfast?"

"You want to give me some?"

"I run a café," Tracy said and, losing patience, walked off. Dean had no option but to seat himself. He sat at his usual table and, long after the breakfast rush had died down, he was still sitting there. Finally he was forced to broach the subject of his hat himself.

"Hey!" he called over to Tom who was shining up some of Tracy's prettier wrought-iron chairs. "Tom, isn't it?"

"Yeah," Tom called back.

"Well, Tom, what do you think of my quiff? I got it back you know, won it back in a game of cards."

"Yeah I heard," Tom said. "It looks good."

"Not the looks I'm too worried about – they do just as well as they should and that's not so well at all – it's all the rest of it that counts."

"The rest of it?" Tom asked, dropping his cloth and walking over to Dean. "What's the rest of it?" he asked and sat down.

"Why the rest of my life," Dean explained, happy that

177

someone had asked him at last. "I told you the story didn't I? About the crone and the cards and the chicken, the whole story, you know that don't you?"

"Yeah, you told me that."

"And I was right about it all. Now that my hair's back my life is finally happening for me. Trouble is, lad, I think I'm a bit too old to take up the offer."

"Ah, you're never too old," Tom said with all the patronising gusto of youth.

"Think I may be a bit too old for her, though," Dean said happily and produced a glossy studio photograph of a woman in her thirties.

"Well you can never tell," Tom said without conviction and Dean laughed

"Oh, I can tell right enough. This girl's looking for a husband, says she fancies having children."

"Do you know her?"

"No lad, I found my hair too late. Do you not see? She was one of my might-have-beens, now that my hair's back they're all coming crawling into my life."

"What?" Tom asked. He was getting a little worried now. Looking Dean straight in the face, seeing his ridiculous, lacquered mohawk towering over his patches of grey hair it dawned on him, surprisingly only for the first time, that the poor man may really be mad.

"Ah yes," Dean said leaning back in his chair, a smug smile of satisfaction spread over his face. "Ah yes, there's a lot of living that old Taylor witch did me out of and the proof's in the amount of women who want to marry me now."

"And are there?"

"Yes lad, there's a fierce amount of women want to marry me now." And he produced four letters all with photographs of attractive women, all proposing future meetings.

"I just love a man who is as active as you are," Tom read,

"and please rest assured that your money is of no interest to me. I plan to always maintain my independence; I don't believe in being dependent on a man, no matter how rich he may be."

"Yes, I too love mountain climbing and horse riding. If you take me to your villa I'll take you to heaven."

"I've never done this before, it sounds so silly, but I do think we could be wonderful for each other. How do I know without meeting you? I don't know. Will I be sure after meeting you? There is only one way to find out. Meet me in Havana."

"But," Tom managed to stutter "But you don't, you haven't, are these letters yours?"

"And that's only a few of them. They're the letters from the prettier girls. I'll write back to them, let them down easy, explain how my life was held up by a witch." Dean folded the letters back into their envelopes and tucked them into the inside pocket of his jacket. "I must say though that it's nice to see what I would have been capable of. Even if I never got to live my life it's good to know that it was something worth missing. I did always say that I'd like to see Havana and I was a grand hillwalker as a boy and do you know, lad, but I always felt as if I was supposed to be rich."

Jason felt a bit guilty when he first heard Dean's tale buzz down as far as his shop, but Joe soon set him right on that one.

"Sure we all only believe what we want anyway," Joe said.

"I suppose the man's happy anyway," Jason said.

"He is that," Joe agreed emphatically. "And wouldn't it have been a sight worse if he had found out that he'd wasted his whole life waiting for nothing?" Jason nodded. "Sure he's bursting with pride. Cock's comb! The man will grow himself a peacock's tail yet," Joe finished triumphantly and Jason was convinced.

"Did you ever hear the like?" Mavis Bradley asked Jean Taylor and Jean, still sitting in her dressing gown, had to ask, "What?"

"Well let me in and I'll tell you." And this time Mavis didn't waste her trump card on the doorstep, or wait for an invitation to bring her bike in, this time she just wheeled her way right through the Taylors' street door. "You put on the kettle and I'll put this out of sight," she said and Jean hadn't the energy to stop her. As it turned out though she did appreciate the visit.

"Well who would have thought," she said. "The old guy believing all that nonsense."

"And him strutting around the town with that thing on his head."

"And for all these years it was right here in the house — you know that fair gives me the shivers."

"If it hadn't been for the jumble none of this would have come out. The shock of seeing the thing must have un-balanced the man. Do you know but I feel a bit responsible, you know, having the hat stall and taking all the poor man's money." And then, without feeling the need to explain the link between her guilt and her question, Mavis asked, "So where's our Melissa this morning?"

Jean had enough family pride to bristle at Mavis's inference and so she answered sharply.

"Up at Elm House as usual. And that's a thing I've been meaning to say to you Mavis. The girl spends too much time there by far. Day and night she's up there without a moment to spare for anything else and really that old woman is your responsibility."

"Well, technically."

"Technically nothing. You told Father Leary, who

probably told Mrs Levine's daughter, that you'd be keeping an eye on her and have you been up there once?"

"Oh, I would go but I've been so busy."

"And Melissa has things to be busy about too."

"Well then, I suppose we cannot have her good deeds impinge on her domestic or professional duties," Mavis said huffily and Jean ignored the tone and took the words at face value.

"No," she agreed, "we cannot. Would you like some more tea?'

"Thank you, no," Mavis said and left swearing to herself that she would never set a foot in Elm House.

"To help out that enormous lump of a girl and me so busy, I don't think so. Do the child good to do a little soul work and the mother might get the work done on her own if she got up before midday and stayed sober at night! Such a pair and such a fuss over a bit of parish visiting, I never heard the like, and likely as not will not see the like unless it has a twin, as father used to say." And she kicked herself off the kerb and swung herself astride her bicycle.

Across in The Continental Tom watched her pass and vaguely thought that she would do very well as a knight. The black knight astride his steed, battling obliquely with life and then, before he could make a note of that, Tracy appeared with his lunch. As was usual she served him before the lunch trade started and so the café was quiet.

Just Tracy and Tom in the place and nothing between them except a plate of pale gold and ripe red quiche, nothing between them except the forest green smell of wild garlic.

"I mixed sweet basil and lemon balm in with the hens' grain during the whole of last week," Tracy said. "I was priming them to lay for today's cheese quiche."

But Tom didn't respond; he barely heard her and, as she swept her dish down before him, he had to blink past the plate to even notice the woman behind it. Tracy didn't mind though; she was smiling.

CHAPTER 19

Mavis Bradley was true to her word. She didn't set foot in Elm House, but she did worry about what Jean had said. She was probably right, she thought, the woman was her responsibility, and so she rang again. Rang twice and no one answered, rang the third time and got Melissa.

"Oh no," Melissa said. "No, everything is fine, of course I can manage. My mother said what? Well I do call up a good bit. No, really she is doing fine. She's out at the moment. Just taking a walk." And that was that and that was just what Mavis wanted to hear. She thanked Melissa quite sincerely and Melissa put down the phone and smiled at Mrs Levine who was standing right in front of her smiling back.

"Are we evil, dear?" she asked.

"Not at all." Melissa said, "we're just keeping everyone happy."

"And what can be evil in that indeed ? But maybe, just to keep the books straight, I should go for a little walk around the garden. Nothing like a bit of honesty to work up an appetite."

"Eggs for lunch?" Melissa asked.

"Five for lunch," Mrs Levine answered slyly. "But maybe eggs for two."

"Guests for lunch?" Melissa asked happily. She knew by Mrs Levine's tone what type of guests they would be.

"I knew you wouldn't mind, dear, and shall we dress?"

"For visitors, of course."

"And perhaps we could eat in the orchard."

"A lovely idea."

By now, almost three weeks after she started regularly visiting Elm House, Melissa and Mrs Levine had slipped into a routine of sorts. Melissa spent a couple of hours most afternoons at Elm House; she did a bit of light grocery shopping for Mrs Levine and prepared some meals for her. But around those mundane basics Mrs Levine wove a web of ceremony. She not only insisted on china and garden teas but on proper conversation and definite rules of etiquette. She also insisted that Melissa wear the clothes she found in the giant wardrobe on her first day there.

"Forgive me," Mrs Levine had said on Melissa's third visit. "But you look too hot for June. Black is a terrible waste of youth and beauty; are you in mourning perhaps?"

"No, I just find it comfortable."

"And there you are with your polite untruths again. You will give yourself heartburn, Miss Taylor. We both of us know that you find your costume hot and bothersome but think it slimming, though why you should wish to camouflage your body I have no idea. My mother was blessed with your proportions and her clothes are still in her wardrobe. If you wish you can try them on and wear them while you visit but I am terribly sorry that I cannot give them to you as a gift. My mother was a most terrible woman. She is fifty years dead and I have only recently managed to persuade her to rest quietly in her grave. I cannot risk doing anything that may rouse her in anger."

"Of course," Melissa had said. "I couldn't accept them anyway."

"But you will wear them?" Mrs Levine asked hopefully and Melissa did.

She went straight upstairs, up to that huge wardrobe, and stayed there for almost a full hour. She tried on high-waisted skirts that clung tight to her stomach and hips and thrust her chest forward. She tried on blouses loose with lace that dripped from her throat or scooped low over the rise of her breasts. And she swirled and danced through a selection of heavy silk dresses, and warm velvet wraps, and beaded shimmering gowns, and every outfit she fitted on turned her into a beauty.

That first time Melissa finally chose a white cotton dress, yellowed in parts and brittle in others but perfectly suited to the day. Melissa pulled it on over her head, twisted her hands behind her to fasten the round pearl buttons, smoothed the fall of the skirt down over her hips and stepped in front of the full length mirror that fronted the wardrobe. After seeing herself in all the other outfits she was expecting to look well, but she was astounded by what she saw in front of her.

The dress worked a magic on her: it lengthened her neck, accentuated her waist, highlighted the gauze of hair that blurred her edges and turned her dark and wildly exotic looking. Her eyes flashed deep brown-black and her hair, which she usually wore brushed forward over her face, had been ruffled by all her changes. It was swept off her face now and fell as far as her shoulders in thick dark curls. She looked like a woman, like someone who confidently re-defined the usual concepts of beauty. She looked like someone new. That day Mrs Levine had applauded Melissa's appearance and every day afterwards she took the trouble to compliment her on some detail.

"Your eyes match that colour blue perfectly," she would say or, "Your waist is beautifully defined, you should wear fitted clothes more often."

And then, dressed and beautiful, Melissa and Mrs Levine would eat lunch together, stroll through the gardens together and play tunes on the piano together. Sometimes Mr Levine would make an appearance and Mrs Levine would leave to spend some time with him but mostly she devoted herself to Melissa. She talked a lot; she said that she was filled with a lifetime's words and couldn't be expected to contain them.

"My frame is too small," she said. "That must be why you are so quiet: your frame can accommodate your experiences to date." And Melissa didn't argue with that. She didn't want to admit to how limited her experience was – she felt that it was growing though. She felt that every day with Mrs Levine was stretching her and so she was looking forward to eggs and visitors for lunch in a way that she had not looked forward to anything in years.

She ran upstairs to change with her head filled with choices of clothes and recipes for eggs. She was worried about Mrs Levine's appetite; her friend was so frail, so tiny, and she barely ate a thing. Melissa chose a pale blue light wool skirt and a white handkerchief linen blouse with a soft lace collar. As she changed, she watched Mrs Levine tour the lawn. She looked like she was being blown by the soft summer breeze: her brown skirt and jade green cardigan fluttered wide of her delicate body and flapped sail like around her. She just seemed to follow where they led.

Melissa made an omelette for lunch. She loaded a tray with the almost-good china, made a large pot of tea and carried everything out to the orchard. She set up five chairs around two wicker tables and arranged all the furniture under the low sweep of two apple trees. It was a beautiful setting, quiet and deep green. Melissa was just ready when Mrs Levine arrived, swept along by the light breeze, her two arms pulled back as if leading two reluctant guests forward.

"I see Mr Levine is here already," she said smiling at one of the chairs. "And may I present Mr Alexander Fitz-Simmons," and she dropped one arm. "And Mr Edward Browne," and she dropped the other. Melissa raised her hand, palm down, to the two patches of air and then everyone settled themselves around the tables. Mrs Levine sat close by Melissa and, under the guise of helping Melissa serve the omelette, managed to whisper, "Of course, they are all in their prime. That is the wonderful thing about the dead, they are so very vain. Not that anyone would expect poor Teddy to turn up at a lady's luncheon in the state in which he died, all inside out he was with limbs missing. But Alex there died in his seventies chronically overweight and there he is in his twenties. As for dear Mr Levine, why he didn't have that much hair when I met him first."

Melissa stared at the empty chairs as hard as she could without upsetting Mrs Levine. And it seemed to her, if she tried very hard, she could see the portly Mr Levine with more hair and less bravado than his picture on the piano showed him to have. And she could see the clean, handsome man whose portrait was on the stairs. He was wearing khaki in that picture but Melissa saw him dressed in cricket whites. And Alex, well he was easy, he was the roguish-looking chap with black hair and a broad moustache who was in the middle of one of the group photographs that were scattered around the friends parlour. Melissa smiled around at the gathering.

"Tell Miss Taylor one of your college stories, Teddy," Mrs Levine said. "Tell how yourself and Richard Manning turned up drunk at the temperance meeting. It is a story far more suited to a summer lunch than those grim war stories you always insist on telling. I am sorry, Melissa dear," and she laid her leaf light arm over Melissa's shoulder, "but these men do insist on telling unseemly tales. Alex! Your language, dear, and with a young lady around." And then she laughed and lapsed into a listening silence.

And that was how their lunch party passed. Melissa stayed quiet for most of it, desperately listening to the sounds of the orchard, straining to catch whatever it was that was being said, whatever it was that was causing Mrs Levine to laugh or scold. And soon it seemed to Melissa as if her concentration began to work on the wind itself, soon it seemed to her as if she could hear the breath of words and laughter humming around her. She closed her eyes and concentrated on the men opposite, and then she concentrated on the summer noises of the orchard, and then, without barely noticing the transition, she heard those noises separate into words and build into stories.

Teddy's stories were always solemn, almost morbid. He had to be cajoled into good humour and even then it didn't last for long; he would always return to his war stories, stories of valour and ignominy, other men's stories.

"But it wasn't your fault," Mrs Levine said over and over and then said to Melissa, "He never listens but it wasn't his fault. He was dropped behind enemy lines in a very inept way. He got picked up by a crosswind and was killed almost immediately. He was supposed to have carried out a great mission that would have saved a great many lives but of course he never did. He is still meeting people who died because of that failed mission and he still thinks he is to blame for it. Poor Teddy."

And poor Teddy picked up where he left off with a story of trenches and mud and aged young men struggling towards the comfort of death, but Alex was the complete opposite. He twirled his moustache, winked at the women and told great and marvellous stories. Stories of hunts and races that thudded through your head and quickened your heartbeat. Stories of love that soared over time and lingered still in the rooms and gardens of Elm House. Stories of men with good and evil in their hearts, like every man, but whose circumstances forced a choice. Some died saints and slept easy. Some died devils and they still strode angrily around their estate, frustrated beyond rest in the knowledge that death had rendered them ineffectual.

And Mr Levine's stories were different again. He sat beside his wife, holding her hand or touching her hair while his deep, confident voice rolled out stories of fair days and holidays, of neighbours' weddings and children's picnics, and every story was told in detail. He described clothes, and food, and horses, and sunshine, and beauty and Melissa sat wide eared and open mouthed listening to it all.

Eventually though it had to come to an end.

"Must you, dear?" Mrs Levine sighed to Alex and, "You too?" she said to Mr Levine and then, ignoring Teddy, she waved them off. Melissa copied her, waving her hand in the direction of the stables, and then she loaded the tray full of the remains of the meal and carried it back to the house. On the way Mrs Levine linked her and curled her sweet face up to Melissa's.

"And what did you think of my Alex?" she asked, breathing close to Melissa's ear, as soft as the wind. "Not a word to Mr Levine, though, old jealousies die hard, but tell me what did you think of my Alex ?"

"Very handsome," Melissa said.

"And wasn't he charming?"

"Yes, very charming," Melissa agreed.

"Oh, I knew you would understand," Mrs Levine said happily. "Some people find him common but I always found him charming. He is my cousin, you know, he and

Teddy both, but I think he was always my favourite, even before he kissed me."

"He kissed you?" Melissa asked enviously; she knew that much was expected of her.

"Oh yes, shall I tell you about it?" Mrs Levine asked, and then continued on immediately without waiting for Melissa's nod. "I was sixteen and wearing a dress of sky blue, so light it seemed sewn from the sky itself. It was my birthday and as a treat some friends were asked around and Teddy played tunes for us on the piano while we danced. Teddy was a very happy chap back then," she added quietly but then, after a moment's pause, continued on as happily as before.

"I had drunk my very first glass of wine at dinner that evening and Alex was as handsome as he was this afternoon, so you see what happened wasn't his fault at all. I had not the will nor the wish to stop him. He danced with me for most of the evening and then, when it was dark, he danced me out into the garden. Out one of the French doors and in the other, and then he did it again. I was laughing and twirling in his arms and all around us the night sky was doing the same. I was staring up at starbursts and stardust and then he kissed me. Oh, it was just the slightest kiss, but it was on my lips and he was a man in his twenties. For so long after I had such a crush on him and then he married that awful Myrtle who had an enormous bust. But he is not drinking tea with her these days, is he? And that is a dreadful thing for me to say, but I cannot help it – he is still so charming."

Mrs Levine's story stopped just as they reached the kitchen and that grim little room dragged their conversation down to more mundane topics.

"I must go home," Melissa said. "I am sorry to but I have quite a bit of work to do."

"And I am sure your mother must miss you. I take up too much of your time."

"You could never do that."

"Oh, I could, the old can be every bit as clingy as the dead. But you will visit again soon?"

"As soon as I can," Melissa said and ran off to change.

CHAPTER 20

Melissa ran most of the way home as well. She was busy. It seemed that every woman in Seeforge needed at least two new party dresses and Melissa herself was trying to rework her wardrobe. She didn't mind, though: as had always been agreed between herself and her mother, she was working for a wage now and she was spending as she earned. Suddenly she seemed to need such a lot. Suddenly her few possessions, her bleak little workroom, her shoddy mis-sewn clothes, all seemed inadequate.

She had started with her workroom. After spending so many afternoons sitting in the worn luxury of Elm House Melissa felt displaced in bare discomfort, and so, remembering what Mrs Levine had told her about her home reflecting herself, Melissa began fleshing her surroundings out with pieces of herself, with small scraps of comfort: deep blue and milky cream paint for the walls, some thick, ruby red brocade for cushions and two terracotta pots planted with two quite mature yuccas. Melissa had slipped all these things into her room while her mother was out or busy. She didn't want her mother's snide comments associated with her new sense of home. She wasn't secure enough in her choices yet not to be affected by her mother's scorn, but she felt that she soon would be, when she was dressed for the part.

Since first day at Elm House Melissa had studied the clothes she had found there in detail. She discovered they were structured and that that was where she had gone wrong. She had been so busy trying to hide her bulk she had never thought to address it properly. She realised that she had never even measured herself before, that she had never made clothes to fit herself, only clothes to hide herself in, and no wonder they had always turned out wrong. No matter what words she had sewed them up with they could never be anything more than an apology, and so Melissa ripped them all apart and started again. And this time she made clothes to fit her and she ran their seams up with powerful words: confidence, capability, authority, strength, ability, success, skill. Good words that Melissa felt were better suited to her potential than the softer words she had always aimed for.

It was a lot of work – cleaning, painting, moving furniture, sewing and visiting Elm House – but Melissa was enjoying it. She was proud of herself. She felt that she was growing into the words she was sewing into her clothes, and she felt that the clothes she was making for her clients were benefiting from her new sense of confidence and independence. And that was why she was so angry with Jean for criticising her that day.

"That you Melissa?" Jean called out from her back room as soon as Melissa came home after her lunch with Alex and Teddy.

"Yeah," Melissa said and went to go straight up to her own workroom. She had two dresses to finish by the next morning.

"And what time do you call this?" Jean asked quietly,

tight-lipped with anger. She had suddenly appeared before Melissa, blocking her way to the stairs.

"I don't know, fourish?"

"Fourish? It's ten past five, where have you been?"

"Elm House," Melissa said.

"Doing what?"

"Nothing," Melissa answered shrugging.

Jean sighed. She had tried. God knows she was always trying but what kind of answer was "nothing"? It wasn't like she was some kind of monster of a mother; she had never hit Melissa, well only the once, never gave out about much at all, so why did the child act like this? "Nothing" one way or another was all she ever said and all Jean was looking for was the tiniest "something". One piece of gossip, one anecdote and even if either contained sex, drugs, tattoos and motorbikes Jean wouldn't have scolded; she would have understood. Herself and Melissa were two women now. Two women living together and working at the same business and not a shred of fun between them. Never mind that they were family! Never mind all that Jean had had to give up! And for what? It just wasn't fair!

Drunk she would have started crying but, being sober, she just started shouting.

"Nothing!" she said, starting low but building. "Nothing! Gone all day long with not a thing to say for yourself at the end of it. You're a spineless creature, Melissa Taylor, and that woman up in the big house is just taking advantage. Her and Mavis Bradley between them making a mock of you in front of the town. Do you not think people are noticing and laughing at you? A young girl roped in with the likes of Mavis Bradley: advertising your unpopularity, that's what you're doing!" And then, because that sounded so good, Jean repeated it. "Advertising your unpopularity and everyone knowing that you've nothing to be doing with your life but running here and there, doing errands for anyone who asks. Is that what you want from your life? To grow into a Mavis Bradley? Is that what you want? Do you hear me?"

Melissa had stopped listening and so she didn't answer.

"Do you hear me?" Jean roared and for the first time Melissa stood her ground when facing her mother.

"How can I not, you're shouting."

"And can you blame me? Can you, eh? With all I have to put up with?" It was Melissa's detachment that pushed Jean further than she wanted to go and, once she was there, she couldn't stop. She was hearing herself, hearing all the cruel things she was saying, but still she couldn't stop. "You upstairs spreading your fat arse over the whole of the house, moving and bumping and grinding God knows what at all hours of the night. You sullen, ungrateful girl and not as much as a 'thank you' for the work I'm giving you or the business I built up for you, not to mention the life I had to give up just to have you. Too hoitytoity full of yourself to even say a hello to the neighbours. It's no wonder you don't have any friends, never mind boyfriends, when you don't even make the effort to wax your arms. And as for your conversation! God, but you're boring! All day out in the world and you come back to me with a 'nothing' and I have to ask for that much."

And that was all Jean could manage without having to stop for breath. She stopped, gasped and Melissa never said a word. The room around them was suddenly large and quiet. Melissa was looking wide-eyed at her mother and Jean was trying desperately to regain her composure. She knew that her outburst had sounded stupid, cruel and vindictive. She knew that she needed to apologise but she couldn't bring herself to. In a desperate effort to normalise the situation she tried slotting her wild vitriolic ramblings into a more structured, maternal lecture.

"I say this for your own good, Melissa," she said softly and Melissa almost laughed in her face. "I am your mother and I care about your happiness. You cannot possibly want to spend every afternoon nursing some old woman and, really, your work here is slipping. I don't want to have to dock your wages."

"My work is perfect," Melissa said firmly.

"And we'll see how long it will maintain any standard if you are toing and froing like this. I don't want you going back up to Elm House any more and I've already had a talk about this with Mavis. I'll tell her tomorrow that she is to take over from you."

"You will do no such thing," Melissa said coldly. "I will arrange my time as I see fit and you will treat me with that much respect. In future I expect you to limit your criticisms to specifics. You may complain of my work, or of my behaviour, only when you have just cause. Until then I will thank you to take your loneliness and your boredom out on someone else."

It was all Melissa had ever wanted to say to her mother and, once the words were out of her, she was left feeling hollow and tired. She stood staring at her mother who was staring back at her. Stunned by her daughter's sudden anger and eloquence, Jean was only just grasping her meaning when the door behind Melissa opened and Louise, Lou, Melissa's old school friend, popped her pretty blonde head around and chirped out an awkward little greeting.

"Hiya," she said.

"Louise, isn't it?" Jean said ever so sweetly and, still staring straight at Melissa, she pulled her mouth back on smile. "See who it is, Melissa?" she said. "It's Louise, isn't this lovely?" she said, stepping around Melissa and over to the door. "Come in, come in, dear." And so Louise did, but she was very nervous.

Melissa turned then and said hello and, when Louise

saw her expression, she started talking, started darting her eyes around the room and started fiddling with the cuffs of her shirt. Louise had grown into a nice girl, with a trim, even figure, good posture, clear skin and a liking for outdoor activities. She was a kind girl too and so, although she had been too weak-spirited to carry the stigma of a fat, hairy friend through adolescence, she knew well that she had behaved badly towards Melissa. That was why she specifically wanted Melissa to come to her going-away party. She wanted a chance to be nice to her old friend in front of everyone, and so she had called around on purpose to ask her to come. She hadn't thought it would be so hard though; she had expected Melissa to be grateful not angry.

"Well, hiya Mel, Mrs Taylor," Louise said, talking too quickly and keeping close to the door. "Lovely day wasn't it? Cool summer we're having, well, not cool like cold but you know. Whatcha at Mel? Haven't seen you about at all. I've been swimming a lot down by the Dell. You should come down – it's cool. Well anyway, the reason I called around is about my party. I'm just checking that you're both coming. You got your invitations, didn't you? And you will come, won't you?" And Louise looked to the two women, including them both in her appeal.

"I would love to," Jean said. "Thank you, Louise dear, and thank your mother. Tell her her skirt will be ready by Saturday."

"I will Mrs Taylor. And Mel? You're coming too, right?" Louise looked her old friend straight in the eye as she spoke. Looked all Melissa's hurt and anger straight in the eye and Melissa did appreciate her courage. But still, after the sausages, and Louise had been right there and had seen everything, after that Melissa felt she just couldn't do it. She blinked, breaking eye contact, and then slowly shook her head but before she could answer Louise started again.

"Please. Please, Mel, it won't be the same without you. Remember, remember how we used to play at grown-up parties? Remember we'd get all dressed up and pretend that all weird people were coming and we'd play the piano and dance and ..."

"Yes," Melissa said and she knew she was agreeing to everything.

"Well good then," Louise said. "That's just great and Melissa."

"Yes," Melissa said again.

"And could you come a little early, you know to make sure everything looks OK and all?"

"Yes." Melissa knew that that was the ultimate compliment: she was being offered the role of best friend again.

"Good," Louise said and left feeling happier than she had thought she would. She understood now that Melissa's gratitude would have been pathetic but her anger was honest and in that context her acceptance meant something. It meant that Louise had been forgiven.

It was almost six now and The Continental was lit up for its night's business. Its candles and soft wall lights burned uselessly against the still bright summer sky and there, sitting at the window, at the furthest table from the door, was Tom, reading through some sheets of paper, waiting to be served. Louise didn't know him, not at all, but she wanted to. To her and her friends he was still the most interesting man in Seeforge. It was his age more than anything else that fascinated them. There were hardly any men in their twenties in Seeforge, and men in their twenties were deemed very attractive by Louise and her friends. It was definitely worth a try and so she crossed over to The Continental and pushed the door open just as Jason was pulling it from the inside.

"Excuse me," he said stepping quickly by her. Joe

followed immediately behind Jason and Louise was forced to step aside. Still holding the door she nodded to Joe as he passed and then just stared at Dean. He followed close behind the two men, waving his chessboard over the concoction that was balanced on his head; he was calling to them.

"So you don't believe me? So I'll go home and get it then, will I? Thank you, miss," he said to Louise before following his friends across the road. "I'm telling you now like I always told you before, I was supposed to be a pilot. I got the forms this morning and I'd have them with me if I had thought that I'd be forced to prove myself to my own people."

Louise watched the three men cross over to Hardy's before she stepped into The Continental. Tom was alone, laughing.

"What was that?" Louise asked.

"A load of cock and bull," Tom said and they both laughed. After that it was easy. Louise just walked up to his table and said, "Do you mind?" Tom shook his head and she sat down. Tom, who after nearly three months in Seeforge was starved of young company, thought she was very pretty. He stretched his hand across the table, smiled his big blue-eyed smile and said, "I'm Tom."

She took his hand, shook it and said, "I'm Louise and I'm going to have a party. You want to come?"

"Yeah, I would thanks," Tom said and, up to that point, everything was going fine but then the chrome door to the kitchen crashed open and Tom, who had been smiling so nicely at Louise, shifted his attention to a point over her left shoulder and she watched his smile slip into a leer.

Tracy was walking slowly down the length of the bar, stopping now and again to add some some things to the dish she was holding in her left hand and Tom was staring at her.

Staring fixedly at her and leering. Louise turned slowly to see what was having such an effect on him and when she saw Tracy she was disgusted. Tracy had cleared the bar now and was moving down the café, moving her hips around tables and holding her shoulders well back. Behind a veil of steam she was leering, staring fixedly at Tom and leering. It was disgusting, plain and simple, that's what it was.

"Duck with wild berry sauce," Tracy said settling the plate in front of Tom who just stared hard at the food, blinking.

"Thank you," was all he said. He knew the rules of The Continental by now and so he knew not to compliment Tracy, but he couldn't stop himself gasping. It seemed to Tom that Tracy's cooking was getting better by the day. Every day he swore his evening meal could not be improved upon, and today was no exception: it looked and smelled perfect. The slices of duck, fanned out over a bed of thick, red berry compote, were browned and glazed around the edges but swirled into a centre of pale, pink flesh and then, over them, Tracy had tossed a lattice of shredded lovage.

"Well, hello Louise," Tracy said cheerfully just as she turned away from the table. "Are you staying? Would you like to see a menu?" Louise shook her head and turned back to Tom but her moment was gone. She waited until Tracy was out of earshot and asked, "Are you and ...?"

But she didn't finish her question. She had expected Tom to be watching the broad swing of Tracy's bottom as she swept down the length of the café, but he wasn't. He had shifted all his attention onto his dinner. His head was down and Louise couldn't see his expression, but something about the way he curved so close to the table and something about the way he inhaled the steam off the food struck her as almost explicit. Something too personal to witness. She stood up.

"See you at the party then," she said putting an invitation down on the table but she didn't wait for an answer; she didn't expect one.

In her kitchen Tracy heard her go and nodded to herself. She was stirring the ground, crystallised leaves of angelica through the passion-fruit torte she had prepared for Tom's dessert.

Across the road Melissa leaned forward to peer down from her attic window; she watched Louise run the length of Hephaition Way before she settled back to her work. She was unpicking an old pinafore of hers. An old pinafore that was shaped like a tent but was made from a pale blue linen so soft it felt like the sky itself.

CHAPTER 21

Melissa stayed up late working but got up the next morning as soon as Tracy's cock crowed, long before Jean even woke. She wanted to get to Elm House, to Mrs Levine, before her mother decided to carry out any of her threats. Melissa knew her mother well, had spent years studying the woman's moods, and usually could tell the difference between her intentions and her bluffs. But she had never seen her mother so stripped down and angry as she had seen her the day before, and so she couldn't be sure what kind of outcome that kind of tantrum would produce. To be safe she wanted to warn Mrs Levine.

It was still very early when Melissa arrived at Elm House and so she decided to wait in the gazebo until a more reasonable hour. But she had only just settled herself in one of the wrought-iron chairs that were stored there when Mrs Levine joined her. She slipped in through the door that Melissa had left open, fluttered down on to a seat and then coughed politely to alert Melissa who was already almost asleep.

"I saw you from the house, dear," Mrs Levine said. "I thought I was imagining things but it is true. What a wonderful surprise to see you here so early. I have always found that there is nothing that cheers a day quite so much as breakfast with a friend. It sets such a hopeful tone for what is to follow, do you agree?"

"Of course," Melissa said sitting up straight as Mrs Levine had taught her to. "But I thought it was far too early to disturb you, I thought you would be asleep still."

"Goodness, child, how you flatter me. Do you think for a moment that a lady of my age can sacrifice a moment more than necessary to sleep? I'll be sleeping soon enough, and for long enough, but for the moment I will be taking breakfast with my dear friend. Come along, let's make some horrible tea and use the best china. But, oh, dear me!" And Mrs Levine fluttered back into her chair, her rust brown robe falling heavily around her. "I never thought to ask! Have you come for a reason? Is there something wrong?"

"Well," Melissa said and stopped. Well what could she say? How could she describe her mother and her mother's venom and how persuasive it was. How could she explain that all it would take was a phone call from her mother and Melissa's part in Mrs Levine's world would be shattered. "My mother ..." she tried again and then she just broke down. She cursed her mother and burst into tears. After a moment Melissa looked up. She had expected some show of comfort or concern from her friend but instead Mrs Levine was looking at her quite sternly.

"Curses are most unladylike, usually most unnecessary and I am certain that to curse one's mother must be quite a tremendous sin. Also, dear, and I'm sure this has been explained to you before, crying does dreadful things to the delicate skin surrounding the eyes. Please stop crying, for that as well as so many other reasons. It sounds horrible and brings forth all kinds of discharges that, well really, I would not like to witness." Surprised and hurt Melissa did what she was told. She stopped crying and as soon as she had Mrs

Levine leaned over to her, smiled, picked up her hand and whispered, as sweetly as she had ever whispered anything, "But I do understand, really. It is just that I have to say such things out loud in case my mother is listening." And then, in her normal voice, she continued, "But Melissa, my dear," and any remaining trace of bad feeling faded when Melissa heard how gently she used her name. "You are old enough now to understand that people, especially women, are very rarely born mean. Life makes them mean and mean people are never happy. It sounds to me, dear, that your mother is never happy and so she doesn't deserve your anger just your understanding and, if that fails, your pity. From what you tell me I would say that your mother's problem is that she lost her love, or maybe she never did love, and we all need love to help shape our worlds. Did I ever tell you, dear, how I came to fall in love with Mr Levine?"

Melissa shook her head and settled back into the cushion of leaves that had pushed their way through the lattice of the gazebo, ready to let the story carry her away.

"I knew him as I knew a lot of young men," Mrs Levine said slowly, solemnly, perfectly matching her tone to the dark beauty of her surroundings. "We would meet at dances and dance; he would take me for drives and we would talk. In the summer we would play tennis and at Christmas he would take me skating over the Dell, but still I never really noticed him. He isn't much to look at as you know, not even now, and he was older then with less hair and more flesh. Way back then I was too young to appreciate anything other than good looks and charm. I never knew that he loved me. I never questioned why he was always there when I needed him and I never questioned why I always turned to him when I needed anything. I just assumed that that was the way it was supposed to be. You see, I must have always known that we were in love, but the night I realised this was the night he was supposed to collect me from the train station.

"I had gone to Dublin on the evening train. I was to stay with some friends and, as Mr Levine was up in town on business, he said that he would collect me and deliver me to their door. It was a job that someone had to do – my mother would never have allowed me negotiate my own way through city traffic. But Mr Levine was late, which was very unlike him, and so I went into the railway café for a cup of tea.

"Now, Melissa dear, you must understand that back when I was a girl young ladies did not frequent railway cafés alone and at night. But it was cold and I was thirsty so I braved all the staring eyes and sat down by the window. I was wearing a very stylish hat and coat, I remember, with the daintiest pair of gloves and a hairdo that had just been done the day before. I drank tea, when the waitress brought me a cup, and I sat quiet, nervously looking out for Mr Levine.

"Everybody else in the café that night was eating cheap teas: the air was fat with the smell of lard – fried eggs and chips. They all seemed to be factory workers of some sort, eating while waiting for their trains home. They were all tired and smudged. It was a very dirty sort of night. The filth of the trains lay heavy on every surface in that dirty little café and my gloves were grubby even before I touched my cup. My hair was falling out of shape, the greasy air was pulling at it and I felt so sad, so sad like crying, and all around me tired factory workers waited for their trains, and their tomorrows, and I waited for Mr Levine.

"Then he came. He was wearing a white raincoat that swirled around him as he rushed across the platform and he was carrying a huge bunch of flowers, a fresh smelling splash of colour for his lateness. He burst in through the café door and I rose to meet him. He made such a noise," and Mrs Levine stopped there to smile but Melissa didn't say a word: she was waiting, holding her breath, waiting for the end. "He was loud," Mrs Levine continued in a much lighter voice. "Loud and vibrant and apologetic and commanding. He over-tipped the waitress and I hugged him, a most unladylike thing to do. I took the flowers and he took my arm, we left the train station together and we haven't been apart since.

"You see, Melissa, he rescued me. He validated me, he took me higher than egg and chips, and ever since then I knew that that was how I wanted my life to be. To be higher than the mundane. When Mr Levine walked me out of that café I was a film star, functioning offset but still in black and white."

She stopped then and Melissa took her hand. They sat side by side in silence for just a moment before Mrs Levine sat forward and, in her usual tone of voice, drove her point home.

"You see, Melissa dear, your mother may never have felt like that, not even once. She may never have realised that her world could be raised beyond fried eggs and chips in a dirty little café."

It was a novel concept and Melissa sat silently for a while trying to assimilate it. She had never considered pitying her mother before. Jean Taylor was thin and hard, she laughed on the phone and with the neighbouring men, but maybe even that was pitiful, maybe that was egg and chips.

"I never thought of it like that," Melissa said finally.

"And that is because you are young," Mrs Levine said holding her hand out for support. "I feel a little musty," she said. "All these leaves get in on the lungs eventually. Come walk with me in the gardens for a little while and we will talk about our favourite breakfasts."

And that is exactly what they did. They walked through

the orchard and across the breadth of the lawn and slowly back towards the house and all the while Mrs Levine talked about kippers, and scotch eggs, and devilled ham, and shamefaced looks passing between houseguests. Later they drank horrible tea and toasted some stale bread and after that Mrs Levine lay down for a nap in the friends parlour.

"Will you be here when I wake?" she asked and Melissa nodded.

"If you will have me I will be here all day."

"I could think of nothing nicer. And, dear, don't bother to change for lunch: I don't think mother's wardrobe can match the outfit you have on." Melissa blushed. For the first time she was wearing one of her re-stitched dresses, it was russet red with tight three-quarter length sleeves and a fitted waist. "And we cannot have such an outfit wasted, can we?" Mrs Levine continued twinkling. "So I shall ask Alex to join us this afternoon?"

And she shut her pale pink eyelids over her bright blue eyes and settled her head on one of her faded chintz cushions. Melissa sat by her side and was still there when she woke. She had decided not to waste a moment of that day with Mrs Levine. She sensed that it was to be her last afternoon in Elm House.

They ate lunch together on the lawn, cucumber sandwiches and water flavoured with lemon balm. They were alone for the meal – Mr Levine and Alex only joined them once it had been cleared away. It had begun to rain and Melissa and Mrs Levine were in the friends parlour watching the weather through the open windows.

"Well here they come at last," Mrs Levine said looking up from the magazine she had been flicking through and Melissa smiled out into the rain.

"They'll get wet," she said and Mrs Levine laughed.

"If you're not careful you'll catch your death of cold," she called into the garden and Melissa could almost hear the laughter that roared with the wind in through the room.

"Play us a song, Melissa dear?" Mrs Levine asked. "Play us all a song to cheer us up and I will sit close by Mr Levine and Alex can turn your sheet music for you."

And so Melissa sat at the piano and started playing. She sang:

> Baby loves dancing,
> Baby loves romancing.
> Everybody loves baby,
> Baby doesn't love me.

And when she was finished Mrs Levine laughed and clapped and called for another.

"Sing us another, Melissa dear," she said. "Sing us one to cheer away the rain." And so Melissa sang:

> They said she'd marry Lacey
> And if not she'd marry Jim,
> She said I'll not give chase
> For I don't want to catch him.
> She said I'll take the chap
> With the stars bright in his eyes,
> And with that I doffed my cap
> And she led me down the aisle.

Mrs Levine tapped her feet and Mr Levine tapped her knee. Alex twirled his moustache and leaned close to Melissa breathing through her hair and whistling out her tune and they all had a wonderful afternoon, but it did have to end. Melissa did have to go home.

"I should go," she said finally and, as usual, Mrs Levine politely apologised for keeping her.

"A whole day together," she said, "and I'm greedy for more. How do you tolerate me, Miss Taylor?"

"If it were up to me," Melissa said seriously, "I would never leave but there's a party this Saturday and everyone wants a dress for it, and I have to make one for myself too, you see I have to go to it."

"Have to go! Dear me, child, but you make it seem like you don't want to go." They were sitting side by side on the sofa facing the piano. Melissa's hand lay on Mrs Levine's and their knees were touching. Alex and Mr Levine had already left.

"Oh, but I don't!" Melissa wailed.

"Why on earth not?"

"I'm fat and ugly out there." Melissa waved at the world beyond the friends parlour and ranted on, but she made a huge effort not to cry. "I'm fat and ugly and hairy and I just don't know what to say to people, even the ones who are being nice to me, I get all sweaty and shy and ..."

"Goodness, child, how awful. But you are intelligent, aren't you? You did well in school, didn't you?"

"Well, yes."

"Well then it is easy, it is all a matter of applying your wit to your world. In my day we were all taught this long before we were subjected to our first dance. I had a French lady come all the way over from Paris just to teach me exactly how to wear my face while listening to a bore. Has no one ever taught you anything like that?" Melissa shook her head. "Well then I must," Mrs Levine said decisively. "It is a disgrace to let a young girl out in the world without the proper training. Why it must be an agony for you not knowing how to curtsy or what to do with a bread roll or who to talk to during the soup." Despite herself Melissa laughed.

"Well, things are very different now. I don't have to know those things."

"Of course not – I am not quite so lost in my youth – but

I do know that some things never change. For instance," and Mrs Levine sat up a little straighter, cleared her throat and continued in a mock lecturing tone. "Lesson one: in any social group always be convinced that you are well worth knowing. No one will appreciate your worth if you do not appreciate it yourself. Lesson two: assume a superior stance every now and again – sometimes it helps to have your peers work for your approval, it stops them taking you for granted. And finally lesson three, and I promise this guarantees popularity: compliment lavishly. My life-long rule has been an enormous compliment on first meeting someone. Something along the lines of, 'I don't think I have ever seen such beautiful hair.' Then, ever after, whenever you meet you toss away a few minor compliments, something like, 'That colour suits your eyes to perfection.' Of course with men you have to compliment differently: refer to their intelligence and the thickness of their hair and you will be fine.

"Trust me, dear, this really does work because it plays on people's vanity. You know even the cleverest people are stupid enough to believe themselves special, and even the most particular people will accept someone who tells them that they are. People like that, which is really all people including myself, can believe you to be a fool, a traitor, a murderer or a thief and still forgive you because of what they see as your impeccable good taste."

She laughed then and so so did Melissa, thinking it was a joke.

"But I could never do that," Melissa said getting up to leave. "It would never work for me."

"And how will you know without trying? Oh! Oh, dear girl, I have had just the most wonderful idea. When is your party?"

"This Saturday."

"And today is Tuesday, yes, I think we have time. But

hush, we must be sly." And she linked Melissa, drew her across the big, square hall and through the heavy front door and she only spoke again when they had reached the start of the elm avenue. "We must be careful not to let Mother hear us but I have a plan. We will have a practice party for you on Friday evening. I can invite all my friends and, as you will not meet any of them again, and as they are all so long dead they are, for the most part, past caring, you can make as many social blunders as you wish, just as long as you remember to learn from your mistakes. By Saturday I promise you you will be ready to enjoy any party. Please say you think it a good idea – I would so love to go to a party again."

"It is a wonderful idea," Melissa said.

"It is, isn't it? But Mother must not know about it before hand or she will not lie easy until I lie beside her. She never liked parties but she hated public scenes more, so once the party has started, she will do nothing to stop it and will only be angry after the last guest has left, and I will have had too lovely a time to care by then. But it means I cannot really prepare for your party. I am sorry, dear, but if I do too much out of the ordinary Mother is sure to wake and notice."

"Don't worry," Melissa said, smiling so hard the words were bubbling out of her. "I wouldn't want to put you out anyway. I will come on Friday with everything we will need, trust me."

"Oh I do, dear, with my life." And she pressed Melissa's hand and turned to go but Melissa stopped her.

"Mrs Levine," she said awkwardly. "I just wanted to know, and of course I don't mind, but lesson three, you know, about compliments. Well, was that what you did to me when we first met? You know what you said about my skin and bone structure."

"Goodness, child, no, not at all! Use up three compliments on someone of no social standing! No, child, what I told you was true."

And then, on impulse, Melissa bent and kissed Mrs Levine's cheek. It was as soft as the breeze and smelled as fresh as the surrounding green trees.

CHAPTER 22

Jean Taylor never did tell Mavis Bradley to take over Melissa's duties at Elm House. She had fully intended to, was quite looking forward to standing her moral high ground, but then something happened. Melissa suddenly melted into quite a manageable, good-humoured girl. Strange though it seemed to Jean, something about her and Melissa's last argument had triggered something in the girl. And for the life of her Jean couldn't figure out how one shouting match had worked where years of bickering had failed. Of course the change hadn't taken place immediately but still it was immediate enough to count as a miracle in Jean's eyes.

As soon as Louise had left that evening Melissa had stormed up to her workroom without as much as a glance in Jean's direction and, as far as Jean could tell, had stayed there all night. When Jean got up the next morning Melissa was gone and it looked as if her bed hadn't been slept in. Jean had checked the sheets and they were cold. It was a long day.

Jean knew that sulks and disappearances were common enough amongst teenagers, but Melissa had never acted like a common teenager before. She had no friends to share her drama with, no tradition of independence to fall back on. She was just gone and that was so out of character that Jean did think of phoning the police. She knew she would be laughed at though and so she just waited. She tried working for a while but her mind kept wandering back to that horrible argument. She knew that it had been her fault, that she was the adult and that she was the one who had lost control. But still, she couldn't help thinking she had been driven to it. There was nothing about her daughter she understood, so much that just didn't seem normal.

Take Melissa's bedroom for example – and then, to prove her point to herself, Jean did just that: she stood in the middle of Melissa's little bedroom and took it for example.

It looked just as it always had looked, neat and tidy and totally characterless. The bed was made up with white sheets and a blue duvet cover, the curtains were yellow, the wardrobe and chest were pale brown and the walls were bare. Under the window a low bookcase was lined with a selection of books that Melissa had gathered from around the house, but even they were bland: a few classics, a broad collection of period romances, a couple of old books on etiquette kept, Jean supposed, for their curiosity value and a few textbooks – nothing. Jean left the door open when she left, just like Melissa always did; there had never been a reason to close it. And then, just to convince herself further of her daughter's complete lack of character, Jean climbed the narrow little iron ladder that led up to the attic boxroom.

Jean hadn't been up there in years. The last time she had seen the room it had been filled with boxes and bags of rubbish and had smelled of damp and dirt. Ever since she had given Melissa the option of using it as a workroom she had felt guilty – thinking about her daughter stuck up there between some split old floorboards and the weather, but her guilt and pity had been misplaced. That tiny little space

214

lodged tight under the eaves was beautiful. It was blue and cream with deep ruby-red trimmings. It was rich and opulent and though so small it looked shrunken it exuded an air of wealth and space.

It took Jean only six steps and she had crossed the room. Two hothouse plants framed the little window, there were no curtains and below Hephaition Way was spread out in miniature, sustaining the impression of a shrunken world. It was a fairy land. The worktable running the length of the room was stacked with all the bits that Melissa was working on. Jean didn't look too closely but it seemed as if Melissa was well up to date and doing some good work. Hanging on the back of the door was a sky-blue dress loosely tacked together. On the way out Jean took the time to look at that up close and marvelled. It was a beautiful garment, cut with precision. It reminded Jean of the work her grandmother used to do for all those old matrons who were willing to pay any amount for a suggestion of youth. She carefully closed the door to the boxroom when she left.

Melissa arrived home that evening quite early. Jean heard the street door open and recognised her daughter's step. She dropped the skirt she was working on and held her breath. She was as tense as if a stranger had just walked into her home and that was even before Melissa had popped her head around the door. She was wearing something new, a very well tailored dress that Jean had never seen before. Her hair was swept back and was bouncing off her shoulders – and she was smiling. She was standing up straight and smiling at Jean.

"Hiya!" she said. "Busy?" she asked.

"Bit," Jean answered. "And you?" she asked.

"Not so bad. I was up at Elm House. I hope you don't mind but I still have time enough to finish what has to be done before Saturday." It was more than Melissa had said to her mother at a sitting since as long as either of them could remember and, "Good," was the only thing Jean could say in reply.

The next morning, though, she found it easier. Herself and Melissa sat down to breakfast together and chatted. Melissa spoke a little about the new dress she was working on.

"It's sky blue, Mum," she said enthusiastically. "It used to be a smock but I'm going to make a tight bodice out of it with quite a low neck and I found some beautiful buttons. If it's ready I'll wear it on Saturday."

And Jean told Melissa all about how Jill Daily had phoned in some fictional measurements for a skirt.

"She thought that she'd lose weight by the time it would be ready but when she came for the fitting she was fatter than ever. Sure it was as obvious as a nose that she was pregnant."

And they both drank an extra cup of tea each before disappearing into their separate rooms.

"Oh, by the way," Melissa called after her mother from halfway up her ladder, "I meant to say your hair looks really well like that." Jean patted the loose bun she had pinned together and surprised them both by blushing.

"Thank you, dear," she said, "and I like your top."

Melissa worked hard that morning; perched high over her world she sang and sewed and watched all the little people below bustle about. She saw Tom stroll up and down Hephaition Way, two hands stuck deep in his pockets, his head down and his shoes kicking at loose stones. She saw Joe Hardy cross over to Hardy's and then just stay there in the porch, spitting occasionally, and she saw the breakfast clientele pour in and out of The Continental. She ate lunch with her mother and didn't go to Elm House: she was too busy.

"Go if you want," Jean said when Melissa told her she was staying. "Maybe you should if Mrs Levine expects you."

"She doesn't and really I am too busy," Melissa said stacking the lunch plates and, just for a moment, the two women stopped what they were doing, went so far as to stop what they were thinking, and smiled at each other. And that was that; neither of them ever mentioned their argument again. Melissa went back to her room and Jean walked straight out onto the street. She felt like she needed a walk.

Jason Last watched her go, watched her tight little bum wiggle down the road, bouncing on her still taut calves. She had always been good looking and she still was. Still well groomed and sparkling bright. He wondered how many people settled for second best, how few men would consider the likes of Jean Taylor second best. And then, just as if she were answering a call, Tracy walked into his shop. He wasn't surprised although Tracy very rarely came calling. He had seen the way she had been looking at him recently and he had been expecting her. She stepped into the shop, closed the door behind her but stayed standing beside it.

"You busy?" she asked but she talked over his answer.

"Not –"

"I mean busy doing anything other than drinking your life away and taking the piss out of poor old Dean Kelly? You planning on keeping this business up, are you?" And she gestured about her. "You planning on retiring already? I always hoped for more from you, Jason Last. Up until now I was always proud of you."

"Proud of what?" Jason asked flinging his arms wide. "Proud of this? Proud of being the best little shopkeeper in the west?" But, although his words were bitter, his tone was honestly questioning.

"Proud of you being a good man."

"I was never that, Tracy. What do you think makes a good man?"

"I don't know, good stuff; you're just talking shite now."

Tracy was beginning to feel deeply uncomfortable. She had come to give Jason a bit of a lecture about drink. She had come to ease her conscience about prioritising Tom. She had not come to talk some nonsense about the definition of good.

"I'll tell you what makes a good man," Jason said ignoring Tracy's discomfort and her dismissive tone. "A good man is honest and brave and I always thought I was that. I was proud of being that." And he slumped down on his counter. Tracy stepped up to him and awkwardly laid a hand on his shoulder.

"You are that, Jason," she said.

"I'm not. I've been lying to myself all my life and the reason I did was to give myself an excuse to take the easy way out."

"But I don't understand," Tracy said, and she didn't. "This wasn't easy, this business."

"I don't know, Tracy, but I think it was easier do this than find something else to do." And he lifted his head and shook it. "I don't know what to do with any of it now, Tracy. I don't know why I have it. Life's just become real to me and I don't know what I'm doing in it. I'm not laughing at Dean at all, you know. I think I'm jealous of him."

"It's not that hard, Jason," Tracy said after a short pause. "All you have to do is find something in life to hold on to, something that holds on to you."

"Like you have?" Jason asked and, for the first time, there was a suggestion of malice in his voice. Tracy could think of no answer to that and so she just smiled and said, "Dean Kelly thinks they want him to train as an astronaut now."

"Wonder where he got that idea," Jason said.

CHAPTER 23

By Friday Melissa had finished her sky-blue dress. Knowing that it was going to be worn at Louise's party she had sewn it through with a special combination of words. She had put in all her new, powerful words but she had diluted them a little with some softer ones and then she had run the whole back seam of the skirt up with one specific wish. She had also finished Samantha's dress and Mrs Hardy's blouse and skirt. It had been a busy week and she hadn't had a chance to visit Elm House at all, but she didn't mind: she still had Friday night ahead of her.

By Friday night Jean was no longer surprised by anything this new daughter of hers said or did, and so she didn't question her when she said she was going out.

"Somewhere nice?" was the only comment she made and Melissa had nodded enthusiastically.

"Somewhere very nice."

And that was when it hit Jean. The girl had obviously found herself a boyfriend. To Jean's mind nothing but a boy could have brought about such a change in Melissa; the new way she walked, the way she pulled her shoulders back, the shine in her hair, all pointed to some new source of confidence, and wasn't that what boys were? But Jean knew only too well that it takes more than words and kisses to sparkle up a girl's eyes and clear up her complexion. Recently Melissa had been looking a bit too bright eyed and smooth skinned for virtue.

"You know," Jean started nonchalantly. "You know you don't always have to give boys exactly what they want when they want it." The comment sounded so out of context to Melissa that she laughed, a noisy wet kind of laugh, and then Jean laughed too. Ah, what was she worrying about? she asked herself. After all, things were different than in her day. Melissa was a smart girl and anyway wasn't this the kind of worry she had been wanting for years?

"The nice ones usually hang around long enough to ask twice," she said and that was the end of her advice but still, once she had given it, she felt a little closer to her daughter, like they had something in common at last.

Melissa decided not to wear her new dress to Mrs Levine's party and when she arrived in Elm House she was glad she hadn't. Mrs Levine was waiting for her by the front door wrapped around in soft, twilight blue.

"Do you like it?" she asked twirling for her guest and Melissa nodded.

"It's perfect," she said and it was – and its perfection would have been lessened by a lighter, younger blue.

"My but you have brought so many things," Mrs Levine said looking down at Melissa's bags. "For your own party too. Such a breach of etiquette! I dare say these walls have never seen the like. Do you think it would be possible to unpack without letting the walls see you?" And she laughed and linked Melissa. "We will have the party in the friends parlour, don't you think? It is by far the happiest room in the house," and, arm in arm, they passed through the hall.

Melissa had brought very little really. She didn't think it necessary to supply either food or drink for dead people and so she had just brought a few things for show; some fruit, some little cakes, some cheese sliced onto crackers and a bottle of thick, red wine that she decanted into a cut-glass jug. She arranged the food on the table by the piano, using the very best tableware that Elm House could offer.

"No slur on your food, dear Melissa," Mrs Levine said, following her from kitchen to parlour and back again, "but this is a party." She kept glancing over her shoulder as she spoke. "Looking for Mother," she explained when Melissa asked. "I am sure she must have noticed something by now. What time is it, dear?"

"Half past eight," Melissa said.

"Then you must get changed," Mrs Levine urged waving her towards the door. "Wear the jade silk, but first let it hang out of the window for a while. That should do away with any trace of mustiness and it will scent your skin. Night air and young skin produce the headiest perfume, the perfume of transitory hope. You should wear it well while you can. Oh, but do hurry up. You must be ready for your guests: it is one of the first rules."

And so Melissa hurried. She lit the candles she had brought with her and set them in holders all over the room, turned off the lights, opened the French doors, kissed the enraptured Mrs Levine and ran upstairs.

She picked out the dress Mrs Levine had recommended, a heavy silk gown weighted down with hundreds of glass beads, forced the bedroom window open and hung the dress on the curtain pole. It fluttered slightly as the breeze from the garden caught it and then it billowed out, taking the form of a dead woman out of habit. Melissa threw off her clothes, worked her hair up into a high bun and all the while she imagined her dress absorbing the scent of wild roses and purple light. Mrs Levine was right; she would smell beautiful.

She dressed slowly. She stepped into the cool of the

material, folded it up over her hips, wriggled down into its depths and then stood straight. She was standing in front of the mirror and she was beautiful; olive brown and flowing in curves of silk and shadows of darkest green. Mrs Levine called to her and she ran, ran barefoot over smooth floorboards and soft rugs thickened by dust.

"My dear girl!" Mrs Levine gasped as Melissa stepped off the staircase. "My dear girl, you fill my mother's gown every bit as well as she did when she was in her prime and the envy of every society beauty. Come and take my arm. Mr Levine, Alex and Teddy are already here. We have time for a toast before the rest of our guests arrive."

They crossed the hall together and stepped into the candlelit friends parlour. Mrs Levine led the way straight over to the piano and then, under her direction, Melissa poured five small glasses of wine.

"To Melissa," Mrs Levine said smiling around her. "May you carry the memory of this night with you always and may you collect many more wonderful memories to keep it company."

Melissa smiled and ducked her head but Mrs Levine told her to keep her chin up.

"Another social rule, dear. I do hate to lecture but tonight is about learning, isn't it? You must never let the world see you cower, not even out of modesty. A lady should have the strength of character to look her compliments, as well as her insults, straight in the eye." And so, looking Mrs Levine straight in the eye, Melissa drank her wine.

It was getting dark now and the candles were beginning to come into their own, beginning to dance over surfaces and play along the walls. Outside the stars were just starting to show against the deepening blue of the sky, and Mrs Levine's guests began to arrive. Melissa didn't even have to be told: she could hear them whispering and laughing on the wind. They blew in through the open French doors, smelling of newly mown grass and freshly turned earth. They ran past the candles causing them to flare and flicker and they clustered around Mrs Levine draping her in mist, drawing her close to them, drawing her back through the years. But after a while Mrs Levine pulled herself free and took the time to present everyone to Melissa.

Melissa stood as she was told to stand, upright and proud, a broad smile on her face, and she greeted them all: Harriet Armstrong, Gertrude Lawrence, Mr and Mrs Robert Charter Bowles, Raymond Grace, Ellen Ellis, Catherine Devane and on and on. Most of the names glided straight through her outstretched hand but Mrs Levine called her attention to a few of them.

"Try not to dance with Raymond Grace," she warned. "He tends to grasp too tightly and tell unseemly jokes. I cannot think who could have asked him. And you should look to Harriet and Gertrude when Alex pays you any attention. They are both passionately in love with him and wildly jealous. Neither of them ever managed to attract his attention in this short life but they are both hell-bent on ensnaring him at some stage during eternity. And here come the Fennells. Look at them, doesn't it warm your heart to see them? They must be over ninety years married and they still act like newlyweds."

Melissa was enchanted by it all and, when she was finally left to her own devices, she looked about her with the expression that Mrs Levine had taught her to adopt.

"If you are at a loss in any social situation," Mrs Levine had whispered to her, "never occupy yourself with a task – it smacks of menials and desperation. Instead occupy yourself with your thoughts. That way people may still think you unpopular but will respect you for being aloof."

But Melissa was never left alone for long. For the most

part she stayed close to her old friend and laughed when she did, and listened when the room seemed to settle to the quiet of an anecdote. After a while she told a story of her own, the story of the sausages, and the room gusted with laughter. She was a success.

A little later, after everyone had been offered food and drink, they danced. Melissa played some waltzes on an old record player that crackled out the tunes and she danced every dance. She danced three times with Alex, twice with the dreaded Raymond and once with Teddy, who managed to rise to the occasion with a smile. Mrs Levine kept calling for some brighter music, some ragtime, but the only records Melissa could find were waltzes. She was pleased about that – she didn't know the steps to any other dances – and she loved how the men, even Raymond Grace, held her and moved her as if she was just as light as Mrs Levine.

The night wore on and the candles burned brighter – pinpricks of light breaking up the dark, just like stars. Dancing in the middle of the room Melissa watched them swirl about her. She noticed that the wine was almost gone but most of the food was still there and she thought it strange that the ghosts had managed to drink but couldn't eat. She supposed it was because they were spirits. She whispered that to Teddy, whom she was dancing with, and they both laughed.

It was Alex who sobered her up. He called for silence and announced to everyone that Melissa was a talented musician with a beautiful voice. He said that she would, if encouraged, play for them. There was a rush of approval. The candles flickered, the French doors rattled and Melissa could feel gentle currents push her towards the piano. She looked up at Alex and his black eyes twinkled and she looked to Mrs Levine who nodded and so she sat at the piano and played and sang:

Goodness gracious
My man's at the races,
He got paid on Friday
Won't have time for me.

Then she sang:

Baby loves dancing,
Baby loves romancing.
Everybody loves baby,
Baby doesn't love me.

Then she stopped and rose to go but gentle currents pushed her shoulders back down and a strong breeze blew emphatically at the candles. So, in that fiery darkness, Melissa played and sang as slowly as she saw fit.

If I were to lose you, if you were to go,
Tell me where would I find you ?
How would I know ?
How would I know which stars were your eyes?
Which were the stars that looked down as I cried?
And how would I know which corn grew your ears?
Which field I could trouble with my whispered fears?

When she had finished there was a moment's silence and then a heavy gust of wind blew through the room, blowing some of the candles out as it swept by. Melissa got up to relight them but was stopped by Alex.

The slow, sad strains of that simple love song still hung heavy in the air as Alex pulled Melissa close to him and began moving her around the floor. He danced her once around the room and then out one of the French doors and in the other. And then again – out one of the French doors, and then he stopped. Behind him Melissa could see the stars swirl together, starbursts and stardust, and then she felt Alex's mouth on hers. His moustache tickled her cheek and his large, black eyes with stars for pupils tenderly held her gaze. It only lasted a moment and then they danced back into the friends parlour and broke apart without anyone, except Mrs Levine, noticing them.

It was almost midnight and amidst much joking about the witching hour the guests began to leave. Melissa could feel their gentle kisses and the whisper of their best wishes play across her cheeks. But when it came to Teddy and Mr Levine she could see their kind faces smiling gently behind their words before they followed the others out through the French doors. Alex waited until everyone was gone, and then he waited until Mrs Levine tactfully withdrew to the kitchen, before fading slowly into the night. He stood by the open doors not saying a word, just smiling – just staring down at Melissa with the full force of his black, starlit eyes and smiling. Mrs Levine came back into the room just as he faded into nothing. She was laughing.

"I suppose we have something spiritual in common now, don't we, Melissa dear?" she asked and Melissa blushed by way of an answer. "Tell me, dear, did you enjoy yourself?"

"Oh, Mrs Levine," Melissa said, still blushing, "I had as lovely a time as you had when you were sixteen."

"And no one could have a better time than that. I am delighted for you but I am afraid that I am also exhausted. It is very late and I am sure your mother will want you home. Wasn't it delightful that mine stayed quiet?" Melissa nodded and then took the hand that Mrs Levine was holding out to her. "Would you do me a favour, Melissa dear?" she asked. "Would you walk me to my room? It has been so long since I have been minded to bed."

Melissa folded her hand over Mrs Levine's elbow and slowly they moved across the hall, through the patches of red, yellow and blue moonlight, up the sweeping staircase and down the corridor to Mrs Levine's bedroom door. They stopped there and Melissa bent her head intending to kiss Mrs Levine's cheek, but instead Mrs Levine spread her cobweb hands on either side of Melissa's face, holding it firm and straight. Melissa was left staring straight into a pair of deep blue eyes pierced by starlight, eyes very like Alex's.

"My dear," Mrs Levine whispered, "after tonight, after all these weeks, do you think that you are a little less sad? Perhaps a little closer to discovering what makes you happy?"

"I think so, yes."

"So you have a dream for your future?"

"I suppose I can always dream," Melissa answered.

"My dear, it is most important that you do."

"But it is only a dream," Melissa said, smiling at the thought of her dream coming true, of being able to exist in the world as easily as she could at Elm House.

"But dreams are essential," Mrs Levine said brightly. "Reality alone is nothing, a construct dependent on some very dubious senses. Everyone, every wise one, bends their reality a little to suit their dreams. It is our dreams we have to be sure of; so many people go chasing the wrong ones. If you know what you want you can easily fashion a life to contain it." And then she shook her head sadly. "And then there are those like Teddy," she said. "Those poor people who have allowed their disappointments, their nightmares, shape their lives or, in Teddy's case, their deaths."

And she smiled a little, and then she said goodbye. She pulled Melissa's lips down to meet her own. Melissa closed her eyes, felt a brush of dust and heard the bedroom door click shut.

CHAPTER 24

Melissa wore her new blue dress to Louise's party. She had based its design on the white cotton summer dress she had worn that first day she had dressed up at Elm House, and it suited her just as well as the original dress had. It was very old fashioned, so old fashioned that it looked antique and so it couldn't be criticised in contemporary terms. It was sculpted and lavish and projected a powerful image of femininity, a role that Melissa had quite successfully sewn herself into. She stood in front of her mother's full-length mirror and, for the first time, recognised her spirit in her clothes.

"I'm strong," she whispered at her reflection. But she was more than that. She was tall, broad, full-figured and wrapped around with light.

"You look nice," Jean said when Melissa presented herself in her mother's workroom.

"Thanks," Melissa said and smiled. Jean smiled back awkwardly; she still wasn't used to this cheerful child. "I'm going to head off now," Melissa said. "I'll see you later."

Louise Hardy lived close to the river in a relatively new bungalow, centred on a heavily landscaped mound. It was a cheap, sprawling house and, the minute Melissa stepped on to its tarmacadam driveway, all her nerves melted away. After all the glory of Elm House she was beyond being intimidated by such bland ugliness.

"You look wonderful," Louise called from the side of the house where she was pinning balloons to a tree. "You look really grown up." And, compared to Louise dressed in a tiny, shiny yellow sundress, Melissa did look very mature.

"Thanks," she said and then, remembering Mrs Levine's third rule, said, "and you look beautiful. Your dress compliments your skintones perfectly, but then you have great skin." Louise simpered a little and Melissa shifted the focus of her attention onto Mr Hardy. He was standing behind Louise fussing over a barbecue "Hello Mr Hardy," she called out, "that barbecue looks great. Did you design it yourself?"

"Designed and built it myself," Dick Hardy said proudly stepping back from the stone plinth that supported the grill.

"And built it too?" Melissa echoed as if too impressed to comment further and Louise linked her friend and whispered, "You've just made Dad's night."

After that Melissa helped Louise with the decorations, helped Mrs Hardy with the food and sewed a tuck in the waist of Louise's dress so that its skirt sat a little smoother. By the time the party began Melissa felt very much in control of her situation.

Just as the first guests started arriving Melissa left what she was doing in the kitchen, patted her hair down into place and joined them. The boys and girls of her age were strung across the lawn in twos and threes and their parents were gathered in larger groups around the barbecue and the makeshift bar. The atmosphere was crisp with politeness and Melissa, with her stomach turning slightly, stepped out onto the lawn. For a long while no one noticed her, no one spoke to her and so she had plenty of time to calm herself.

She strolled down the length of a flowerbed and concentrated her mind on the black depths of Alex's eyes. It worked to a certain point: she was still alone but she was no longer the sort of girl who would be called on to carry a pile of firewood.

Eventually Melissa was discovered by Louise who made a great play of befriending her in front of everyone. She linked her, and whispered to her, and took the time to explain all the gang's references to her, and soon Melissa almost felt herself to be back in the comfort of the friends parlour, standing by Mrs Levine, laughing when her friend laughed and listening when the crowd settled down to some anecdote. Eventually she felt so comfortable she told an anecdote herself: she told the story about the sausages and all around her all her peers laughed and laughed. They wiped their eyes and held their sides and added their own touches to the story.

"I thought you'd gone mad!" Samantha squealed

"You did! Imagine what I thought!"

"And Tom of all people! Did you see his face?"

"Well, at least he doesn't have mutant fingers?"

And that was how Jean first saw her daughter. All dressed up like someone's grandmother but surrounded by a laughing group of friends. She just couldn't understand it.

"Children!" she laughed up at Roy Lyons. "Can't live with them, can't kill them." And Roy was happy to move a little closer and laugh a little too heartily at the joke.

"Indeed, indeed," Mavis Bradley suddenly hissed close to Jean's ear. "Children indeed. May I have a word?" And she smiled at Roy as if to dismiss him. He just smiled back though, and so Mavis was forced to pull at Jean.

"Sorry," Jean said to Roy and, "What's wrong?" she snarled at Mavis. She was mortified. To be dragged away from Roy Lyons by the likes of Mavis Bradley! Well, it was mortifying, that's what it was. "What is it?" she asked again but Mavis, all bristling with drama and importance, wouldn't say a word. She just led Jean over to where Melissa was still standing talking to some girls. "Melissa!" she called out over whatever was being said, and then again, louder, she called out, "Melissa!" This time she managed to quieten the group and all the girls turned towards her. Melissa didn't though; she felt that Mrs Levine would never allow herself be addressed so rudely in public.

"Melissa Taylor, may I have a word," Mavis barked out and this time Melissa did turn, but, "Please," was all she said.

"Please?" Mavis repeated in confusion and Melissa answered sweetly, "Certainly." And she walked away from the girls leaving them gaping after her.

"1 told you she was cool," Louise said triumphantly.

"Now," Mavis said as soon as Melissa was within reach. "Now I have you, missy," she said grabbing on to Melissa's arm Melissa looked down at the old hand gripping her forearm and stood quite still staring at it until it was removed. Jean stepped up beside her daughter and, together, the two women looked down on Mavis. They were draining her of her moment and that made her angrier than her complaint ever had.

"Don't you stand there looking at me like that, you ... you ..."

"What is all this?" Jean asked.

"Ask your daughter, she knows well enough." Mavis was whispering but her body language and the hiss of her anger were beginning to attract attention.

"What?" Jean asked again. "Someone tell me what this is?" She wanted everything cleared up before it erupted into a scene. She hadn't drunk nearly enough yet to cope with a scene and as for one involving Mavis Bradley! Well, drunk or sober, who could recover socially from that?

"I think Miss Bradley must be referring to Elm House," Melissa said calmly, smiling at her mother before turning to include Mavis in her good humour. "Am I right, Mavis?" she asked. "Is that it?"

"That's it all right and that's enough to get the police involved if I and Father Leary see fit."

"Oh, don't be silly," Melissa said laughing as if Mavis had been joking, and then she stepped away, stepped back towards the party.

"Silly!" Mavis squealed. "Silly!" And now people were definitely beginning to take notice. "I'll tell you what's silly! Lying and stealing and God knows what, that's silly!"

"No," Melissa said gently. "That would be sinning." And, despite herself, Jean began to smile.

"There's nothing to smile about," Mavis said suddenly rounding on her friend, "nothing at all. I have a letter here," and to prove that she was telling the truth she pulled a letter from her pocket and waved it in Jean's face. "This is a letter from Canada, from Vera Levine-Loy, who writes to tell me," and here she paused to regain her composure and deliver her trump card with dignity. "Who writes to tell me," she repeated, "that her mother, Mrs Emily Levine, passed away in a nursing home in Canada a month ago. She had been a patient at that same nursing home for more than six weeks before her death." And then she paused again before asking quietly, "So what do you make of that then?" Jean looked at Melissa and Melissa shrugged back at the two women.

"I suppose everyone's time comes around sooner or later," was all she said before making another attempt at returning to the party. This time it was Jean who stopped her, pulled her close and hissed.

"You explain yourself and you do it now." Melissa sighed, as if with the boredom of it all, and did just that.

"I went up to Elm House to check on Mrs Levine as I had been asked to do, but when I got there the house was bare. I checked around in case she had fallen or something and I found that the only open and aired bedroom had obviously been packed up – so I assumed that the woman had gone away."

"But I rang!" Mavis spluttered. "I talked to you on the phone and you told me she was indisposed, or not to be disturbed or something. "

"I think I may have told you that she wasn't at home, which was true. I assumed that if she wanted you to know why and when she had left she would have told you. I wasn't there to spread gossip, or was I?" Melissa asked cheerily.

"But you were up there day and night, trespassing and probably worse!" Mavis's frustration was spilling out of her now, her voice was climbing higher and higher and to hide the ugliness of the scene Jean had started laughing. The two women looked quite out of control and that calmed Melissa right down.

"I popped in now and again to keep an eye on the place. The hall door had been left open. Probably the old woman hadn't used it for years and forgot to lock it. I couldn't find a key for it and so I kept an eye on the place." And here she shrugged again. "So sue me," she said and walked right past the two women. "Check everything in the house against an inventory and sue me if you can."

"Melissa!" Jean called out after her. "Melissa, where were you all the time? Where were you last night?" And, luckily, that was the only part of the discussion that the party heard – that and Melissa's answer.

"Ah, Mum," she groaned. "I was out. You don't want details, do you?" And then, unbelievably, just before she walked away, the child winked. Jean didn't ask anything more and Mavis had nothing left to say. The two women parted right there on the lawn. Mavis did try to spread her story about a little but the telling of it just seemed to wear the facts of it thinner and thinner.

"So she was keeping an eye on the place then?" people asked her when she told them how Melissa had trespassed.

"Why didn't Mrs Levine tell you she was going?"

"But there's no harm done, is there?"

"So poor Emily's dead then?"

And after all those questions were answered there didn't seem to be any story left at all. Mavis went home early.

Huffing and puffing back into town, kicking the pedals of her bicycle down in anger, muttering to herself about the morals of the mother and then what could you expect, she sailed right past Tracy and Tom without even noticing that they were walking arm in arm.

It was a lovely evening, after ten and still warm, still lit by the remains of the day. It was a lovely evening for a stroll and so Tracy had closed The Continental early and had agreed to accompany Tom when he said that he was going to look in on Louise's party.

"Really?" Tracy asked when Tom had told her he was going.

"Yeah, I am," Tom said. "But I probably won't stay too long."

"Well, hang on and I'll walk up with you," Tracy had said before disappearing into the kitchen to speed up her cooking. She fed everyone who was there, closed the door against anyone who hadn't arrived yet and was ready, exhausted and waiting for Tom by ten o'clock. Tom kept her waiting for almost a quarter of an hour and, when he did finally come downstairs, he looked very tired.

"You sure you want to go?" Tracy asked. "You look pretty wrecked."

"Yeah, I'll go," Tom said and Tracy followed him out

onto the street. That was all she could do, but earlier she had done a lot more.

Earlier, when Tom was still talking enthusiastically about Louise Hardy's party, Tracy had started serving him his dinner. She didn't usually give him an appetiser – she thought that that teasing way of presenting a dinner was more suited to older people – but that night she did. She served him with pâté to start. A thick wedge of mushroom pâté on a salad of evening primrose leaves and then, directly afterwards, she set a steak down in front of him.

"Muscle meat," she called it and she grabbed Tom's forearm and squeezed it. But Tom didn't notice, as usual he was just engrossed in his food. "Not that you need it," Tracy said and Tom laughed although he had only heard the tone of Tracy's comment. He hadn't been focused enough to listen to the words: all his attention was centred on the food in front of him.

Tracy knew how to do steak and she had done this one well. She had fried it in butter so it was crisp, golden and still solid with juice. She had served it with a potato, yarrow and camomile mash that she had whipped together with warm milk, and with a lavish helping of caramelised onions that had been boiled in wine before being browned in sugar. Then, just as a finishing touch, she had trickled a little brandy butter sauce over the plate and had opened a bottle of very full-bodied wine.

It was a large piece of steak and it took Tom a while to eat it. Even before he had finished it he could feel himself growing uncomfortably full, a thing that had never happened to him at The Continental before. But he couldn't leave anything behind him – Tracy's food never allowed for that. And so he ate on but, just as he had proudly cleared his plate, just as he wiped the last piece of meat over the last trace of sauce, Tracy appeared beside him with a bowl of trifle.

"They call it trifle 'cos they don't respect it," she said putting the dish down in front of Tom and Tom, who had his mouth open to say that he was just too full, closed it again. It was impossible to argue past Tracy's food and, increasingly for Tom, it was getting hard to see past it. It was filling his world, filling his writing, sending him sound to sleep every night, wrapped round in dreams of Tracy and her dishes, waking him early every morning in anticipation of those dreams come true. And so, instead of sending his dessert away, he made an effort to focus on the woman behind it and smiled at her.

"Eat that and then talk to me about respect," she was saying, rubbing her hand across the breadth of his shoulders.

"Get back to me on that one," Tom said picking up his spoon and Tracy laughed as if he had said something improper.

Tracy very rarely made trifle. She thought that it was too heavy, that it tended to outweigh what went before. She also thought that sometimes, when what had gone before fell short of expectations, that was a good thing so she tended to associate trifles with failure. She remembered that later that evening and cursed her choice in dessert but, even then, she knew that it wasn't really the trifle's fault.

And it wasn't: the trifle had done everything a trifle could do and had done it well. It had tasted wonderful, had juxtaposed textures and tastes perfectly and, long after Tom had finished it, the sherry and the sugar were still reacting in his bloodstream producing a mild feeling of intoxication.

Tracy expected Tom to want to sleep after such a dinner and so she was surprised when he said that he still wanted to go to Hardy's.

"Really?" she asked and then cursed herself for forgetting how the feeling of mild intoxication manifests itself in young people.

"Yeah, I am," Tom said. "But I probably won't stay too long."

And so, a couple of hours later, after Tracy had closed up and after Tom had changed into his new Taylor-made shirt, the two of them walked arm in arm up to the Hardys' place.

It was an ugly place and, because Mr Hardy was so proud of his barbecue, it was full of ugly smells and rude lumps of food. The only good thing about the party was the cake, and that was high and flamboyant, just like Tracy remembered Louise when she was a child playing dress up with Melissa Taylor right across from The Continental. The two of them trailing generations of Taylor glamour up and down the dirty footpath. The cake was beautiful, three tiers of strawberry sponge topped with a meringue crust and decorated with mint-green bows, but the rest of the party looked awful. Tracy relaxed immediately she stepped on to the tarmacadam driveway – she could see nothing threatening in such bland ugliness – but then she looked up at Tom.

He was staring straight ahead with that same locked expression he usually saved for his dinner.

It was late now and Melissa was tired. She had been good for hours and she was tired. She had been a success, she had chatted and joked and had been sadly disappointed by everything and everyone. She was tired but she didn't feel right about going home without her mother, and Jean was nowhere near ready to leave.

"But why isn't anyone dancing?" she was asking swinging her hips from side to side stretching her two arms out to Roy Lyons. Melissa stepped away. She moved out of the bright frenzy of the party and leaned up against the narrow trunk of a cordeline, and that's where Tom saw her.

He had just stepped on to the Hardy's driveway and there was Melissa leaning up against a tree with her back to him. She had slipped one foot out of its shoe and was rubbing her bare toe up and down the length of her shin. The first thing Tom noticed about her was the sheen and colour of her hair and then he dropped his gaze and stared, fascinated by the fall of her skirt. He was still staring when she turned and when he moved his eyes back up to meet hers he had to blink past her elegance before recognising the rather plain girl who had measured him up for a shirt.

For a moment Tracy watched Tom watch Melissa. For a moment she watched all her stupid dreams crumble away. She couldn't understand it herself, an arse too wide and a sight too much hair, but she understood that Tom saw something more. Tom saw something even more wonderful than her stuffed goose, and she couldn't compete with that.

Nobody noticed her going. She just slipped backwards away from the party, back towards town, to the one man who had always been happy to focus all his attention just on her. By the time she reached Hephaition Way she had herself convinced that she was doing the right thing. After all, she knew what she wanted and she was going to get it: it was that simple. She wanted a solid little business and a husband. She had the former and she was going to get herself the latter.

CHAPTER 25

Jason had been invited to the Hardys' party – he was always invited to everything – but he didn't go; he didn't see the point. He was sitting at home, sitting upstairs over his shop, thinking that he might go for a drink and wondering what the point of that would be, when Tracy came calling. She pushed her way into his sitting room and then just stood there staring around. Just her, just her with no cake and no conversation. Just a broken version of herself come home, just as Jason had always known she would.

"Sit down," he said to her and she did. She sat facing him in the newer of his two armchairs and all around her the carefully arranged clutter of his life threw her into stark relief. If Jason hadn't been sure of it before he was certain of it now: there was no place for Tracy in his world. "You want a drink?" he asked and she said, "If you're having one, yes." He poured two glasses of whiskey and handed her one.

"You OK?" he asked and she nodded, drank a stiff gulp and then smiled through her tears, pretending they came from the sting of the alcohol.

"Yeah," she said. "I just came by. I was up at Hardys' and, Christ, but what a God-awful bunch. I guessed you wouldn't be going: more sense, eh?"

"Was Tom there?"

"Yeah, I left him up there."

"I see."

"So, anyway, I just came by to see if you wanted to go back up with me, or maybe go for a drink, or maybe ..." And she let her tone slide a little towards innuendo.

It was the most encouragement Tracy had ever given Jason and two months ago it would have been enough. Two months ago and one more glass of whiskey and all of Jason's dreams would have come true, but now he just sat across from his friend and didn't say a word. He was wondering whether he could forget the last few weeks. He was thinking how much he wanted to and how he would never be able to. He looked over at Tracy where she sat staring at him, sat close to heartbreak hoping in him, and he knew what he had to do.

"This won't do, Tracy," he said slowly, quietly, dipping his whole broad bulk over the tiny rim of a shot glass. "This won't do, Tracy, " he said again and she said nothing. For a long time she said nothing and then, so quietly, she whispered to the top of Jason's bright red head.

"I always thought it would," Jason sat up and the two friends stared straight at each other.

"You're right," he said. "It would do and that would be all. But you're better than that. You deserve better than that, you deserve better than me."

"But ...!" she wailed.

"But I'm not saying I'm a bad man," Jason said and laughed. "I'm just saying I'm not your man." And he shook his head.

"I should be going then," Tracy said trying to keep the high pitch of broken pride out of her voice.

"OK, but wait a bit," Jason said holding her by the shoulders and pushing her gently back into her chair. "I've something to show you." And he turned away from her and started rooting through the bottom shelves of his bookcase.

He was kneeling on the ground with his back to Tracy and all the time he was talking. Chatting away a bit too breezily.

"You know I saw it here just the other day," he said ripping through albums and folders. "Help yourself to another drink if you want. This shouldn't take too long. It's definitely here. I saw it just the other day and God but it made me laugh! You know I had bought it to give to you as a present on our wedding day," and behind him Tracy got up to pour herself another drink. "Then I saw it the other day and realised what an insult it would have been! What was I thinking of at all? You and me and children makes God knows how many and you with my present hanging on the wall taunting you all day long. 'Cos you know I would have insisted you hang it up: it was that expensive and I was that stupid." He stood then and turned. He was holding a cardboard tube that he offered to Tracy.

"Happy wedding," he said.

"Why are you doing this?" she asked holding a drink in one hand and keeping the other close by her side. She was thinking that maybe, over the years, her indifference had worn her friend bitter. She was wondering if he was taking this opportunity to hurt her, and he was smiling so broadly it seemed like he was enjoying himself.

"Open it," he said prodding her a little with the tube. "Remember what you said to me about having to find something in life to hold on to, something that holds on to you, well hold on to this." He said and prodded her again. After one long moment she did just that. She took the tube and pulled a thick, rolled-up sheet out of it. Jason cleared his coffee table and she unrolled the paper on that. It was a map, drawn on linen, showing an unrecognisable landmass, and it was beautiful. Rivers and mountains were painted on in blue and brown inks, sweeps of valleys were coloured green and red – emerald and burnt sienna – and the ocean was dark green, with tufts of white surf curling at its edges, and then swirling black and wild before rearing up in the shape of serpents and dragons.

"Remember?" Jason asked but Tracy didn't answer him. She was tracing her finger along the line of a river. "No husband would ever be able hold you the right way, Tracy," Jason said, almost whispered.

"There be monsters," she said finally, and when she looked up her eyes were shining bright. "I'll send you a postcard," she said and Jason nodded, nodded twice and then kept his head lowered. She laid a hand on his shoulder but he didn't answer. She let herself out.

Within a week Tracy was gone. She packed up enough stuff for a two-week break away and told herself, and everyone else, that that was as long as she was going to be gone for, but no one, not even herself, believed that.

Jason was the guest of honour at the going-away meal she cooked for herself and her friends: ten people, champagne truffles, Hungarian goulash, black forest gâteau, the best a mature wine cellar could offer and Tom holding on tight to Melissa Taylor. It was a fine night and Jason left long before it was over. He didn't want to say goodbye to Tracy; he thought that they had said all they had to say and she obviously felt the same. She left the next morning before her rooster crowed and she left the key to the back door of The Continental in Jason's letterbox. It came wrapped around a note asking him to take care of the chickens and telling him how to – and it was signed with love.

"Grain on top shelf over fire. Change their water daily and clean them out every second day. The eggs are worth the trouble, love Tracy."

That morning, as soon as he got the note, Jason went around to The Continental and let himself in the back door. He wanted to see for himself that Tracy was gone; he

wanted to start feeling the hurt he knew her absence would
have to cause. He felt that the anticipation of that hurt was
almost worse than the real thing but, since the night she
had come calling on him, all he had felt was an anticipation
of loss. He needed it to start; he was ready for it.

"I'm ready for this," He said aloud to himself as he
stepped round back and into the yard behind The Continental. He hadn't been there in years but he remembered
it as soon as he saw it, a long chicken run, a broad vegetable
patch bordered by herbs and the big black door with shiny
iron hinges that, as a child, he was never allowed enter. It
was only as he was turning the key in the deep lock of that
ancient door that he realised he had never been inside the
kitchen of The Continental before, never had as much as
peeked in.

The door opened, surprisingly easily for such a heavy
weight of wood, and it snapped back on itself as soon as
Jason stepped through it, leaving him staring into darkness.
For a long time darkness was all that Jason saw, felt, heard
and smelled. A pitch blackness that pushed on his nerve
endings, that forced its way into his ears and up through his
nose, a hard blanket of nothingness and then, just as he was
opening his mouth on the scream he knew would be forced
down his own throat, he saw the fire. It was beating with a
strong pulse, growing stronger with every beat, brightening
and dimming, breathing in the void and exhaling itself,
growing out of nothing and eventually filling that whole
dark space with itself. It spilled out from a hole in the centre
of the room, rose up through a squat stone cylinder that was
positioned under a series of grills, hooks and grids; there was
no other method of cooking in Tracy's kitchen, but Jason
didn't notice that.

All Jason saw was the fire and in that he found everything he had never known he was looking for. He didn't

know how long he stood staring at it but when he finally stepped away his eyes glowed with an echo of the flame: they were burned bright orange and yellow. For the first time Jason understood everything his father had tried to teach him about metal; he understood it all and more. He understood that molten metal was so close to the element of fire it had first to be returned to that form before it could find its proper shape. The deeper he looked into the fire the clearer it all became. He saw organic licks of life flare up and die low, he saw colour and movement separate into line and form and he felt that the whole movement was being driven by a pulse that included him.

Eventually he pulled himself away. He walked past the fire, through the kitchen and out into the café. He was holding a card, a handwritten notice that read, CLOSED FOR HOLIDAYS. He put it in the front window of The Continental and then went back to his fire.

Upstairs Tom had heard Tracy leave and Jason arrive. Tracy had told him that that would happen, that while she was away Jason would be in charge, and Tom was a little nervous about that. He pulled on his jeans and walked downstairs. Everything was quiet. Already the café looked worse than deserted: it looked derelict.

"Hello!" Tom called out and there was no reply, only a clang of metal ringing off metal that came from the kitchen. "Hello!" he called out again and walked around to the open end of the bar. He was only halfway to the chrome door before it was flung open and Jason suddenly appeared with the door closed firmly behind him. Tom took a step back. Ever since his first day in Seeforge he hadn't trusted Jason and he didn't now. The man looked wild, broken free and random. His expression ran loose all over his face and his hair was ripped through with energy; his eyes were burned bright orange and yellow.

"Good morning," Jason said and his words sounded so normal that Tom laughed.

"Breakfast's off I take it," Tom said and Jason nodded.

"But I'll feed you if you go down and put the kettle on." And he tossed the key to his flat over to Tom before he started advancing on him. Tom caught the key and then, keeping one eye fixed on the bigger man, started retreating. They walked like that, face to face and in silence, as far as the café door and then Jason reached around the boy, pushed a couple of bolts aside and before Tom knew it he was standing out on the path, bare foot and bare chested. Across the road Melissa, who was just getting up, leaned close to the window and watched Tom run the two doors down to Last's Hardware. She was smiling – it had been almost a full week now and she just couldn't stop smiling.

Jason followed Tom within minutes. He thumped up the stairs to the flat over the hardware shop singing a drinking song he had found somewhere in his head.

"I'll drink to the girl whose eyes shine so bright,
And I'll drink to men that I drink with tonight.
And tomorrow will come and we'll all be dead,
But I'll drink to the dawn and I'll drink to the lead."

"Tom! Tom lad!" he called and Tom, who had been waiting awkwardly beside a boiled kettle, stepped out of the tiny kitchen. "Tom lad, I have you all packed up and sorted out," Jason said, and dumped all of Tom's possessions down in the centre of the room. "The Continental's no one's home now and you need a place to call your own. 'Bout time you got a job too and I can give you that – that and a room. What do you say?

And after a good breakfast and a hearty, spit on the palm handshake, Tom said he was well pleased with the arrangement. He was to work most mornings and every afternoon in the shop and he was to sleep in Bill's old room. A nice square white room with a heavy iron bedstead in it. It was a good room to write in and, more importantly, it kept Tom close to Melissa.

When Melissa heard the news her smile spread a little deeper. Tom told her immediately. As soon as he had finished his breakfast he ran straight across the road, headed straight for Melissa and that fold of elegant comfort that epitomised everything he loved about her. He ran through the Taylors' reception room, up the stairs and up the ladder. Melissa, hearing the rattle of his approach, was ready and waiting for him, standing by the door of her workroom, smiling.

Down in the kitchen Jean heard the clatter of commotion on the ladder and stepped a little closer to the open door, straining to hear what was being said. For the past week she had been looking at Melissa's smile and understood it to mean just one thing and now, as if she needed proof, here was that lad running all over her house at unsuitable hours the very morning that Tracy was due to leave.

"Come to say his goodbyes, I suppose," Jean snorted to herself.

But upstairs, up high over Hephaition Way and deep in the comfort of Melissa's room, Tom was holding on tight to his girl and talking out all his plans for their shared future.

EPILOGUE

Three months later there is still no card from Tracy but no one is waiting for one. The Continental is closed now and looks like it always has been. Black smoke belches out from the kitchen chimney day and night and Jason is rarely to be seen. Whenever he does come out, though, he blinks and smiles and talks with a deeper rumble to his voice. He has grown into a much more solid man. A man with a lot more to say for himself.

"It's about form," he tells people. "It's all to do with tracing the metal's form back to its origin and then moulding it in answer to the flame that creates it. Do you understand?" he asks them and, although some people nod, nobody encourages him. He doesn't mind, though; he knows that once he produces something that translates his meaning into the concrete he will be respected.

"No time for his old friends," Joe Hardy says sitting in one of the booths in Hardy's, hunched over a game of chess that he knows will end in stalemate.

"Never trust a man who can't take the time to drink a pint of an evening," Dean Kelly says and then, just because it is a great thing to say, he adds, "They want me to buy Elm House now, you know Levine's old place."

"Ah they do, do they?" asks Joe.

"They do," Dean states firmly, bobbing his cock's-combed head up and down. "Sent me out a big glossy brochure and all."

"Well it's a good job you would have had the astronaut's salary for that then."

"Aye, it needs some upkeep. I went up to have a look at it. Think it would have suited my wife down to the ground, though."

"Jane?"

"No, I think I would have married Marie."

"Marie?"

"Likes winter sports."

"Ah, I remember her now."

Tom, up at the bar, leaves half his sandwich behind him. For the past while he hasn't been too fussed about food: his appetite has all but disappeared; the action of eating makes him feel quite uncomfortable. Trouble is, though, he can't stop thinking about food. He sees it, and smells it, everywhere and it always sickens him slightly. He pays for his half-eaten sandwich, nods at Joe and Dean and leaves. Outside the air is heavy with the weight of too many lunches, heavy winter lunches. Passing Taylors' the air thickens, becomes fat with the smell of lard – fried eggs and chips. He crosses the street and unlocks the door to Last's Hardware.

"I'm home!" he calls out and from upstairs Melissa answers, "Be down in a minute."

She is sitting in the room she created for the two of them, a luxuriously comfortable room, and is sewing Jason a shirt written through with her prayer for him. "Honesty," she sews, "truthfulness, candour, integrity" and down one whole seam she repeats "self awareness," over and over again.

Downstairs, sitting at the old portable typewriter he found in the back of the shop, Tom continues his writing from where he left off that morning.